Number

CW01095198

BRUTAL
BOY

SELENA

Brutal Boy

Willow Heights Preparatory Academy: The Exile

Book Two

Selena

It is nothing to die; it is dreadful not to live.

—Victor Hugo

one

Harper Apple

Just walk in, I tell myself. *It's no big deal. You did it yesterday. Anyone who has anything to say can fuck right the fuck off.*

I stand next to the bike rack outside the towering stone building of Willow Heights Preparatory Academy, ironically named since there's not a spot in Faulkner, Arkansas, that could reasonably be called the heights of anything but degradation. I squeeze my hands into fists, reminding myself that I am stronger than anyone in this fucking place. I want out of this town, and this is my ticket, and I'll be damned if a bunch of entitled pricks are going to take it from me.

Still, I can't seem to get my feet to move, even when thunder grumbles in the dark clouds overhead, threatening to unleash cold drizzle in response to my cowardice. I'm frozen next to the expensive-ass bike one of those assholes got me, which I'm still riding because fuck if I'm not going to get something out of what they've done to me. Since I couldn't stop the video from being leaked, a bike is all I've got.

I can do this. I know I'm strong enough.

I walked in the other day, after Royal Dolce the royal asshole fucked my face while his brothers stripped me naked and held me on my knees on the stone floor of the basement. I walked in the next day, not knowing everyone had seen the video of me blowing my old math teacher. I walked in the day after, thinking it would start to die down. But it's gotten worse every day, and now it's Friday, when all the football players will be treated even more like gods than usual, and their Dolce girls all wear little jerseys with their numbers like those boys wouldn't do the exact same thing to them they did to me, and I just… Can't.

The bell rings, a soft little chime that sounds so sweet you'd never know what monsters lurk in the halls of Willow Heights.

Yes, I'm strong enough. I could go in.

I just don't want to. I want to turn and walk away.

No, I want to run.

I want to turn and run away from this fucking place and all the bitches in it—the girls who have made a point to make my life hell since I arrived wearing all the wrong clothes, the dangerous psychos who tell the teachers what to do and treat girls like dogs, and the asshole administration that does nothing to change it because those assholes' daddies pay the salaries of everyone in this place.

I want to run back to Faulkner High, where being coerced into blowing a teacher was the worst thing that happened to me. Where I may not have had friends, but at least the entire school wasn't full of enemies.

It doesn't matter what I want, though.

As Gloria reminded me, I'm not a runner. I'm a fighter.

But all the fight seems to have been sucked out of me this week, and there's no cheerleader to give me a pep talk today. I reach for the bike I put up when I still thought I could face the leering crowd.

"Skipping school already?" drawls a male voice behind me.

I nearly jump out of my skin, my heart pounding and my fists raising automatically as I spin around, light on the balls of my feet.

Colt Darling—tattooed rebel boy and the closest thing to a friend I've got—stops on the sidewalk, brow quirked as he takes in my fighting stance. At first glance, you'd think he fits right into the world of wealth and privilege inside these halls. Designer shades perch on top of his longish blond hair, his dress shirt probably costs more than all the clothes I own, and his left hand rests casually in the pocket of his Diesel jeans.

A critical eye picks up all the things you don't see when you skim over him, assuming he fits in. Above the collar of his expensive shirt, his neck is tatted right up to the chin. The hand hidden in his pocket it tattooed as well, the ink covering burn scars that stretch across his hand and over his wrist to his forearm. A finger is missing. The first two fingers on his right hand are tinged with tobacco stains.

"Fuck," I snap when I see his slightly amused smirk. "If you want to walk away with your balls intact, don't sneak up on a girl like that."

"Care for company?" he drawls in that refined Southern accent that's so posh you'd think he stepped out of an Antebellum movie. Colt talks slow, strolls slow as he moves toward me, brow raised with bored indifference. But under the carefully cultivated blasé exterior, I know he cares about something. I'm just not sure that it's me.

"What you got in mind?" I ask, dropping my fists and tossing my hair back. I stare him square in the eye, daring him to say something about the video the Dolces released.

"I said I'd give you some clothes," he says, letting his gaze do a lazy sweep over me. "You can come to my house, and I'll give you a makeover."

I can't help but laugh at the image of bad boy, fighting-ring coordinator Dynamo giving me a makeover like some chick in a bad 90s movie. "Are we going to braid each other's hair, too?" I ask. "And paint our nails?"

"Maybe," he says with a little shrug, cracking a smile back at me. "Do we get to have a naked pillow fight?"

"I don't think pillow fights happen while naked," I point out. "Too much would be flopping around."

"I feel like I should be offended," he says. "But I'll settle for underwear and a T-shirt, no bra."

I gesture to my chest. "Again, flopping."

"Those tiny things won't flop," he says. "They bounce. I'll show you."

"No promises."

"Then you can't braid my hair," he says, shaking his head solemnly.

"A real tragedy."

Low, distant thunder sounds somewhere in the distance, and Colt jerks his chin toward the parking lot. "So, how 'bout it, Appleteeny? You coming over? My parents aren't home."

He wiggles his brows, as if this should entice me. Sometimes I forget people have functioning parents and actually worry about that stuff. I only care about my mom being home if she and one of her tweaker boyfriends are going to be banging the headboard against the wall. But then, it's not like I ever bring friends over, anyway.

I take one more look at the building and then turn away, tucking my thumbs into the straps on my backpack. It was one thing to walk back in after blowing Royal. Yeah, the Dolces made sure everyone saw them drag me down there, so I'd be publicly humiliated when I walked out. They wanted the audience, either to show me that no one would stop them or to show everyone else that no one is exempt from the royal treatment, as Duke called it. Even so, if half of what I've heard is to be believed, just about every girl at Willow Heights has had a Dolce dick in her mouth at some point. Hell, most of girls would drop to their knees and open wide if they got the chance to do it again.

But walking into a school where everyone has seen me sucking gross old, wrinkled dick? That's different. There's no way I'll ever be invisible now. This week has proven it. I'll always be the school slut, the scandal, a disgusting freak. It's a weird sex thing, so everyone's obsessively fascinated with it. It's a miracle I lasted until Friday, since the video got leaked on Tuesday.

No, it didn't *get leaked*. That makes it sound like no one is responsible.

The Dolces leaked it. On purpose.

By the time we reach the parking lot, I'm pissed again. Fat, cold drops of rain begin to pelt our shoulders as we hurry across.

"Hey, hold up," I say, grabbing Colt's elbow. I pluck the keys from his hand and make a little detour toward the primo parking spots at the very front of the lot where three black cars sit—a sleek little Tesla, a Range Rover, and a giant Hummer that I'd say was compensating for something if I hadn't already seen Duke's dick and could testify that he has nothing to compensate for.

"What the—" Colt protests, but I'm already winding one of the keys off his ring. I take the path between the Rover and the Tesla, a reckless thrill rising in my chest as I dig the keys into the paint on either side of me and stride down the length of the cars. I close my eyes for a second, holding onto the sheer satisfaction of the moment. That's some ASMR level shit right there.

I step past the cars, wind the extra key back onto Colt's keyring, and toss them back to him.

"Whoops," I say, a spring in my step that wasn't there a minute ago. I hop up into Colt's Denali, barely registering the cold drops of rain running down my scalp, and toss my bag onto the back seat.

"You're fucking crazy, Teeny," he says, hopping up in the driver's side. The wipers go on, and my heart does a little skip when I see someone standing outside the school. But it's just someone buzzing in late, not a Dolce coming to murder me.

I turn on the radio, spinning the dial until I hear the aptly timed "November Rain." I turn it up, but Colt jabs the button, shutting it off altogether. He frowns at me, resting one arm along the steering wheel. "Harper, the Dolces are dangerous. Not in some cute way that's a game."

"You think I don't know that?" I ask, glaring back at him. "What am I supposed to do, Colt? Get on my knees and blow them every time they ask? Roll over and die? Look at me. I have nothing. I *am* nothing. I fight dirty not because it's the only way to win, but because it's the only way I can fight back, period."

"You can't fight them," he says quietly. "Believe me, I know. You're one girl. They took down my whole family—the most powerful family in town. And it wasn't a small family, either. What do you think they'll do to one person?"

"Here's the thing, though," I say. "You think I'm playing to win. I don't care about winning. I care about surviving."

"If you know you'll lose either way, why make it worse on yourself by retaliating?" he asks. "If you do what they want, yeah, they'll have their fun with you, but they'll get bored if you don't fight back, and they'll leave you alone."

"Like you?" I ask.

He just stares at me, his jaw hard, his lips sealed.

SELENA

"After they took everything from you, they left you alone," I say. "After they took your football career, your finger, your girlfriend, your friends…"

"I'm still here, aren't I?" His voice is hard, and I know I'm pissing him off.

"Tell me it's worth it."

We stare at each other a long moment, and then he shifts into drive, and we leave the parking lot, the wipers sluicing water from the windshield with each stroke.

"You're making it worse for yourself," he says after a minute.

"And you're making it too easy for them," I say. "If they're going to kill me either way, why not give them a taste of their own poison before I go?"

He shakes his head and doesn't say anything. I turn the radio back on, turning it up and singing along. After a few lines, Colt shakes his head and grins at my antics. Then, he joins in, belting out the dramatic anthem with me. A swell of exhilaration builds inside me as we share this moment, even though I know he's right. They're going to make me pay for that. But why shouldn't I make them pay for what they did to me? They deserve it. I'm not just getting revenge for me. I'm getting it for Gloria, her sisters, Quinn, and all the other girls they've hurt.

Right now, I don't want to think about the consequences. I don't want to think about anything. I want to do what I did on Halloween night, when I drove away from a party with Royal. I understand my mother too well in this moment.

I understand the siren song of a bottle, like standing on the edge of a cliff and suddenly being filled with a rush of daring, an irresistible urge to leap. I know giving in would leave me right where Mom is, stuck in this hellhole town with a kid she doesn't want. But god, what I wouldn't give to get high as a kite and fuck my brains out just to forget for a moment, an hour, a day, with a boy who doesn't matter.

We drive north out of town, further than the Dolces' neighborhood, down a winding two-lane road and then a section of gravel, until at last we pull up in a gravel parking area beside a house. I can see the back deck from here, complete with what looks like an outdoor bar, and the front porch. As we stare out the windshield into the rain, a weird feeling of *déjà vous* runs through me like a shiver.

"We can sit here until the rain lets up," Colt says. "I can think of a few ways to occupy our time."

"Like smoking a joint?"

"Sure," he says, lifting his hips to dig in his jeans pocket, which leave me staring right at his crotch. "Or you could give me a BJ."

I glare at him. I heard that shit all week, an incessant, exhausting parade of guys leering at me and asking for head. "Please tell me this has nothing to do with that video."

"Oh, I saw the video," he says. "Everyone saw the video, Teeny. But nah. I wanted you to suck my dick way before I saw that."

I shake my head, but I can't help but smile. Gotta love the honesty.

He lights a one-hitter and inhales before handing it to me. "Smoke up," he says, a cloud billowing out of his mouth as he speaks. "Maybe you'll get horny and change your mind."

"Never gonna happen," I say, taking a hit and passing it back.

He reloads, and we smoke in companionable silence for a while. It's still raining when we step out, but we're too stoned to care much about the icy drops streaking down from the grey sky. I grab my bag, and we run across the gravel onto the front porch, where Colt unlocks the door and pulls me inside. We're both breathless and laughing a little, and Colt's sparkling blue eyes are so damn inviting, I want to jump in. I want to be my mother, do something stupid, something easy and uncomplicated, something that would mean nothing to either of us.

"Come on," Colt says, taking my hand and tugging me up the stairs. "I'll show you my sister's stuff. You can take whatever you want."

The house is big and a hell of a lot newer than mine, but it's not outrageous, like something out of a TV show about celebrities flaunting their wealth.

"Are you sure she won't mind you giving away her clothes?" I ask as we reach the top of the stairs.

"She never comes home," he says, opening a door and pulling me inside the bedroom. It has a sterile smell, like no one has been in here for months. It looks like a guest room, with everything tidy and unused. There's no bulletin board with pictures of Mabel Darling and her friends and family, no trophies or awards, though Dixie told me she was smart and involved in a lot of school activities. A digital picture frame lays flat on the dresser, as if it were taken down before the batteries even went dead. No posters of movies stars or athletes or *Just 5 Guys* adorn the walls. It looks like the room of a girl who left, never planning to return.

"I'm sorry," I say to Colt, but he's already strode past me into the room. He throws open the double doors of the closet, and my first thought is a less than grateful one—why the fuck would he think I want these clothes?

It's not that they aren't new or nice, it's that they aren't *me*.

But then, I guess that's the point. I don't fit in at Willow Heights. He's trying to help me. This is why he called it a makeover. He's not just giving me some new clothes that I'd choose for myself. He's giving me a new look, the chance to start over. To be a girl who doesn't give old men blowjobs in the back of cars.

The clothes hang in neatly organized, color-coded order. I think of my own dresser with the drawers pulled out at odd angles, t-shirts spilling from them; my closet with shirts hanging halfway off the hangers and old shoes kicked into the back corner to hide my stash of money.

I reach for the pants section, which contains several pairs of white pants, a handful of khakis, then a few tan, two shades of brown, a handful of navy, and a handful of black. Talk about a wardrobe of neutrals—or zero personality. Pulling out a pair of khakis, I hold them up against me and fight back the urge to laugh. Either these clothes are from a long-ass time ago, or Mabel Darling is built like a child. There's no way my fat ass is fitting into these.

I put the khakis back and pull out a pair of black pants. Same straight cut.

"I don't think these are going to fit me," I admit. "Your sister was a lot thinner than I am."

"She did like to complain about her lack of ass," Colt muses. "And you've got that in spades. But I bet something in there will fit you. Try a top."

He reaches past me, his other hand resting on my lower back, his body brushing against mine as he stretches an arm in to grab a shirt. I startle at the contact, and he chuckles before holding the shirt up against my front, still standing so close I can feel the heat of his body all up my back. It doesn't make me crazy the way Royal's touch does, but it's not unwelcome, either. I like Colt, maybe not the way I like Royal, but he's sexy and easy and I don't feel like I'm drowning every time he's near me. It's nice to feel wanted, to feel sexy, instead of being told I'm a worthless whore by the guy touching me.

I take the shirt from his hand and step over to the mirror, holding it up and ignoring what he just did. My head is foggy from the pot, and I know I'm making terrible decisions today, but I can't seem to stop. From leaving school, to keying the Dolces' cars, to being here alone with a boy I hardly know… I'm on a real fucking roll today.

"Maybe," I say doubtfully. Not because it won't fit—I have no tits to speak of, so that's not a problem—but because it looks like the exact opposite of something I'd wear. She's got a few more colors of shirts to choose from—pastels as well as the neutral colors of her pants—but they're all button-up dress shirts, with a few simple blouses at the end.

"Try it on," Colt says, grinning at me.

"With you here?" I ask, cocking a brow at him.

"Dude, I've seen tits before."

16

"Uh huh."

"Seriously," he says. "We used to be just like the Dolces. I've seen about ninety percent of the tits in the senior class."

I bite back a smile. "I'm not in the senior class."

"I've seen ninety percent of the junior tits, too," he says. "Trust me, Teeny, yours are hardly something to write home about."

"Doesn't mean I want to show them to you."

"You're wearing a bra, aren't you? It's no different from me seeing you in a swimsuit. I'll even sit on the bed like a good boy if you're afraid I can't keep my hands to myself. You need a second opinion on what looks good, anyway."

I glare at him until he goes over to the bed and flops down with a grin, tucking his hands behind his head. "Showtime, baby," he says, adjusting his hips on the bed like he wants to make sure I notice he has a hard-on.

"I'm not hooking up with you," I say, swallowing and tearing my eyes away from his groin.

"Okay," he says, a smug grin on his face.

"I mean it," I warn. "If that's why you brought me here, just take me back to school and forget it."

"I know you've got a lady boner for Royal Dickwad," he says. "But he got what he wanted from you, and now you're fair game for everyone else."

"Way to make a girl feel special," I say, rolling my eyes.

I turn away and peel off my shirt, dropping it on the floor, keeping my back to Colt. The truth is, I don't want to be special to Colt. That wouldn't be fair. I like him, but not that way, and if he liked me that way, things would be awkward. I don't want to hurt him. I like that his feelings don't go deeper than friendship and lust.

"You've got more ink than I realized."

"Yep," I say, pulling my hair over my shoulder and turning the other way to show Colt the ink running up my side and onto my back, over my shoulder blade and shoulder. I flash him a smile over my shoulder, and he moans and grabs his dick.

"Fuck, Teeny, you're such a tease."

"I told you up front there would be no sex," I say. "You're the one who wanted to watch me undress."

"I can't decide if the torture is worth it."

"Oh, it's worth it," I say, smiling where he can't see it this time. I pull on a shirt from Mabel's closet and start buttoning it.

"Hey, I'm just saying," Colt drawls. "I'm at your service in case that weed made you horny, Queen Teeny. Teeny Queenie? I'll have to think on that one."

"You're so fucking high right now," I say, laughing as I reach for the skirt section, since they're a little more forgiving than pants.

"Want to know the name of Royal's oldest brother?" he asks. "King. His name is fucking King."

I snort at that. "Seriously? Their family sure thought highly of their sons. Probably sucked being the only girl in that family. Surprised she wasn't named Queen or Princess or something equally unfortunate."

I find a skirt, undo my jeans, and slip out of them. Colt groans behind me. I bite my lip to keep from smiling. I'm not the type to usually care what guys think of me one way or another—I'm not dressing for them. But it's still flattering when one does notice me or thinks I'm hot, especially when he looks like Colt Darling.

When I turn back around, he grins and runs a finger slowly along the ridge in his pants. "Wanna ride, cowgirl?"

I smile back and spread my arms wide. "Do I look like your sister?"

"Dude, that's so wrong," he says, squeezing his eyes shut and pressing his palms into them. "You legit just killed my boner. It's dying as we speak. A slow and painful death, I might add."

"It's your own fault. It was your idea to watch. I tried to warn you. You brought this on yourself, *cowboy*."

He mimes plunging a knife into his chest and twisting. "Does your cruelty know no bounds?" he asks dramatically, throwing an arm over his eyes.

I can't help but laugh. "I'm going to try on a few more if that's okay. You can go in the other room if it's too much."

"Can I jerk off it's too much?"

I sink onto the bed beside him and pull my knee up. "Colt…"

He stares at my knee, then sits up and grabs my leg, pulling it up onto the bed. "God Lord, woman, don't you ever shave your legs?" he asks, running his hand along the bristles on my shin.

"It's winter," I protest, slapping his hand away. "And I've had a lot of shit going on this week. Keeping my legs silky smooth was near the bottom of my list of priorities."

"Okay, Sasquatch," he says, giving me a little shove. "Go get some more clothes. If I start popping a boner, I'll just picture the natural disaster that's probably growing on your Congo Basin right now, and I'll be fine."

I'm laughing too hard to be embarrassed as I step back into Mabel's closet, ready to unearth some skeletons. Colt is already giving me so much, but I can't walk away without getting what I can from him. He's one of the only people I know who was there the whole time, when it all went down, after the Dolces arrived in Faulkner. He knows shit, insider information that might be exactly what Mr. D needs to take down the Dolces. And it's not just Mr. D who wants to take them down. For a while, I was torn, feeling like a snitch for airing their dirty laundry to whoever is on the other end of the messenger app. I don't feel guilty anymore.

Whoever Mr. D is, I'm with him one hundred percent. It's time for the Dolces to taste their own medicine.

*

The Royal

The royal waits
Atop his throne
For his Brutus to show his face
For his court to turn their daggers on him
But he is not afraid
Neither they nor their daggers
Can defeat the monster
That lurks under his disguise
Or pierce a heart
That's harder than their steel blades.

two

Harper Apple

"So, where is your sister, anyway?" I ask as I rifle through the clothes in search of something else that will fit my curves.

"I dunno," Colt says, his voice serious as he lays back on the pillows again, an arm folded behind his head. "She changed her name and disappeared after graduation last year."

I wonder if this is the first time anyone's been in her room since then. If, for six months, no one's even stepped into the room to think of her and wonder where she is. For some reason, it makes me sad, though I'm sure the second I'm gone, Mom will put a pool table in my room and convert it into a bar. I don't care. It won't be my room anymore. It'll be just a thing.

But somehow, the emptiness of Mabel's room feels forlorn.

"She didn't tell you where she was going?"

"Nah," Colt says. "We weren't close. She hated being a Darling, and I was wrapped up in it. I cared about my image, about how the town saw me. She hated that."

"She sounds cool to me," I say, setting aside another shirt that fits.

"Mabel's my half-sister, same dad. Dev was my half-brother, same mom. I was always closer to him and Preston than her, even though we were raised together. Everything's just easier for guys, I guess. The town loved us. We were the golden boys."

He sounds wistful, and my heart aches for him. In a small town like this, there are plenty of washed-up old football dads who still talk about high school as the glory days. But Colt isn't even out of high school. The best years of his life shouldn't be behind him.

"Your sister wasn't a golden girl?" I ask, unsure if I should be ransacking the closet of a girl who blew away like a ghost.

"Nah," he says. "She probably could have been. Preston's sister is royalty at Faulkner High. But she didn't want any part of it. The Darlings were the backbone of Faulkner, and she hated this town more than anyone you've ever met."

"I wouldn't count on that," I mutter as I pull on a pair of linen pants with a drawstring that actually kinda fit.

"Even before the Dolces, she couldn't stand it," Colt goes on. "To her, the Darling name was a trap. And once the Dolces got started, she found out just how right she was."

"They targeted her just because of a name she didn't even want?"

"That's the fucked up part," he says. "They didn't care what kind of person you were. Mabel didn't even want to *be* a Darling. She probably would have helped them take down our grandpa if they'd let her. But no. If you were a Darling, they had to make sure you wished you were dead before they were through with you."

I let out a low whistle. "Damn. That bad, huh?"

I try to imagine a skinny, nerdy, female version of tatted up, smooth-talking Dynamo, but I can't picture her. All I see is a faceless cutout of a girl who hated her name so bad she changed it on her way out of town, never looking back at the hellhole she was leaving behind. Though I've never met her, I feel a strange kinship toward her, and instinct tells me that's exactly how she'd want me to imagine her.

Poverty's not the only trap in this town.

"I sound like a broken record warning you about them over and over," Colt says, flexing his scarred hand in the air above his face as he talks. "But yeah, they're that bad. They tortured her, physically and mentally, until she snapped."

I've always liked figuring people out, seeing what makes them tick, and yes, what makes them snap. It's not just morbid curiosity. Growing up, it was survival.

It was knowing that Safe Mom was the obnoxiously affectionate drunk who came home at two in the morning breathing her vodka fumes in my face as she insisted on snuggles that invariably led to her falling asleep on my twin bed, leaving me pressed against the cold wall and unable to pull the blanket around me because she was lying on top of it.

Unsafe Mom was the cruel dragon who woke in the morning breathing flames of hatred, reminding me that I ruined her life, so I owed her some goddamn respect, and if I didn't figure out real fucking fast exactly what she meant by that, I'd get my fingers smashed with a pan or my knuckles whacked with a wooden spoon or spend the day locked in a closet to think about it.

"Snapped… How?" I ask, my voice barely more than a whisper. I could have asked what they did to her, but I won't make him say those things aloud. Even if they weren't close, she was his sister. And last night I woke in a cold sweat, the fear holding me so tight I couldn't move, the ache of the hard stone floor under my bare knees so real I couldn't breathe. I know what they did to her.

I just don't know what comes next.

"I wasn't there," Colt says. "I guess no one really knows but her and Royal."

Suddenly, I wish I'd never asked. There comes a point where the desire to figure someone out becomes just plain masochistic.

Even though I recognize that I've reached that point, I also know I'm not a dumb bitch who walks away from answers because ignorance is bliss. Yeah, the truth fucking hurts. I'm a big girl. I can take it. I'd rather take the pain than sit in the dark like a dumbass because I'm too afraid to turn on the light and see the monster under the bed.

"It was Royal," I say flatly, yanking my jeans back on. "Not the twins."

Colt sits up on the bed, swinging his legs off the side. "I only know what she said, but by then, they'd fucked her up so bad I don't know if she knew what was real and what wasn't. And it doesn't make sense to me, after all they did to her, that Royal pulled her out."

"Pulled her out?"

"She said she jumped in the river, and he pulled her out," he says. "But he said he didn't."

"What does he say happened?"

Colt chuckles darkly. "Have you ever tried to get a straight answer about anything out of Royal Dolce?"

"Fair point," I admit.

"He's never going to lay it all out there for you," Colt says, turning on his side and patting the bed in front of him. "But I will. Story time and cuddling at *mi casa* any time, babe. What do you say?"

"I say that offer's hard to resist."

When I sit down on the bed beside him, he gets up onto his knees and pulls me onto the bed fully, arranging my legs and stuffing a pillow under my head before sliding down beside me. He props himself on an elbow and grins down at me, and my heart fucking breaks a little. This is the kind of boy I should be with, the kind every girl wants, who could give a girl the world.

But it's not my world.

"Colt," I say, my voice low with warning.

He traces his fingers in a slow circle on my belly. "Yeah, Teeny?"

"I'm still not fucking you."

"How do you feel about hand jobs?"

I laugh and shake my head. "I feel like you're shameless as fuck, that's for sure."

"Come on, baby," he says, pushing his erection against my hip. "I'm dying here."

My thighs clench the way they always do when I feel a hard dick. Maybe I'm the whore everyone says I am, my mother's daughter through and through. Or maybe it's just that I'm still relatively inexperienced, and I've felt few enough penises for it to be purely sexual when I do.

Colt takes my indecision for an opening and leans down and kisses me. His lips are warm and soft and inviting. Kissing him feels good, just like his arousal feels good. I like Colt, and I'd like to keep being his friend, and I don't want to damage his pride by outright shooting him down, especially right in the middle of his act of kindness. But just because he was nice to me, that doesn't mean I owe him access to my body.

Still. I'm not kissing him because I owe him or because he gave me nice clothes. I like kissing him. It's nice to be treated the way he treats me. Not like someone he cares about, but like I'm an equal, like we'd be cool to hang out again. It wouldn't be awkward, and he wouldn't spread rumors about me. We'd smoke a joint and maybe hook up again sometime if the time was right and we had nothing better to do. If one of us brought another guy or girl around, the other would respect that and be cool and not cause drama.

But I've been down that road. I've got the ink to prove it.

I push him away gently, almost reluctantly. Because I'm not my mother. I'm too smart to make the same mistakes I've made before. I don't regret Maverick, but I don't want a repeat, either. That's not my style anymore.

"Colt…"

"Come on, Teeny," he says, nuzzling my neck. He pulls my body toward him, pushing his thigh between my legs. "I'm so hard it hurts. My sister disappeared, too. Doesn't that warrant a pity fuck?"

"You think I respect myself so little I'd trade my body for some old clothes?"

"They're Ralph Lauren," he says, rocking his hips against mine, his fingers hooked through my belt loop. I laugh, and he grins and nips my earlobe. "The sheets are, too. Let's get under the covers and you can feel them for yourself."

"We're in your sister's room."

"We can go to my room," he says, still grinding against me. "Just let me put it in. Hell, just slide that pussy down over the head, and I'll cum."

"Wow, you're really selling this," I say, but my voice comes a little breathy. He's pushing against me in all the right ways. I wonder if it would be as good as Maverick. I wonder if his dick would be as magnificent as Royal's. And most of all, I wonder how much it would piss off Royal. Would he even care? He told me he didn't want me talking to Colt. Would he lose his shit if he saw me right now, with Colt between my legs, grinding his cock against me? Or is he afraid of what Colt will tell me, how much he knows, things Royal doesn't want me to find out?

Maybe that's all he cares about. He said he didn't want me talking to other guys, but he's ignored me since the video leaked and he choked me out in the hall and basically told me I could never trust him. He played me even after I obeyed. He had ammunition, and he was going to use it either way. Getting me to kneel and suck his dick was just a bonus to make the pot that much sweeter when he defeated me.

But I'm not defeated.

He may have won the battle, he may be done with me, but I'm not done with him.

"I'm so close," Colt says, grinding his hardness between my thighs. He rolls us over so I'm straddling his hips. He grips my hips and thrusts up hard against me, his head dropping back and his eyes squeezing closed. "Tell me how wet your pussy is, baby."

I feel guilty for what I'm doing, but the poor guy's worked himself up into a tizzy, so I give him what he wants. I mean, I'd be lying if I said having him grind against my clit for ten minutes didn't feel good. But I'm nowhere close to where he is. "I'm so wet," I say, making my voice all breathy for him and rocking my hips over his length. "But you feel so big, I don't think you'd fit."

Bingo.

He grabs my ass with both hands, his hips jerking under mine, his teeth biting down on his lower lip as his eyes screw tightly closed. Watching a guy cum always makes me feel slightly powerful, but also oddly detached, like it wasn't really my doing at all. I'm not part of this orgasm, after all. I've actually never been part of the orgasm. But I enjoy the part before it, and I enjoy the sense of accomplishment when he gets there, like I've done my job.

I wonder if that's how Royal feels. Maybe he never cums because he can't, either. But I seriously doubt it. I get the feeling it's more about him being a control freak. He wants to control everyone and everything, right down to his own body.

And it's not like I *can't* orgasm. Guys just generally don't try because they're too busy chasing their own orgasm, or they think it's too much work. To his credit, Mav did try, but I got bored of him trying to figure it out and faked it once, and then he thought that move did the trick, and he kept doing it every time. So, I kept faking it. It was easier just to let him get his and take care of myself afterwards. Plus, it was cute how proud of himself he was.

"Fuck me, that was hot," Colt groans, rolling us over so he's on top of me. "You made me make a mess of myself."

"I think you did that all on your own."

"I had help," he says, moving his hips in a slow circle so I can feel he's still got a semi. "Want me to eat you out? I've been told I'm good at it."

"I'm good," I say quickly, not really wanting to go into the whole explanation of how that feels more personal to me than sex, and I don't want just any rando's face down there, getting up close and personal with my snatch.

"Oh, yeah, you've got a jungle situation going," Colt says. "Hey, I've got a razor you can borrow. What do you say we take this to the shower and clean up, and then I'll return the favor when you're done clearcutting?"

"We're really sticking with this metaphor?" I ask, pushing him off. "And I'm good. Really. I already came. Before you."

Colt narrows his eyes and gives me a look that says he knows I'm full of shit, but he doesn't push it. He shrugs and hops up, adjusting his jeans. "Well, I'm going to get myself cleaned up.

Grab the clothes you want and wait for me in the kitchen, okay? I'll make us some lunch."

My jeans are still dry, thanks to the position we were in when he came, so I stuff as many clothes as will fit into my backpack and head downstairs. It seems a little weird that he didn't have me wait in his room, but whatever. Maybe the guy's private, or maybe he only lets girls go in his room if he's fucking them. He did offer to take me there to fuck, after all. Still, almost as soon as I step into the kitchen, I hear tires on the gravel outside, and I wish I'd asked to wait in his room. Though I don't know the house well enough to know where his parents will go when they come in, I have the absurd urge to run and hide nonetheless.

I'm not the kind of girl that guys bring home to meet their moms. I'm the kind they take all the way out of town and park beside bridges with. The kind who gives blowjobs in cars down by the tracks behind the tampon factory. I don't usually have to hide because guys hide *me*. And that's fine by me. It's a small town, and people gossip, and I don't want to be the subject of it any more than they want the town knowing they're slumming it with a girl like me.

SELENA

A broad-shouldered man gets out of the SUV that just pulled up. He takes a leather briefcase out of the car with one hand and grips a cane in the other as he starts across the gravel. He looks too young to walk with a cane, his hair still mostly dark blond, his solid frame clad a suit like he's working a good job and not retired.

My mind races with excuses for why I'm here, for why Colt is home in the middle of the day. I haven't come up with one when the guy lets himself in. I pray he'll go into a study or something, but he comes right into the big, fancy kitchen instead.

He sets his bag on the island and shrugs out of his sports coat, watching me like I'm supposed to say something.

"Um, hi," I say at last, hooking my thumbs into my jeans pockets. "Mr. Darling?"

My mind flashes to the texting app that led me to this moment. Is this Mr. D? There are a lot of Darlings in this town. How would I know which one has been texting me? Does he look like the kind of guy who pervs on teenage girls online?

"Yeah, that's me," he says, giving me a halfhearted smile. His eyes are like Colt's—cool, blue, guarded. "Guess you're a better reason than some for him to be skipping school."

"Oh—Colt's upstairs," I say, as if that explains anything. "We were just about to have lunch."

"Lunch, huh?" He says the words like they're a code for sex. I'm tempted to sniff the air and see if I somehow filled the room with the scent of what we've been doing. Or maybe I'm reading too much into it because I have a guilty conscience, or too much experience with grown-ass men who just screwed my mom all night leering at my legs as I race from my room to the bathroom in the morning.

He could totally be the perv. Yeah, he looks normal, but what do I know about the guy? He's got money—maybe not an ungodly amount, but enough to float an extra scholarship at WHPA. Beyond that, I know what car he drives, that he walks with a cane because of some injury or disability and not age, that his daughter disowned his family, and that his son is beautiful and broken and fun and wonderful.

"Hey, Pops," Colt says, strolling into the kitchen with a towel still hanging around his neck. His blond hair clings to his ears and neck, and his tats are on full display below the sleeves of a plain white tee, which he wears with a pair of low-slung Levi's and…

"Are those… Cowboy boots?" I ask.

He gives me an aw-shucks grin and leans an elbow on the island, tipping an imaginary hat. "Why, yes, ma'am, they sure are," he says, laying the accent on thick.

I shake my head at him. "Well, who woulda thunk it," I say, exaggerating my accent, too. "Our tatted up rebel boy is a goat wrangler at heart."

He grins and pushes off the counter. "Guess y'all met," he says, grabbing bread and sandwich stuff out of the fridge.

"Not officially," Mr. Darling says, reaching out a hand. I swallow hard, trying not to be sick when I take his hand and shake. He's missing a finger, too.

three

Royal Dolce

"Dude, she's not here today," Duke says, elbowing my arm and making me drop my sandwich, which falls all to pieces on my plate.

"What the fuck," I say, pushing back from the table.

"Want me to get you another sandwich?" asks the freshman girl who brought my first one.

"Sure, whatever," I say, barely sparing her a glance before she scurries off to serve me like I'm a fucking king. I don't even remember her name. I never cared about any of them. Baron chooses the girls. I'm sure my brothers will fuck her if they haven't already. She's pretty and blond and wears no makeup, but I wouldn't care if she was a fucking Kardashian.

I glower at the empty chair at the table where the nosy bitches sit. If she's out talking to Colt under the bleachers again…

"You hitting that on the DL or what?" Cotton asks.

I turn to him, satisfied by the way he stiffens, even though he pretends he's not afraid of me. "Who?"

"You're not exactly being subtle," Gloria says. "You've been glaring at her table like you want to murder the whole lot of them for the entire lunch break."

Everyone else at the table stops to listen. I'm so fucking sick of them all watching, waiting, like they're just here to see what I'll do next. Waiting for me to snap. I'm sick of being the boy who was kidnapped, the boy who might castrate you if you cross him. The boy who killed his sister. Everyone has an opinion. Like Baron says, you can't stop them from talking. You can only turn the conversation in your favor, if you're clever.

"Well, where the fuck is she?" I demand of Lo, as if it's her fault that Harper isn't here. As if she's the one who made sure Harper would never feel anything but hate for me again, and not the girl who went to check on her for me when I couldn't do it without ruining everything.

"The real question is, why does it matter?" Baron asks.

"Yeah," DeShaun says. "You do you, man, but don't leave us in the dark."

Right. They're all looking to me, waiting for me to put in the final word on Harper. They've been waiting all week for their QB1 to call the play. If I say she's off limits, no one will lay a finger on her. If I say she's the enemy, they'll destroy her. If I say she's cancelled, no one will ever speak to her again.

It's fucking ridiculous. Sometimes I want to tell them all to jump off the bridge just to see if they're really a bunch of fucking lemmings.

But they're my boys, and I'm being an asshole. I need to give them something.

I did what I did, and I can't be sorry about it. If I didn't make her hate me, I'd be tempted to do something I can never do, or never undo, I'm not sure which. Maybe both. When she's in my head, nothing makes sense. All I know is that I had to get her out of there, and if I couldn't, I had to make her hate me enough to take herself out of the picture.

"She's done," I say. "We're done with her. She's nothing."

"Then you won't care about this," Lo says, sliding her phone across the table to me.

On the screen is one of the social media accounts of the meddling, Darling-worshipping bitch Dixie Powell. Not her blog, but *Rumor Has It*, one where she posts little gossipy tidbits throughout the day for vultures like the Waltons to pick up and spread like a disease. If Baron didn't remind me on a regular basis of her usefulness as an instrument that helps us stay where we are, I would destroy her life with more enjoyment than I would a Darling. I fucking hate Dixie and everything she stands for.

Rumor Has It… a notorious loner boy and a girl who's gained sudden notoriety this week were seen leaving campus together before school. Have these two lonely souls found a friend in each other, or is it something more?

My blood boils as I read the post. It was posted only two minutes ago, but I see people bent over their phones, eating up her gossip like it's ice cream and not dog shit. I see her basking in the glow of admiration at her table, eating that shit up as eagerly as everyone around her is eating up her idiotic, uncreative words.

In a few weeks, no one will care what Harper's doing. But this week, she's in the spotlight, and Dixie'd be damned before she'd miss out on an opportunity to insert herself in the drama. She's a master at grabbing the headlines, keeping her finger on the pulse of the school, and using it to her advantage. The only person better at it than Dixie Powell is my brother.

That's not why I hate her, though. I hate her because she inserted herself into my family's life, because she used her friendship with Crystal to her advantage. I hate her because she encouraged my sister to pursue things with a Darling, because she helped her sneak around, and then my sister ended up dead while Dixie played the grieving best friend. I hate her because she used the sympathy to build a platform for herself, because she is now popular by association with the tragedy that is my fucking family.

And I hate her because she'd sell out the guy she supposedly loves and the girl whose empty chair is two spots down at her own table just for five minutes of attention.

When she gets up to go to her Friday meeting, I follow. She's scurrying down the hall when I step out of the café, but my stride is twice as long as hers, and it takes me no time to catch up to her. I grab her shoulder and spin her around, slamming her up against the lockers.

Her eyes widen, darting around as she licks her lips, and for a second, she looks like that freckly little freshman I dismissed as harmless back then. I should have seen her for the snake she is. "Hey, Royal," she says, a tremor in her voice.

I brace my hands on the locker on either side of her, caging her in. "Where'd you get that bullshit you just posted?"

"It's not bullshit," she says. "And I can't reveal my sources. People would stop coming to me with information if I ratted them out."

Footsteps echo in the hall behind me. I don't have to turn to know who followed.

"You are a rat. You've built your little empire of shit on it." I speak slowly, so her little brain can comprehend. "You can cover it with glitter and call yourself a gossip girl, but it's still shit, and you're still a rat. So spill it or admit you fabricated the whole thing to get attention."

"I didn't make it up," she insists, her eyes widening when she takes in my posse behind me. They're not all here, but enough of them followed me to threaten her reputation if I say something in front of them.

I know I've got her. I have more power in this school than she does, though I'm a monster partly of her making. But she knows I can destroy her with a single word. I can tell everyone her posts are not authentic, that she's making shit up, and their trust in her will evaporate overnight. At the end of the day, she's more worried about her reputation, about me exposing her as a fraud, than she is about protecting her sources.

"You already know you're going to tell him," Duke says, leaning on the locker beside her with a bored expression on his face.

"Okay, okay," she says, lifting a hand to stop us from going on. "I'll message you his name. I don't want to say it in front of all these people."

I lean down until I'm almost nose to nose with the bitch. I can see her pulse racing on the side of her neck. I want to wrap my hands around and squeeze until her eyes pop out of her head. "Cut the pretense and get it over with before this becomes more unpleasant for both of us. You know your face makes me sick."

"A sophomore coming in late saw them leaving in Colt's Denali," she says in a rush.

"When?"

"Like, five minutes into first period. That's all I know. I swear."

I push away from her, but Baron leans in to have the last word. "You think you're high up on the food chain, but you're a scavenger," he says to her. "You're lucky the ecosystem needs scavengers to survive, or the apex predators would eat your ass for breakfast."

She nods mutely, then scurries off down the hall, glancing back over her shoulder like she thinks we might follow. She should know we don't chase snakes. If we wanted more, we would have gotten it already.

When she's gone, I turn to my crew. "Why the fuck is she with Colt?" I demand.

"Maybe because you were an unforgivable asshole to her, and he's not?" Lo volunteers.

I stare her down until she shrugs and drops her gaze. She's not wrong. That's exactly why. Wasn't that the entire purpose of what we did to her? She needs to know who we are, that she can't fuck with us, that she needs to stay out of our way. But she also needs to obey, and I told her to stay away from Colt Darling.

"Is it just because she's with Colt?" Baron asks, narrowing his eyes at me. "Or because she's with anyone?"

"You just told everyone she was nothing," Duke points out. "I get why you're pissed about Colt, but if she's nothing, you wouldn't care if I fucked her, right?"

I swing around and glare at him. "Don't. Touch. Her."

"Got it," he says. "But you might want to tell the guys because they're all back there talking about running a train on her at the next party."

My fists clench involuntarily, and I glare at my brother. For whatever reason, Harper is my challenge. She fucked with the wrong guy, and now it's personal. Now, it's my job to break her. Maybe I finally did, and she won't come waltzing through the doors on Monday morning like none of it affects her because she's above it all. Maybe she won't walk around all day like she doesn't care that she knelt for me after all that talk about how she never would, like she doesn't care that the whole school knows she's trash who sucks off old guys in shitty cars in parking lots.

But I don't think so. I think she's with Colt because she knows it pisses me off. Because she's showing me that despite what we did, we can never control her. That she'll do whatever the fuck she pleases, no matter what we do to her.

She has no idea what she's asking for.

I could let my brothers at her. Sometimes, they're such psychos that they even scare me. But no. She's not theirs to destroy. Not even my brothers get Harper. They had Mabel. This one is mine. This time, I'll do the dirty work. I'll make her suffer, and I'll savor every moment of it. And when she breaks, when those walls around her shatter like glass, I'll crawl inside and eat out her soul like it can replace the one I lost two years ago.

four

Harper Apple

Colt turns into the small faculty lot and stops beside the bike rack, whistling "Back to Life" under his breath. The rain has let up for the moment, but fat little drops still sprinkle down at random. "Well, this was fun," he says, shutting off the wipers. "Next time you want to make a dude cum in his pants, remember, I'm your guy."

I laugh and grab my backpack off the floorboards. "Thanks for the clothes. And smoking me out, and the sandwich… Damn, I'm starting to think I really do owe you a BJ. At least a hand job."

"I mean… I'm not gonna argue with that logic," he says with a grin.

A car engine roars behind us, and his smile vanishes, replaced with a flash of fear.

SELENA

I twist around to see a black Range Rover barreling toward us.

"Get out," I yell, yanking the handle and literally diving out the door of the car. My backpack spills from my lap, tumbling to a stop against the bars of the bike rack as I somersault across the concrete walkway and I roll up to my feet. I throw my hair out of my eyes just as the Rover slams into the back of Colt's truck without slowing.

A sound escapes me, but it's drowned in the grinding of metal and shattering of glass. The back of Colt's Denali caves in, the wheels askew so he can't drive away. They must have busted the rear axel. Black smoke billows up from the tires, and for one second, I'm reminded of the drag race. But this isn't a race. It's an attack.

I started bringing a knife to school the past few days, but my fists are still my best weapon, so I don't reach for it. I'm more worried about Colt than myself, anyway. I run for the cab of his truck, yanking the passenger door open just as Royal yanks the driver's door open. For one second, our eyes meet, and I see not the dark, dead eyes that meet mine when he's hurting me, but a rage so deep and raw it makes my soul quake.

"Did you fucking touch her?" Royal asks, his voice low and lethal. "Because if you did, I will cut every single one of your fucking fingers off this time."

"She was on her own all week," Colt protests, fighting to free himself from his seatbelt and the airbag, which deployed when he was hit. "I thought you were done with her."

"I decide when I'm done," Royal snarls, ripping Colt out of the car by the front of his shirt and throwing him down. For a second, I can't see anything but the fucking airbag. Heart racing frantically in my chest, I race around the front of Colt's vehicle, cursing these guys with their big-ass trucks that make it so hard to see. When I reach the other side, Colt's on his back, and Royal's on top of him, punching him in the face while Duke and Baron stand back and watch.

"Did you fucking touch her?" Royal demands, his fists landing in quick succession.

"Leave him alone," I scream, diving for them. But Duke cuts me off, grabbing me around the middle and pinning my arms. I stomp his foot, thrashing to free myself. Under Royal, Colt shouts something, but his words are cut short by a chilling crunch as the bones in his face give way. Blood sprays from his nose, flying up to splatter Royal's arms.

Baron strolls over, rocking back on his heels as he watches his brother demolish Colt's face. "See, Cherry Pie," he says, his voice a condescending taunt, as if he's completely unaffected by the brutality unfolding in front of us. "This is what happens when you keep pushing. Eventually, something's gotta give. You don't get to pick what that something is."

"Are you fucking crazy?" I scream. "You're killing him!" I throw my head back, slamming it into Duke's chin. I hear teeth snapping together, and he curses savagely and shoves me forward so hard I fall to my knees.

"Did you fucking touch my girl?" Royal asks Colt, his voice coming in short burst between blows, as if Colt can answer. All I can see where his face used to be is blood. Baron steps in and kicks him while Royal straddles him, his knees trapping Colt's body, his fists raining down on his face. They're going to kill him.

They're going to fucking kill him because I went to his house, because I dared talk to him after they told me not to. And he doesn't deserve any of it.

Baron said something's gotta give, and that something is me. I have no chill. No plan. Only desperation and pure, raw hate. I scramble up from my knees, and this time it's *my* rage that makes my insides quake. A scream burns up through my chest like a fireball, and I dive forward, putting everything I have behind it. My fist connects with the side of Royal's head so hard that blindness sweeps over my vision, and for a second, I don't know what happened. For a second, I think someone hit me.

I fall back, and Royal falls back, and no one moves.

Pain races up my arm, hitting my brain like a brick wall. No one hit me. I just hit him so hard the pain stunned me senseless. My fist is a throbbing bundle of agony.

"Come on," Duke says, grabbing my arm and dragging me to my feet. I start to fight him, but Baron comes up on my other side, and they lift me off my feet and shove me in the back of the Range Rover. I'd have thought they loved their car too much to let trash like me grace the seats, but that seems forgotten. Baron hops up next to me and grabs my knee in a death grip.

"Keep fighting this, and you know what's going to happen to Colt," he says. That's all he has to say. I don't want to lie down and roll over for these assholes, whatever they have in mind. But I also don't want to get my friend murdered, and right now, fighting back looks like a good way to make that happen. At least I can get them away from here, and if he's still alive and his skull isn't crushed into a pulp, he can call for help. I pat my pockets, thinking I can dial 911 on the sly when they drive away, only to realize my phone is still in my backpack, where it's been all day.

Fuck.

I didn't KO Royal, but he must have the headache from hell right now. He doesn't show it, though. He slides into the driver's seat, and Duke runs around the far side and hops in the passenger side.

"Get my bag," I say, lunging for the door. I can't just leave Colt there without even calling for help.

"Don't worry about your bag," Duke says as Royal backs up, metal grinding on metal as the Rover separates from the truck.

"It has my laptop," I say, yanking frantically at the door handle. "It'll get wet."

Baron grabs me around the middle and reaches past me to slam the door, almost smashing my hands when I throw them out to block it. Royal engages the lock, and the handle won't budge. I can't tell them what I'm really after is my phone. They'll think I'm trying call the cops on them instead of an ambulance for Colt.

"Forget your fucking laptop," Royal says. "We'll buy you a new one."

Suddenly, I'm sure he's going to run over Colt's body, which is sprawled on the ground outside the open door of his truck. The cabin light shines dimly inside the truck in the blue evening, spreading just far enough to reflect off the pool of blood spreading across the wet asphalt. I think I'm going to be sick.

I've seen plenty of fights, and I've punched plenty of people, but this wasn't a fight. It was a beating, the kind of thing gangs do to their rivals. There's a reason I stay away from the gangs in Faulkner, despite the protection and community and employment they offer.

I enjoy using my fists as much as the next girl, but for me, it's a sport, a rush, and a payout. It's almost never personal. I don't want to fight someone who threw shade and insulted my pride. Pride is overrated already. I'd rather put food in my mouth. And I don't give a shit about territory or guns or drugs or any of their business operations. Getting out of town is more important.

And unlike these assholes, I don't fight to hurt people. I'm not a sociopath. I don't take pleasure in other people's pain.

As Royal pulls out of the lot and roars off down the road, my stomach begins to settle, and I'm glad I distracted them with babble about my backpack, so they didn't get any ideas about running over Colt's body while he lay there unconscious on the road beside his truck. But now that the shock is wearing off, anger takes its place.

"What the fuck is wrong with you?" I demand. "You could have killed him! You left him in a ditch to die."

"Calm the fuck down," Royal snaps, touching his head with his fingertips. "You gave me a headache, and your screaming isn't helping."

"He won't die," Baron says, patting my knee and then leaving his hand there. "We have an agreement with Colt. He bends over and takes it in the ass like a bitch, and he gets to live. He even gets to stay at Willow Heights. He's got it good. Hell, we didn't even take his letter jacket."

I gape at him, a hysterical laugh bubbling up inside me. They let him keep his fucking letterman jacket? As if that fucking matters after they took his family, his friends, his life away. They think a letter jacket matters to him? These guys aren't just monsters. They're so far removed from humanity they have no idea what they've done to Colt, how their actions affect people.

"What is wrong with y'all?" I ask, my voice laced with disbelief. "What happened to you?"

The wipers go on as drizzle begins to fall, and the only sound in the car is the mechanical swish of them moving back and forth across the windshield. No one says anything for a long minute. I really think about my question, about what I know. Yes, they're rich as sin, but they still have problems. Their dad is maybe in the mafia, no one seems to really know for sure. Their mother abandoned them in some way. Their sister died.

But is it enough to explain this?

Most of the kids at Faulkner had stories like that. None of my friends had two biological parents. The only people I knew who had good families, at least from the outside, were people in my periphery, the upper echelon of Faulkner's social order, like Lindsey Darling or even Maisy Gunn. And no one at FHS was like this.

"You don't get to ask questions," Royal says, breaking the heavy silence in his low, accented voice that reminds me all over again that there is so much about this family I don't know, that I can't begin to understand. "You answer questions. This shit doesn't go both ways. Got it?"

"Got it," I grit out. "Let me guess. Next thing, you're going to tell me women should be seen and not heard?"

"No," Royal says, pulling up to a red light. "I want to hear what you have to say for yourself. Why were you with Colt Darling after I specifically told you not to talk to him?"

"What are you so afraid of?" I ask. "That he spilled all your dirty little secrets?"

"No questions," Royal reminds me.

"Fine," I say, sitting back and crossing my arms. "I was with him because he's my friend. I didn't know that carried a death sentence."

"I warned you to leave that guy alone," Royal says flatly. "You disobeyed."

"Yeah," Duke says, twisting around in the seat with a gleeful smile as we slide through the wet streets of Faulkner. "We told you what would happen if you talked to him, and you talked to him. So, this happened. We can't just let you get away with it."

"Because then someone else might dare disobey the kings?" I taunt.

"Exactly," Baron says, squeezing my knee. "You're not as dumb as you look. So it should be easy for you to figure this out. What we say goes. What you say doesn't matter. And when you act like the rules don't apply, you see exactly how wrong you are. That's what just happened back there. Consider it a friendly reminder."

"Yeah, but here's the thing," I say, slapping his hand away. "I tried the whole obedience thing, and look where it got me. Nowhere. So what's the point in obeying, if in the end, I'm fucked either way?"

"You've never played by our rules," Royal growls, sounding equally frustrated and wounded by that affront.

"Except I did," I say. "I got down on my knees and sucked your dick, just like everyone else."

"Not like everyone else," Royal mutters. But I'm too pissed and adrenaline-fueled to care whether he's trying to insult me or compliment me. I can't believe I ever cared, that I ever dreamed of being one of these psychos. They crossed a line, and there's no going back. I fucking hate these boys. I hope they burn in hell for eternity.

But I won't show them how much they've affected me. They don't get to win everything.

"You said you wanted me to suck your dick, so I did it," I say flatly. "And you went out of your way to make damn sure I didn't like it, too. To remind me it was a punishment. But I stuck it out to the end—okay, maybe not the end, because apparently you have some hang-up about ejaculation, but until you were done. I stayed on my knees as long as you wanted me there, like an obedient little servant. And what did I get for falling in line and obeying you? Nothing, that's what. I didn't get to disappear into the masses of other girls you face-raped in the basement. You still released the video. So remind me again, what's the point in obeying?"

In the front seat, Duke's turned toward the window, his shoulders shaking. It takes me a second to realize he's holding back laughter. Guess my fury amuses him.

"Oh, now I raped your face?" Royal asks, jerking the steering wheel as we veer off onto a side road out of town. "The way I remember it, you were licking my dick like a fucking ice cream cone."

"Oh, I'm sorry, was I supposed to bite into it like a Tootsie Pop?" I ask.

Duke loses it, throwing back his head and howling with laughter, falling against the door in his fit of mirth.

Royal shoots him an annoyed glance. "When a chick's slobbering all over my dick like a bulldog, I'm pretty sure she's enjoying herself."

"And you just couldn't have that," I say. "Is that why you made it as ugly as possible? To make sure I didn't get any pleasure whatsoever out of it? Or were you more worried about how much pleasure *you* were getting out of it?"

Baron's watching me with that intense focus he had in the basement when Royal said he wanted me all to himself, like he's barely keeping himself from pouncing on me. I scoot away from him as subtly as I can.

"I don't give a shit about your pleasure," Royal snaps from the driver's seat. "I was worried about you biting my dick off."

I shrug and turn toward the window, watching the grey blur of tears slipping by. "You call me a slut because I dare to enjoy sex. Is that why it pisses you off so much? Because I have the nerve to enjoy sex when you can't?"

"My dick was in your mouth," Royal growls, sounding beyond irritated. "I had you on your knees like a whore, right where you belong. Trust me, I was enjoying it."

"But were you actually enjoying the blowjob?" I ask. "Were you enjoying the way my tongue moved, or the way my mouth suctioned around your cock? Did you like it when my teeth grazed your skin? Did you even feel what I was doing?"

"Dude, pull over," Duke says. "I want in the backseat with her. I'm getting hard just listening to her."

Royal adjusts the rearview mirror so he can see me. "What the fuck are you getting at, Jailbird?"

The truth is, I'm not sure. I feel almost shaky with the power I have right now. I can feel it coursing up inside me, the certainty I'm so close to something, some deeply buried truth.

"Do you actually enjoy sex?" I ask again. "I mean, it's still fun even if you don't cum, but isn't that kinda the end goal for most people?"

"Just shut up," Royal snaps. "Your ridiculous babbling makes my head hurt worse."

"Did I hit a nerve?" I taunt, feeling reckless, high with the thrill of unraveling the mysterious Royal Dolce. I like figuring people out. It's a sickness, really. Or maybe I'm poking the beast because I get the feeling he'll be my undoing either way, so why not figure out why before he eats me alive? "If you don't enjoy sex, then what are you getting out of it? Is it just a power trip for you? That's why you enjoyed me sucking your dick, right? Not because I'm good, because then you would have let me do my thing. You just liked seeing me on my knees, knowing I was powerless, that you could do anything you wanted to me, and I couldn't stop you. Did it make you feel like a big man to see me on my knees for you, Royal?"

"I said, shut up," he says, his voice low and hollow. I can see one hand on the wheel, his knuckles white under the scrapes and blood on them.

"I'll shut her up," Baron says with a shrug, reaching for his belt. "I thought you didn't want my dick in her, but if you're good with it…"

I lean across the seat and give him a wolfish grin. "Aren't you afraid I'll suck your secrets out through your dick, too?"

"Okay, psycho," he says, his dark eyes positively feral behind his glasses, though his words are cool. "Anatomy lesson—there are only two things that come out of a man's penis, and the truth ain't one of them."

Duke snorts with laughter again.

"I'm just curious," I say, "how it's possible for men to feel powerful in a situation like that. Are you really so caught up in your ego that you can't see how small that really makes you? I mean, sure, you took all my clothes and my dignity. You put me on my knees. But I didn't kneel and worship you. It took three men twice my size to physically force me into a posture of submission and get a dick in my mouth. And you were still so afraid of me that you had to immobilize me while you asserted

64

your dominance. Tell me, how does that make you feel powerful, not tiny and weak and ashamed of yourselves?"

"Put your dick in her mouth or I will," Duke says, his voice edged with flint. "She obviously needs a pacifier to suck on."

"Yeah, Baron," I say, running my nails down his bicep. "You better protect your brothers. They're getting awfully jumpy, and can you blame them? After all, there's nothing scarier than a girl who speaks the truth."

"Where the fuck are you going?" Baron barks.

I jerk back, confused for a second when I think he's talking to me. But then I see his gaze has snapped to the bridge ahead. It's a one-lane bridge, the same one where Royal took me on Halloween night, when we started hooking up before he abruptly put the brakes on.

"I was just driving," Royal mutters. He's still staring straight ahead, still gripping the wheel with white knuckles.

"And you just drove *here?*" Duke asks incredulously.

I want to ask what's wrong with here, since it seems like a good place to rape a girl and toss her body in the river, but instinct stops me. I may goad them like a brat when I have a point to make, but here's the thing. I'm not a brat. I know when to keep my mouth shut. You learn to read the room real young when your mom's a peach like mine. And whatever was happening in the car a minute ago, it's over. Something else is happening now, something that's sucked the air out of the car and dropped the temperature ten degrees, like a ghost just squeezed into the seat between Baron and me. The hair on my arms rises.

Royal doesn't answer. I figured this was where he brought his hookups, but that can't be it. The others wouldn't care if he parked us in a make-out spot. They made it pretty clear they're down to fuck me.

"Do you come here a lot?" Baron asks.

"No," Royal snaps. "I'll turn around past the bridge. Calm your tits."

The big car lumbers up onto the bridge, and for a long, tense moment, the only sound is the tires on the wooden boards of the bridge. On the other side, the tires sink into the wet shoulder as he starts to swing the car around. I can see deep ruts further down the bank, grown over with grass now, like someone in a truck went off-roading here a while back.

"Do you come here... Ever?" Baron presses.

"No," Royal snaps. "Do you?"

"But dude," Duke says quietly. "Why would you even come here by accident?"

"I made a wrong fucking turn, and I wasn't paying attention because some bitch was running her mouth," Royals says through clenched teeth. "Now I told you to fucking drop it."

No one speaks while he rights the car and slams on the gas, the Rover lurching forward and roaring across the bridge so fast it makes the whole structure tremble. The silence is heavy and grey, like an Arkansas winter.

I remember someone telling me they pushed Mabel Darling off a bridge. I remember someone saying she jumped. Colt didn't say there was a bridge. He said she went into the river, and Royal pulled her out. Was it here? Is that why they don't want him returning?

I also remember the story about their sister being swept away in a flood, but that can't be this place. There was no bridge in that story. And Royal wouldn't bring me to the spot where his sister drowned when he wanted to hook up. Even he's not that sick.

When we're back on the other side of the bridge, the side towards Faulkner, the twins let out a breath, though they don't speak.

Just when I think Royal's going to keep going like this never happened, he taps the brake. The driver's side wheels sink into the shoulder as he pulls off the road.

"Stay in the car," he says, shutting off the engine.

"What are you doing?" Duke asks.

"Just stay in the fucking car," Royal says, and he gets out and slams the door.

"Where's he going?" Duke asks, twisting around as Royal walks behind the car. For a second, I think he's going to do something revealing, some kind of penance. But he circles around and yanks open my door.

"Come on," he says, his jaw tight, his words clipped.

I glance at the twins, but they look more confused than I am. I was guessing they were going to hurt me here. Why else take me all the way out of town, where there are no witnesses?

I just have to stay alive. If they leave me stranded out here, I can walk back. I've only been out here once, in the dark, and

BRUTAL BOY

I may not know the roads, but I know Faulkner lies to the south.
I could find my way.

five

Harper Apple

Royal stands there waiting, his hand out, the drizzling rain soaking into his dark hair and the shoulders of his shirt. They're all still dressed for school, like they were waiting for me to come back with Colt. Royal's white, button-up shirt is rolled to his elbows and unbuttoned at the collar, his broad shoulders filling it to the seams. If he weren't splattered in my friend's blood, I might still find him irresistible.

I know there's no point in fighting when there's three of them, so I climb out of the car, ignoring his offered hand even though I have to fight gravity to scramble out of the seat, since the car is on a slope. My feet hit the wet asphalt of the road, and Royal uses his hand to steady me, covering the fact that I left him hanging by refusing to take his help.

He lets the car door fall closed, and for a second, we stand there alone on the road, sizing each other up. "We need to talk," he says, his voice emotionless.

"Are you breaking up with me?" I ask sarcastically.

"No."

My heart beats erratically when he grabs my wrist and drags me toward the bridge. I'm not sure if it's fear of the weird, detached way he's acting suddenly or the thought of what he's about to do to me. I race through the possible outcomes.

If he pushes me off the bridge, I think I'll live. The water is brown and flowing faster than the last time I was here, but it's not churning like it might during a flood. There are no limbs or branches from trees floating along to get caught under. It's deep enough that I could jump without hitting the bottom, and though it would be scary as fuck to jump from a bridge this high, it's not high enough to make the water's surface feel like concrete to a falling body. It's November, and I'm sure the water is cold as hell, but this is Central Arkansas, and even this time of year, the water won't be deathly cold, the kind that makes your limbs seize up so you can't swim.

All these thoughts race through my mind as Royal pulls me across the bridge until we're in the middle. He pulls me to a stop and turns to face me. His eyes are dark and intense, his wet hair sticking to his forehead as raindrops trickle down his sculpted face.

He looks like he's waiting for me to say something. "Is this where your sister died?" I ask, unable to keep from pushing just one more button.

"No questions," he says. "That was the deal, remember?"

"Or is it where Mabel tried to kill herself?" I ask. "Your brothers were obviously upset about you coming here, so it must be one or the other. Maybe both? Why'd you pull her out, Royal? That's what I want to know. That should have been your ultimate victory. You didn't even have to do the dirty work. Just push her so far she did it for you."

"Did you fuck him?"

I can't help but let out a little snort. "That's what this is about?"

His expression doesn't change. "Did you?"

"What does it matter?" I ask. "He's right. You've done nothing but tell me I'm worthless, and a whore, and trash, since the day we met. I have every right to assume, as does he, that you're not interested in anything but torturing me."

"I'm going to ask you one more time," he says slowly. "Did you fuck him?"

I open my mouth to tell him he can ask a hundred times, and it's still none of his fucking business. But then I remember Colt lying there on the ground, crumpled like old rags in a ditch as we pulled away, and how I couldn't stand to look at him, so I focused on my backpack because if I didn't…

"No," I whisper, my throat suddenly so thick with frustration I think I'll cry. I could tell Royal to go fuck himself, that I can fuck whomever I choose and it's none of his goddamn business. But if I did, and he went back to finish the job, that would be on me.

"Good," he says, an indulgent little smirk on his lips. He reaches out and tucks a stand of wet hair behind my ear, his gesture casual and leisurely, as if making sure I get the message. He is entitled to touch me if and when he chooses. "That wasn't so hard, was it?"

I fight the urge to slap his hand away. "No."

"Good," he says again, stroking my cheek. "I'm going to make things easy for you, too. I know you like to spy on people, dig around in their lives and try to get your claws in their secrets so you can push their buttons. So let's just get this out in the open, where you can't pretend you didn't know. You are mine, Harper."

I blink at him, wanting to laugh even though my insides are trembling. "What?"

"You are mine," he says slowly, like he's speaking to someone too dumb to comprehend, which I guess I am. What does that even mean?

"I am?" I ask, trying to keep the incredulous from my voice but not quite managing. "So, what, because I sucked your dick, you think we're dating or something? That you're my boyfriend?"

He shakes his head, a little smile on his lips. "No, no," he says. "I didn't say I was yours. If I want to sit in the town square and let the whole fucking parade file by and bounce on my dick, I can do that. But if one guy so much as touches you…"

"You'll cut off his finger," I say, remembering Colt's dad sharing the same disfigurement as his son. Who did they touch?

"He'll lose more than a finger," Royal says.

He takes my wrist again and steps toward the edge of the bridge, climbing through the wooden beams that support the structure. I start to protest, my heart racing as I watch him step onto the narrow ledge that extends past the railing. There's only about a foot of boards extending, and they're wet and slippery. If a car crossed the bridge, the vibration alone would send him plunging into the water if he didn't hold onto the support beams.

"See, I'm a jealous bastard, Cherry Pie," he says, his voice rising a bit as thunder rumbles overhead and the rain picks up. "I don't like people touching my things. And I've decided that you're my plaything. I'm not your boyfriend. I don't love you, or care about you, or want to fuck you. I want to own you. Do you understand?"

"No," I say simply. Because I don't.

"I own you." He grabs me around the waist and lifts me through the beams onto his side of the supports. I fight to stay on the safe side, but it only pushes him backwards, tipping toward the water, and he's still in control of my weight. For a second, I feel the terrifying, dizzying sensation of him reaching the balance point. I suck in a breath, ready to plunge over the side. In some gravity defying move, he tips back in time to set me on the ledge beside him, and I remember the first time we met, when he jumped in front of that train so late it seemed impossible that he wasn't killed. He takes risks like that because he doesn't care, because it doesn't matter to him if he lives or dies. I saw it that night, and I see it again now. He could have died that night, or fallen just now, and it would make no difference to him.

That's why he always wins. Because life matters to me. I matter to me.

"What the fuck," I say, grabbing onto the supports, my heart slamming in my chest. "You could have just killed us."

He smiles, that dead-eyed little smirk. "Now you're starting to understand," he says. "Your life, your body, your soul. They are mine. If I want to kill you, I'll kill you. If I want to fuck you, I'll fuck you. If I want you to kneel, you'll kneel. If I want to show the world that you like sucking cock in the back of a Corolla, I'll show them. It's all mine. Your whole life is mine, Harper Apple."

"I don't remember agreeing to this."

"Tell me who's going to stop me," he taunts. "You? Your mother? The police? Who, Harper?"

My grip tightens as I seethe. He's right. No one in this town can or will stop him. He owns the town I live in, and until I get out of this town, he might as well own me already. "I hate you," I say quietly.

"I knew you were smart," he says. "You'd have to be real fucking stupid to love a man like me, Cherry Pie."

"You're not a man," I say, grateful for the rain running down my cheeks like tears, hiding the real thing, the impotent rage leaking from my eyes like acid. "You're a monster."

"And you, my pretty plaything, are mine," he says. "You saw what happens when someone touches my toys. You like pushing buttons, and I want you to know exactly where mine are so you can do it any time you want to see me lose my shit over you again. If you feel like you aren't important to me, remember that."

He plucks one of my hands from the support beams and steps around me, forcing me to turn. Again, I feel his balance tip, and I'm sure he's going to plunge into the water below. Instead, he presses me back against the bridge, my face against his chest now. I grip the supports behind me, feeling completely vulnerable with the front of my body left open to him. He stands with one foot on either side of mine, not holding onto anything. He tips my chin up and gently pushes my wet hair back from my cheeks.

"Now you know all my secrets," he says, leaning down to brush his lips over mine. "You know exactly how to make me jealous. You know how crazy you make me, my little black cherry darling." He kisses me, his lips cold and wet from the rain. I don't kiss him back, but I don't stop him, either. Something in me feels frozen, as hopeless as I felt at Faulkner, before I started fighting and gambling, before I had any way out of this town.

I don't know what being Royal Dolce's plaything means, but I know I'm going to find out, and I know I'm not going to like it.

He pulls back, cupping my face between his hands. "What are your secrets?" he whispers against my lips. "Had you already figured me out, Harper Apple? Is that why you defied me today? Did it turn you on to watch me beat the shit out of that asshole?

Does it make you hot to know that I'll go to those lengths to destroy the competition when the prize is you?"

"You're disgusting," I snarl. "It doesn't make me hot, it makes me furious. I fucking hate you, Royal Dolce. The only thing that turns me on right now is the thought of you falling off this bridge."

He kisses me again. This time, I struggle against him as well as I can without releasing my grip on the bridge. When my body bucks against him, he reaches up and wraps one huge hand gently around my throat. My neck is still bruised from when he choked me out in the hall after I slapped him, but this isn't an act of violence. His touch is almost tender, as if to reassure me that he doesn't want damage done to anything he owns.

It's also his only anchor to the bridge. His weight rests on the balls of his feet, since his heels are hanging over the edge. Below, the brown water flows, the surface speckled with raindrops. Royal angles his face to deepen the kiss, water dripping from his face onto my skin, his mouth commanding mine to open. When I don't obey, he forces his tongue between my teeth, pushing me back against the bridge harder, his body rocking forward to meet mine.

It's not a passionate kiss, though. It's an examination, like a man who just bought real estate and is exploring his new place to make sure it meets his standards. His tongue moves against mine, slow and arrogant, before skimming over my teeth and teasing the roof of my mouth. He's almost daring me to bite him.

I don't. I focus on my hands holding onto the bridge. Can I let go long enough to push him backwards into the water? What are my chances of escape if I push him? If I don't?

Seemingly satisfied by my lack of defiance, Royal draws back slowly, a smile tugging at his wet lips as he slides them back and forth over mine. He strokes my throat with his thumb, his hand still around my neck. "I could kill you right now, sweetheart," he says, that word sounding like a threat every time he uses it. "Your life belongs to me now. I can decide to end it at any time. You need to remember that when you're with me. Remember that every time I wrap my hand around your neck, I could choose to kill you, or kiss you. And what I do is up to me, not you. I decide for you, answer for you. Do you understand that?"

I glare up at him. "Do you understand that you're the one standing on a ledge, and the only thing stopping you from plunging into the river is your hold on me?"

I expect him to correct that, to grab the rails behind me, maybe slam my head into it for threatening him, but he only cocks a brow. "You gonna push me?"

I release the railing and rest both hands on his chest. In one split second, surprise flashes over his cruelly beautiful face. Then he seizes my head in both hands and slams his mouth down on mine. The kiss startles me so much I grab the railing again, struggling for a second before he overpowers me. He pushes me back against the supports, almost bending me backwards. This time, there's no clinical detachment in his kiss. It's harsh and hungry, the stroke of his tongue rough and demanding against mine.

My mouth responds, my tongue battling his, fighting back against the possession in his kiss. It isn't possessive like a man who thinks he owns me, it's possessive like a demon, like he wants to crawl inside my body and possess my very soul. His chest crushes mine with each quick, sharp breath he takes, and his hands cradle my head with unyielding command. And though this wasn't something I sought or even welcomed, the alpha maleness of the kiss makes my knees go weak and my mouth respond on its own. If I don't, he'll invade me, take me over. My only choice is to fight back, to yield to the demand to return the kiss.

We kiss, and kiss, and kiss, until my cheeks hurt and my lips feel bruised, until I can taste my blood and his, both mingling on my tongue as he slides his against mine, as if trying to lick every drop of it from my mouth before I can swallow him down into my belly, as if he's afraid I'll take a piece of his soul with his blood. I grip the railing with one hand, and I fist his shirt with the other, and when that's not enough, I slide a hand around the back of his neck, pulling him down, arching my body into his. I dig my nails in, feeling them bite into his skin, relishing the growl I feel build in his chest when I hurt him.

The kiss is everything—a battle of wills, a passionate embrace, a fight for control. And more than that, it's an outlet for our rage that smashes together and forms an inferno between us, as if each of us wants to burn the other to the ground but there's nothing left to burn, because our own wildfire has already consumed any ground there is to be gained.

When he pulls back, his eyes are hazy and wild, blazing with lust. It makes me shiver with heat. Without hesitation, I open my legs when he shifts his position, pushing a thigh between mine and gripping the supports behind me for leverage. He rocks against me, his breathing ragged and harsh, his erection biting into my abdomen, the heat of it searing into me despite the cold, wet clothes between us.

"Harper," he says, his voice twisted in something almost inhuman. "Do you need me to fuck you?"

A shiver of raw desire rakes its claws down my spine, and I want to say yes so bad it aches in my throat like a fist. Yes, I need him to fuck me so goddamn hard it breaks me into a million pieces. My whole body is on fire beneath my frigid skin, and I'm so wet that if it wasn't raining, I'm pretty sure my jeans would still be soaked.

But I'm more than my body. I'm made up of a brain that says I hate this boy, that I want him to pay for all he's already done to me, and sexing him up isn't the kind of revenge it has in mind. I'm made up of the nightmares that plague me and the ache in my back from the knife of his betrayal. The memory of him almost killing my only friend because I dared have a good time with him. A heart that knows this boy with all his haunted darkness will destroy me if I let him, and maybe even if I don't.

"No," I say, wishing my traitorous body would stop saying yes so damn loud.

"Are you sure?" The anguish in his voice grips me like teeth, and I feel the darkness inside him calling to mine, luring me in until I know what he's saying under the words falling from his lips. I know that he's asking me to need him. I know that what he really means is that he needs to fuck me, but he can't say it. And I know that if I let him, everything will change. But he already thinks he owns me, and if I fuck him, he won't be wrong.

I've never felt anything close to this with anyone else, but just because I haven't experienced it, that doesn't mean I don't recognize it for what it is. I know myself well enough to know that with Royal, there would be no casual. It's not like with Colt or Maverick. This is something else entirely, something that doesn't come along twice or even once in most people's lives. And if I give in to Royal now, even I won't be able to save me.

Royal slides a hand into my hair, grabbing a messy fistful and pressing his forehead against mine, his breath so hot against my swollen lips it makes my head spin, and I almost forget all the reasons I can't give in. "I'll let you decide this one time," he says, his other hand gripping my hip. "Next time, I'll choose for you."

I close my eyes, feeling the prickle of tears behind my lids and the fluttering, racing pulse in my chest. "I'm sorry," I whisper.

And then I let go of the railing and push him as hard as I can.

six

Royal Dolce

I should have known she'd push me. I should have known she had something up her sleeve when she let me kiss her, when she kissed me back like she fucking needed it. I should have seen it coming. After everything I did, everything I said, I knew she hated me. That's why I said those things, after all. It's why I did them. I should have fucking known.

I don't grab for the bridge or try to recover my balance. I don't pivot and dive into the water to ensure minimum impact. If I really fucking cared about falling, I'd do that. Instead, I wrap my arms around Harper, because if I'm going down, she's coming with me.

I feel her lurch forward, and then her hold gives out, and she's wrenched away from the ledge by my weight. I feel her struggling in my arms, but I only hold tighter, like she's the last thing in the world I have to hold onto.

I had a sister once, but I lost her.

I had a brother who protected me once, but I lost him.

I have two brothers left, and if they're capable of it, they still care. They're required by the laws of blood brotherhood. But I didn't protect them, the way I promised King I would. They're worse off than Crystal, worse off than if I'd been the one who disappeared that night. I can't do anything about that now. Thanks to me, they are who they are. But they'll keep on being that without me.

Harper, though… She won't go on being anything without me.

The water hits us like a slap, and then we're under the surface. She's thrashing in my arms, but I don't let go. I hold onto her like a last breath, and together we sink into the cold dark oblivion of the river.

seven

Harper Apple

He's going to kill me.

That's all I can think as the current pulls us along, keeping us from sinking to the bottom of the muddy banks. I pushed him with both hands, but managed to grab onto the bridge immediately. Everything was going better than I could have hoped—for about half a second. I thought if he fell, the others would run down to get him, and by the time he swam to shore, changed, and got back in the car, I'd be long gone.

Of course I prepared for the possibility that I'd fall, too. That he'd yank me off the ledge, or that I'd swipe for the railing but lose my balance before I got it. The water's not rushing and churning, but it's moving at a good rate, and I knew that even if I fell, he'd have hit the water and been swept along at least far enough so I didn't fall on him and kill one of us.

But no. He's the one who's going to kill us. He didn't just grab me and pull me off, then kick his way through the air like a normal person falling might. No self-preservation instinct made him try to hit the water advantageously. Instead, he wrapped his arms around me and held on like a fucking barnacle, pinning my arms. We didn't hit the water well, but I managed to get a good breath before sinking through the frigid surface, and thank fuck for that.

Otherwise, I'd be dead already instead of struggling as hard as I can against his iron grip. The water is like frozen taffy. I can barely kick out in it, and any contact I make with his shins is blunted by the water. We're pulled along below the surface, twisted by the current until I can't tell up from down. And I can't fucking breathe.

My lungs ache. My whole body aches from the cold, much colder than I expected. My head throbs.

And then, although he must have bigger lungs and is an athlete who should be able to hold his breath until I'm dead and then probably swim up to the surface, I feel him release his air. His arms pulse tight around me for one second, like he's giving me a final embrace, before loosening at last.

I don't waste a second. I grab him and kick as hard as I can, using my other arm to stroke at the water. I move with the current, letting it carry me and do most of the work, letting the air in my lungs lift me to show me which way is up. I'm almost choking on the lack of oxygen. My chest feels like an elephant is standing on it. My head throbs, blackness eating into the edges of my consciousness as I kick and paddle frantically with one hand, not sure I'll make the surface in time. The deadweight of Royal threatens to pull me back down, to the river's hungry bottom.

I want to drop him, but I know I'll never find him if I let him go. The current will take him, and when I dive back under, he'll be gone. Just when I think I'll have to take a breath of water, my head breaks the surface. I suck in a breath, relief making me nearly sob as instinct takes over. Then I'm pulled under again, almost before I can get my mouth closed. I kick hard, breaking through again. This time, I don't fight and flail like a panicked animal.

I force myself to let my body rest low in the water, to take a slow breath, to only kick my legs to keep from sinking under again. I focus on nothing but breathing the air I so badly need.

After I've taken several deep breaths, I'm calm enough to think straight, and I aim for the closer bank, put my face into the water, and swim hard with the current. It seems to take forever, like I'm not moving toward the bank at all but only downstream. I'm sure it's too late for Royal, that I should just drop him and let him join his sister as another casualty of the river.

But I can't seem to unclench my fingers from the shoulder of his shirt, where I grabbed him before I started up. At last, I'm close enough to touch the bottom with my toes, but I still can't get out of the water. The current pulls me along when I try to stand. Frustration and panic claw at me, and I start swimming again.

A voice cuts through my singular focus, and I jerk my head in that direction. Duke and Baron are running along the side, waving to me and calling. When I put my feet down again, I'm able to at least stand without being knocked over. The moment I stop moving, Duke charges into the water. His face is etched with fear as he wades out, reaching a hand toward me when he's still halfway there, as if wanting alone can close the distance between us.

SELENA

For some reason, a vision of Mabel Darling fills my head. Is this how Royal pulled her out, the reason he didn't want to admit it? Duke isn't pulling me out because of any loyalty or feeling. He's doing it because he's a fucking human being, and that's something Royal would never want to admit to. It would damage his reputation to admit he's just like the rest of us, not some vengeful god perched on a throne above it all.

"Where's Royal?" Duke calls, his hand finally connecting with mine. I've never felt relief like I do the moment his impossibly strong hand grips mine, not even when I caught my breath. I was too scared then. Now, I just about pass out with the force of relief. I'm so caught in the moment that my grip on Royal's shirt relaxes and I have to jerk my hand from Duke's and grab for Royal again, this time getting his hand.

"I've got him," I say.

And then I burst into tears like a fucking baby.

Everything happens around me after that, and I know I should jump into action and help, but I can't seem to put myself back in the moment. I was completely absorbed in every moment in the river, but when they pull me out, it's like a part of me was left in the water.

I'm used to giving myself over to the moment in a fight. I relish the way it turns my brain off, and I don't have to think about anything but the goal, the win, the light at the end of the tunnel vision that takes me over in those moments. And even though the practice in honing my ability probably saved me today, I can't seem to snap back to reality when it's over.

Instead, I sit on the bank while Duke and Baron roll Royal on his face and try to bang the water out of his lungs. Then Baron starts mouth-to-mouth, and Duke comes over and wraps Baron's jacket around me. It's damp from the drizzle still falling, but when he wraps his arms around me and pulls me into his lap, he's warm and strong, and I'm so relieved that for just one fucking moment in my life, someone else is taking over, that I don't have to be strong, that I can fall apart and my world won't fall apart with me.

"You did alright, Apple," he says, pressing his warm lips to my forehead. I'm so cold I can hardly feel it.

"I pushed him," I choke out, too tired to care what he's going to do to me for that confession. If he throws me back in the river, I'll give up the way Royal did and just let it have me.

"I know," he says quietly. "We saw."

"I didn't know—" I start, but a shiver wracks my body so hard it chokes the words off.

"I know," Duke says again, and instead of throwing me back in the water, he holds me tighter. "My brother's a complicated beast."

"He didn't even try," I say, wiping the annoying tears from my eyes. They refuse to stop, even when I'm done with them, when I want to say this to Duke, when I want to make him see that I didn't mean to fucking kill his brother.

"You have to understand," Duke says quietly. "Royal's not suicidal. He's not going to jump off the bridge. But if someone pushes him…"

"He's not going to try to save himself," I say, another sob wracking my body.

Duke kisses my forehead again, squeezing me against his chest and letting my tears soak his shirt above the waterline left from when he waded in to get us. "He just doesn't really care if he dies."

As if in answer, Royal starts choking. Baron drags him over, rolling his massive form like the giant it is. Royal staggers onto a hands and knees position and vomits a torrent of brown water, as if he was still in the river, too. Or maybe the river is always a part of him, one that never really leaves no matter how much of it he spews back up, no matter how much his body wants to rid him of it.

"Why?" I whisper. "What happened to him?"

"You don't get it, Harp," Duke says, his voice quiet, for only me to hear. "We lost our sister, but Royal, he lost his twin."

Baron is speaking to Royal in the same low tone a few feet away, two private conversations happening so close but separated by years and miles that can't be crossed. Royal's still on his knees, but he lowers himself to his elbows, pressing his forehead to the muddy gravel on the riverbank, his breathing ragged as a sob. And I think in that moment that Duke is wrong about him. He's lost something more than a sister, more than even a twin. He lost his soul.

"Fuck," he grinds out, his hands balled into fists. He punches the wet earth with the bottom of his clenched fist. "Fuck. Fuck. Fuck." He punctuates each word with another blow, until he's churned up mud from the gravel, until his skin is cut and bleeding, his red blood soaking into the red-brown dirt of the bank.

"Listen, whether he likes it or not, you saved my brother's life today," Duke says. "But never pull this shit again, Harper. You can't push my brother. Just… Stop pushing him, okay?"

I know he's talking about more than pushing him off the bridge. I nod and wipe my cheeks.

"Good," Duke says. "Our job is to help him live, whatever that means at any given time. Remember that. It's your job now, too."

I don't say anything, but I think the same thing I thought on that bridge when Royal told me I was his toy. I didn't sign up for this shit. I didn't ask for this. I don't want the attention. I don't want the responsibility. I don't want the danger.

But in truth, I did sign up for this. I did ask for it.

Not by blowing Mr. Behr in the back of his car or having them catch us. Not by having a video of the incident released. Not even by going to Willow Heights.

I signed up for it when I agreed to Mr. D's conditions. I asked for it when I pursued the boys, when I tried to get in with them. I put myself in the middle of it. I wanted their attention, even knowing it came with a danger I wasn't prepared for.

So I nod, and Baron says we need to get Royal somewhere warm. Duke stands and pulls Baron's jacket tight around me, and my eyes fall to a ring on his left hand. It's a clunky thing, smaller than a class ring and simpler but big enough to catch my eye. Big enough for me to read the clearly embossed D in the center of it.

Again I wonder who I'm actually working for. Maybe it's not a creepy old dude. Baron is supposedly a genius hacker, after all. I have zero doubts that he's the one who hacked into Dixie's blog and put that video up, whether he did it of his own accord or at Royal's direction.

But thinking he's Mr. D is stupid. Why would he want me to spy on him?

I push the thought away and start back to the car with the others. My legs are shaking, my teeth chattering, my whole body quaking with cold. Though Royal keeps shoving Baron away when he tries to help and telling him he's fine, he throws up again halfway back to the car, and he has to stop and rest three times, leaning over with his hands on his knees, just breathing.

When we finally reach the car, I'm so exhausted I don't think I could take another step if I tried. I slide into the back seat.

Royal doesn't protest when Baron takes the keys and opens the back door. He drags himself onto the back seat, looking as drained as I feel. Baron turns on the car and blasts the heat, and Duke turns around in the passenger seat to look at us.

"There's a blanket back there if you need it," he says, seeing me quaking in my seat. I'm clumsy from cold, but I manage to get on my knees and reach behind the back seat to grab a gold and black fleece blanket with the WHPA Knights logo. I wrap it around myself and slide back down on the seat, casting a guilty glance at Royal. He's slumped against the far side of the seat, his forehead resting on the glass.

"You know if you want to get warm, you should get naked," Duke says, flashing his grin at me. But I know there's a real boy under the dirty mouth and the laughter, even if I only got to see him for five minutes when he thought his brother was dying.

"Funny guy," I mutter.

"He's right," Baron chimes in. "That's survival 101. Both of you should toss your clothes and get under the blanket."

"Not happening," I say, glaring at him.

"Then at least cuddle up to share body heat," Baron says, shifting into gear. He pulls the car onto the road, and I'm grateful their attention has turned away from us.

"Want some of this?" I ask Royal, pulling the blanket from under me so I can put it over us both, if he scoots closer.

He doesn't move. I wonder what's going on in his head right now. Is he pissed that I pulled him out of the river? Did he want to die back there? Or just pissed I pushed him?

He sure as hell didn't make an effort to live.

My throat tightens, and I scoot across the seat, knowing he's not going to do it. That he'll never reach out. He'll never give me anything at all. He's locked up tight in his head, in his empty heart, and he couldn't give me what I need even if he wanted to. Still, I'm not a monster. I may have done things to survive that not everyone understands or agrees with, but I'm still a girl, still human. I cover Royal with the blanket, and when he still doesn't move, I move closer, until our bodies are pressed together on the seat. I wrap my arms around him and lay my head on his chest, still clad in the shirt I used to pull him out of the depths of the river.

SELENA

He doesn't move. If it weren't for the heavy thud of his heartbeat against my cheek, I might think he was dead. His skin is cold under the wet clothes, and for a second, I consider unbuttoning his shirt, but that seems creepy, so I only squeeze myself against him, waiting for the warmth to build between our two cold bodies. The car moves through the grey, soggy evening, past the good side of town, down the wet streets glimmering with the reflection of traffic lights in the business section, and then over the tracks.

Though they must know where I live, since one of them delivered my bike, I wasn't with them that time. Now, I see the small, decrepit houses the way they must see them. They look depressing and hopeless. When we turn onto Mill Street, a car sits on the side of the road outside Zephyr's house, two wheels up on cinderblocks, the windows down despite the rain. In another driveway, a trash bag is taped over the window of a car, and kids' bikes and toys are strewn across the brown lawn.

Baron pulls up alongside the curb in front of my house. Though I've never been ashamed of my neighborhood, and I actually like Blue and Olive more than most people, the little plastic kiddie pool full of sand and faded plastic chairs in Blue's yard look as trashy as anyone else's when seen through the eyes of a stranger. Blue stands on her porch in the growing darkness, her porch light burned out, smoking a cigarette. An old, rusty coffee can sits on the steps, waiting for her cigarette butts and adding to the junk.

No wonder these boys, these fucking princes of Faulkner, call me trailer trash. That's exactly what I am.

I'm stiff with self-consciousness as I pry myself from under the steamy blanket spread over myself and Royal.

"Shit," I mutter, sliding across the seat to make a quick escape. "I got your seats wet."

Somehow, until this moment, I didn't take the time to marvel at or even notice that the seats are soft as butter and the interior smells like new leather, that the car moves so smoothly and silently that I could hear Royal's heartbeat all the way home. I've been in Royal's racing car, but this one… Damn. I know zero about cars, but this is a really fucking nice car.

"Trust me, a little river water is the cleanest thing that back seat's ever seen," Duke says, turning around to flash me a grin.

I try not to think about that as I climb out of the car. I wave to Blue and hurry up the walkway and inside my house. I should check in with Mr. D, as is our Friday arrangement, but Mom is home and I don't want to use the computer in the living room. Since my laptop is at school, as is my bike, I can't use that, either. I can't even use the *OnlyWords* app on my phone, since it's also at school.

I'm honestly relieved I have an excuse not to text him. Today was too fucking long, and I just want to crawl in bed and pile blankets over myself and not think about any of it—Colt lying on the road in the rain until someone happened by and found him; the easy fun we had together and how much it cost us both; the helpless hate I feel for Royal Dolce and the infuriating attraction that goes along with it; the way his tortured soul calls to mine and the way mine answers whether I want to admit it or not.

I want to be above it all, to not care what anyone thinks about me, to not care that I'm poor and that people call me a whore and that everyone has seen me sucking a teacher's dick. Sometimes, I pull it off, and usually, I can fake it until I make it to the blissful land of not giving a fuck. But the Dolce boys get under my skin. They make me ashamed of who I am, and at the same time, make me think that I can be someone else. They pull me under their spell and make me want to change, to be better, to be good enough for them. Implied in that desire is the sneaky way they make me feel like I'm not good enough already.

The more I learn about the Dolces, the less I think I know them, the less I have figured out. What scares me most is that the more I get to know them, the less I know myself. I definitely never thought I was the kind of girl who could care about a boy who treats me the way Royal does. But even if he doesn't care if he lives—maybe *because* he doesn't care—I do.

*

A Mother's Love

What were you thinking?
Are you just trying to scare me
After everything this family has been through
Haven't I suffered enough?

Is this some kind of cry for attention
Because I've tried
If you bothered to pick up the phone
Call me back once in a while
But you shut me out
Do you know how that makes me feel?
Do you?

SELENA

And now this
Do you expect me to drop everything?
There's an opening this week
Maria Giancursio has a piece in the gallery
One art class and suddenly she fancies herself an artist
Can you imagine?

Or did your father put you up to this?
So typical
He thinks I'll jump on a plane every time he snaps his fingers
You tell your father
I can't come running every time you swallow a little water
I did that at the Cape one summer
And look at me
It's the Valenti blood
You're tough
Just like me.
It'll happen again
I know how you boys are
So reckless
Just like him.

eight

Harper Apple

The moment I step through the doors of Willow Heights on Monday morning, every head turns my way. I'm so sick of this shit I could puke. If they're trying to drive me back to Faulkner High, this is sure as fuck tempting me. The only thing keeping me going is the knowledge that enduring this for two years will ensure I never have to see a single one of these assholes again in my life.

I wish I could turn and walk out, that I could run to Colt's house and smoke pot and make out and eat sandwiches at the island in the kitchen with light streaming in the picture windows.

But I can't do that again because if I do, they'll kill him.

I run my hand subtly down the back of my skirt, making sure it's not tucked up into my underwear. On Saturday morning, I found my bike and backpack locked to the railing on my porch, and surprisingly, no one had raided the bag and stolen anything. The clothes were wet and the laptop was damp but still alive, since the rain wasn't super heavy. A trip to the laundromat later, I'm walking into school looking more or less normal for once. Well, not normal for me, but at least I fit in with the other rich bitches, if I'm a little on the conservative, preppy side. Mabel's style was more J. Crew than the popular crowd, but that's fine by me. I'm not the stilettos type anyway.

A bitchy voice cuts through my determination to ignore the stares. "Oh my god, what is she wearing now?"

"Oh, bless her heart," squeals the answering voice. "Does she really think this is going to make us forget she's in a literal porn video?"

"Let's go, girls," Gloria says. "Everyone deserves a chance to start over and try again."

I try to meet her eye, to thank her silently, but she ignores my attempt to acknowledge her scrap of kindness.

"Fuck this shit," I mutter under my breath. I'm about to hand them their asses if they keep this up. But I'd rather not be suspended, so I don't react. Instead, I forge ahead and don't stop until I reach my locker. They follow me like bloodsucking mosquitos, their heels clicking down the hall behind us.

When I finish getting my books, those bitches are still standing there, watching me and snickering, probably waiting for me to lose my shit. "Don't you have something better to do than follow me around gawking?" I ask. "I swear you're worse than the guys asking me for blowjobs."

Everleigh scoffs and exchanges a look with one of the other Bitch Pack girls. "You're such a freakshow."

"So, what is it?" I ask. "You want head, or you want a lesson on how to give it?"

"Oh my god," Eleanor squeals, her face twisted up in disgust. "Is she hitting on you?"

"Ew," Everleigh shrieks, grabbing onto Gloria like she's scared I'm going to lunge for her pussy and start eating it in the middle of the hall.

I cock a brow at her. "Don't knock it 'til you try it."

"Are you really such a whore that you don't even care if you're with a guy or a girl?" asks one of their sidekicks, gaping at me. "Would you, like, do an animal?"

I can't help but laugh. "Y'all really need hobbies if you have nothing better to do than obsess over my sex life. Hey, maybe you could try getting one of your own. A good dicking might mellow you out."

"Ugh," Eleanor huffs, flipping her hair over her shoulder and giving me a once-over. "Clothes can't change who you are. You're still a skank underneath."

"Again, why are you so obsessed with my clothes and what's under them?" I ask. "Considering your pursuit of Dolce dick, I pegged you as a straight girl. My bad. But just so you know, you're not my type."

"Oh my god, ew," Eleanor says. "We're not trying to get in your pants, freak."

"Could have fooled me," I say with a shrug, closing my locker.

"Come on, girls," Gloria says, linking an arm with each of her sisters. "I need to talk to Dixie before dance. You would not believe what happened to Royal this weekend."

"Yeah," I say. "It was wild." And then I turn and walk away, just to deny them the satisfaction of doing it first. Yeah, I can be as petty as the next bitch, and I know she's baiting me, trying to get me interested in her gossip about Royal. But fuck if I'm going to chase her down the hall like she did me.

Still, I hate knowing that she talked to Royal, that he told her what happened.

I slide into my seat in class, checking the back table where Duke Dolce usually sits with his buddies. Cotton and DeShaun are there, leaned over a laptop.

I turn back to the front and start getting my stuff out, tuning in to the voices around me.

"Did you hear—"

"…can't believe…"

"… It was random?"

"Have you seen—"

"So sad."

I straighten and set my laptop on the table in front of me. Before I can open it, Dixie comes marching into the room in her kick-ass boots, Quinn hovering like a planet orbiting her cooler cousin.

"Hey, Harper," Dixie says, sliding into her seat opposite me. Quinn takes another seat at the table as usual. The teacher clears her throat, and Dixie lowers her voice to a whisper. "I know you don't like gossip, but you might want to check the blog."

Everleigh comes flouncing in just as the bell chimes softly. I've only been here a few months, but I'm already used to the posh bell. I'd probably jump out of my skin if the harsh, jangling of the Faulkner bell sounded instead.

"I'm not late," Everleigh says, a challenge in her voice.

The teacher sighs and waves Everleigh to her seat. She's a Dolce girl, so even the teachers won't give her much shit.

"We were looking for you this morning," Everleigh says, stopping at our table to address Dixie. "Gloria has tea."

"Spill."

"I can't," Everleigh says, rolling her eyes at the teacher, who clears her throat loudly. "Gloria will tell you in dance. It's about Royal."

She slips back to the table with the other populars, though Duke is missing. I wonder if Royal was worse off than we realized. I mean, the guy stopped breathing. He didn't say a word once we got in the car. Suddenly, my stomach knots. Maybe he wasn't the one who called Gloria. Maybe Duke or Baron called to tell her he was in the hospital. He could have gotten pneumonia or some infection from inhaling all that dirty water. Hell, he could have brain damage or… I know fuck-all about drowning, but I know it can't be healthy to come as close to dying as he did.

I shouldn't care. I should be fucking happy. I pushed him off that bridge on purpose. He deserved it.

But my heart seizes at the thought of anything happening to him. I didn't let myself think about it too much this weekend. After the harrowing ordeal, I slept through the Friday night fight, so I had to play poker all night on Saturday to make up for it. Then I slept all day Sunday and did homework at the laundromat in the evening. Which means I spent as little time as possible awake and dwelling on my thoughts or considering what would've happened if Royal had held onto me just a few seconds longer. We'd both be dead right now.

What would've happened if I hadn't grabbed his shirt? If I wasn't strong enough to hold onto him and pull him up? If I had to choose between letting him go and getting to shore alive, or holding on and dying? What would have happened if Baron didn't know how to do resuscitate him? If I got him to shore, and we had to wait for paramedics to arrive, would it have been too late by the time they got there and trundled down the bank with a stretcher for quarter of a mile? Would we have had to sit there and wait helplessly, watching him die?

I shiver at the thought, wrapping my arms around myself and trying to focus. Thinking about what could have been is pointless. I'm not the sort to dwell on shit I can't control. Even so… I'm not a killer. I know exactly how precious life is. Yeah, I hate Royal, and he did and said some fucked up shit to me, and I was pissed at him. But nothing he's done was as bad as what I did. I could have fucking killed him.

I almost did.

I remember Colt telling me I attacked everything with brute force instead of being patient and letting things work themselves out. That's exactly what I did. I wanted revenge on Royal, so I did something reckless and dangerous, and he almost died. I could have plotted revenge and taken my time, waiting until the moment was right and delivering a soul-crushing blow, the way the Dolces do. They held onto that video for months.

Instead, I went in with all the stealth of a sledgehammer. I wanted to escape, and I knew we could both swim to shore, so I jumped off a fucking bridge.

I'm startled out of my head by the little *OnlyWords* app popping up in the corner of my screen, the black box with boxy green letters blinking at me.

WHGossipGrrl: Did u read the blog?
BadApple: no sry ill check now
WHGossipGrrl: i'm sorry : (
BadApple: y?
WHGossipGrrl: Txt me after u read it
BadApple: k

I make sure the teacher isn't roaming the room before surreptitiously searching for the blog. My stomach is knotted with dread now that she apologized. The last thing I need is more bullshit coming my way. But I seem to be the target of way too many of her blogs, which is why I avoid the thing in the first place. Surely she has better things to blog about than a dramatic wardrobe change, even if it does involve her favorite magnet for gossip. I haven't done anything else noteworthy lately, unless…

My heart flips, and I nearly choke as I shoot her a look. Does she know what I did to Royal?

The entire school will string me up and crucify me if they find out I almost killed their king. I'm lucky the twins were there and relieved enough that I saved his life to punish me for being the one who risked it to begin with.

My hands shake as I click on the link to her latest blog.

Willow Heights Gossip Grrl

Student Attacked

I usually try to focus on the positives, but this week I come bearing tragic news. If you're a normal person who leaves "Local News with Jackie" to your parents, you probably still saw this all over social media over the weekend. If not, you missed a tragic story, and though I hate to be the bearer of bad news, this cannot be ignored. I'm sure we're all equally shocked at the news of a brutal attack on one of our own.

Sometime after school on Friday, Colt Darling was violently assaulted outside Willow Heights in the east/faculty parking lot. A member of the custodial team found him on the ground, unresponsive, when she arrived for work at around 7pm. She called 911, and Officer Gunn arrived on the scene shortly thereafter. Colt was then airlifted to Faulkner Regional where he remains in stable but critical condition as of Monday morning. His family asks for your prayers in this heartbreaking time but also asks that you respect their privacy and do not contact them regarding his condition, details of which they will share as new developments occur. Colt did not attend school on Friday but was seen leaving campus that morning with Harper Apple. His reason for being on campus after school is unknown.

The Scoop: Though the perpetrator(s) remain at large, the police do not think anyone else is in immediate danger. Sources say the attack seems to have begun over a fender bender in the parking lot and escalated to a physical altercation. If you have any information regarding this attack, please contact the police department or call their anonymous tip line.

Must have item of the week: A candle for the candlelight prayer service that will be held Tuesday night at 7pm in the east/faculty parking lot where the attack occurred. First Baptist of Faulkner's Pastor Burton will preside. The Darlings request that all cards, flowers, etc be left there or donated to First Baptist, where Colt attends.

I sit there reading it over and over, wanting to puke. Fragments of conversations I've had about the Dolce boys cycle through my mind interspersed with lines from the news-like blog post.

They're not like the guys you're used to… Prayers in this heartbreaking time… In with the mafia… Perpetrators remain at large… They're criminals… Brutal attack… They ruin lives… Contact the police… They're dangerous… Unresponsive… Airlifted… Critical condition…

I slam my laptop and bolt out of my seat, sure I'm going to be sick. Everyone turns at my sudden disruption, but I barely hear the teacher telling me to sit down as I pass her, throw open the door, and stumble into the hall. My feet carry me out the door before I can stop them. I know I'm fucking up right and left. I should sit through class and pay attention, not go back to my old habits of skipping school and smoking under the bleachers. But fuck that.

Fuck everything.

I don't have anything to smoke, so I sit on the bleachers alone, not doing anything. The day is bright and sunny and cheerful, though inside, I'm being torn apart by a fucking hurricane. This is why I don't have friends.

There will always be psychos in the world. I can't control that. I can only control how they affect me, whether I give them access to my heart.

Friends are dangerous. Friends are a means for them to get to me.

No more friends. That's my first sacrifice.

Because this is my fault. I didn't just let them get to me. I led them straight to Colt. They warned me over and over to stay away from him. They warned me they'd hurt him if I didn't. And I still had to have it my way. They don't give a single fuck about who should have been punished for that indiscretion. They could have hurt me. I can take it. I'd rather they'd hurt me than Colt.

But they knew. They knew that it would affect me more deeply if they went after Colt. And yeah, I could blame them for being sociopaths, for the assault itself, but they've never hidden who they are. I know. They warned me. Everyone warned me. Can I blame a scorpion for having venom? Or myself for reaching in to pet it?

It doesn't matter why they are the way they are. I have to stop trying to understand them and making excuses for them. They are scorpions, and they sting, and I've always known that. They don't care who's the casualty as long as they get the result they desire. No more. I won't risk anyone else I care about. Not by borrowing Blue's car, or talking to Maverick when I run into him, or even breathing the Darling name.

A footstep reverberates along the metal bleachers, and I startle, my heart in my throat for one second before my rational brain catches up and reminds me that Colt won't be joining me today.

Instead, I look up to see Dixie trudging along the row of bench seats toward me.

"Shouldn't you be heading to dance right now?" I ask, resentful of the intrusion. She wrote that blog. She put my name in it. The only reason the cops haven't shown up to ask me questions is that the Dolces had already collected my bike and backpack when the cops showed up, so no one could place me at the scene.

Suddenly, my head swims and my stomach heaves. If they really went back and got my things before the cops showed up, that means they saw Colt. They saw that he hadn't gotten up, that he was lying out in the cold rain, beaten unconscious, and they took my stuff and left him there without even calling for help.

I have to swallow down bile at the thought that I kissed the boy who did that to him, after he did it. Yeah, part of that was to distract him before I pushed him off a bridge, but I kissed him right after he beat the shit out of my friend so bad he might not live through it. I didn't just kiss him, either. I enjoyed every second of it, way more than I should. I felt the kinship of our souls.

Maybe that's the most fucked up part of all. I still feel for Royal. I still see the human boy behind the monster. I still feel a connection, no matter what he does, and I don't know how to break it.

Dixie sits down beside me without speaking, her shoulders slumped, her head down. For a while, neither of us say anything. I imagine what it must have been like for her to write that blog about Colt, to sound all professional, when I know she has feelings for him.

"I do have dance," she says after a long time. She sniffs and wipes her nose, and I realize she's been sitting there silently weeping for the boy who only we mourn. "I just couldn't go in there pretending everything was fine and listen to Lo's trivial bullshit about Royal Dolce and how he called her over the weekend, or whatever she wants me to spread around school so everyone thinks he dumped his older girlfriend and now he's into her. Again."

"Is he?"

"Who fucking knows," she says, the word sounding jarring in her sweet, southern drawl. "I've heard he's into older women, that people have seen him out at fancy restaurants with his secret lover or whoever she is. But every time he sticks his dick in Gloria, she hears wedding bells." She laughs, but the sound is hollow and tired. "And here I am judging when I've been doing the same thing for two long years."

"With Colt?"

"Yeah," she says, wiping tears from her eyes. "I know you care about him, too, Harper. That's why I came out here. I just wanted to sit with someone else who cared about him. Even if it's not the way I did."

"He's not dead, Dixie."

"He's been in the ICU since Friday night," she says. "His parents said they had to put a metal plate in part of his skull. That's how bad they messed him up."

I swallow down the bile again. I don't want to think about it, about how long Royal was kneeling on him, punching him in the face. I must have gone into some kind of shock. It didn't seem that long. I have to tell someone, and not just Mr. D. I have to tell the police. "Do you have any idea who did it?" I ask carefully.

She scoffs and swipes her eyes. "Of course I know who did it," she says. "Everyone who went to school here last year knows who did it. We've all been waiting for it, in a way. I mean, they ruined Preston and Mabel. Why would they let Colt stay, relatively unscathed, forever?"

I think about his hand, the way his skin is so tight he can't extend his fingers—the ones that remain. I think about the sadness in his eyes when he talked about his sister and even the Dolce sister. I wouldn't call him unscathed.

"Do you know why they did it?" I ask.

"Yeah," she says, knotting her fingers together between her thick knees. "It all started about two years ago."

nine

Harper Apple

"It all started when the Dolces showed up," I say. Colt's told me this story.

"No," Dixie says, shaking her head. "On Homecoming night. Which, ironically, is the night I first slept with Colt." She sniffs and wipes away fresh tears. "Royal was kidnapped. They said it was the Darlings, but here's the thing. Before Crystal died, she sent a letter to the police—Officer Gunn. He was a friend of the Darlings. I don't know exactly what it said, but for a while, he was trying to investigate Mr. Dolce because of something she said. Like, maybe they faked the whole thing."

"Why would they fake a kidnapping?"

"To frame the Darlings," she says. "They framed them for lots of stuff since then. But anyway, Officer Gunn eventually gave up, I guess. I don't really believe it, anyway. There's no way

Royal could fake what happened to him. I mean, sure, his dad could have beaten him up and put him in the school basement, but that wasn't the big thing. Royal didn't used to be like that. They found him, but it's like... Did they really?"

"What do you mean?"

"They found someone. Someone in Royal's body. But he wasn't the same person after that."

My heart is pounding hard in my chest. I remember some rich kid going missing my freshman year, but I didn't attend much school that year, so I missed most of the gossip. Even so, I remember a conversation or two about it on the day or days I was at school during that time. I remember Zephyr saying if he disappeared, the cops wouldn't be looking. They'd say good riddance and be glad for the decrease in graffiti. We all laughed because he wasn't wrong, and the truth would be too painful if you didn't laugh about it.

"Their sister wrote a letter to the police turning her dad in?" I ask, because that's the part that's new in all this. I already knew Royal got kidnapped, though I should probably search some local news articles from two years ago to get all the details.

"That was the rumor, anyway," Dixie says. "And if you'd met Crystal, you'd know it's the kind of thing she'd do. She always wanted to do the right thing, you know? Even when she didn't know what that was, she tried."

"You knew her?"

Dixie laughs quietly. "Yeah. She was my first friend at Willow Heights. My best friend."

"Wow, I didn't know," I say, again overwhelmed by just how much history has gone down in the past two years.

"Yeah," she says. "If it weren't for her, I'd never have had the courage to go out for dance or start my blog. She used to blog, too. They found her log-in and stuff when they were searching for her. I still sometimes check, just in case she posted again." She gives a little self-deprecating laugh.

"You think she's still alive?"

"No," she says. "Not really. I mean, if she was alive, she would have contacted her family. She loved them so much. Especially Royal."

"Everyone talks about her like she was a saint," I say. "They barely mention the guy."

"Really?" she asks. "Who were you talking to? Devlin was, like, the darling of Faulkner. The whole town adored him. When he fell, all of Faulkner fell with him. People reminisce about him like he was a god."

"Like Royal," I say, remembering Colt saying they used to be like the Dolces.

"Nothing like Royal," Dixie says, her face darkening. "I mean, yeah, he kept people in line at school. But the Darlings were, like, regular small-town football gods. They got lots of girls and had money. Before I started here, when Devlin was maybe a junior, I remember running into him at a restaurant and my dad honest-to-god asked for his autograph." She shakes her head. "They were loved. The Dolces are feared."

"Did anyone ever check if something happened to her because of that letter?"

"Yeah, they investigated the Dolces and the Darlings both," she says. "Mr. Dolce's crooked as a dog's leg, but he loves his kids. He's a single dad. They're all he has. And the Darlings loved Devlin, like, a crazy amount. In the end, nobody could believe either of them would sacrifice their kid to get rid of the other kid, so…"

"Just seems weird that she wrote a letter incriminating her dad, and then mysteriously disappeared. If he's mafia, maybe the mafia got pissed about her snitching."

As the words leave my mouth, I shiver despite the warm sun. I snitch on the Dolces every fucking week. If they ever found out...

"Actually, I don't think they got the letter until she'd already disappeared. So, like, it hadn't gotten out that she'd accused her dad. People still like to pick it apart, and lots of people have theories that they're still alive, like they're Tupac or Elvis or something. But in the end, I just accepted it for what it was. A horrible tragedy that took my best friend and tore apart the town."

"Sounds like it really just tore the Darlings apart."

"Same thing," Dixie says with a shrug. "I mean, I'm not saying they're saints and the Dolces are the devil. The Darlings are a mixed bag. And it's easy to say Devlin was good and Preston was evil. But everyone's got their dark side, you know? If anyone knew half the things Colt did to me, they'd say I was crazy to love him. But I knew what he was going through, and I forgave him."

"You love him?" I ask, feeling even more guilty about that last afternoon I had with him.

"Well, yeah," she says, like I should have known that. "Since the first moment we met. One day, I always thought he'd love me back. Now, I don't know."

"I'm sorry."

"It's okay," she said. "After Halloween, he said we were done. He's said it before, so I just respected that. But now I think maybe he knew this was coming, and he didn't want me to get caught up in it."

"That's what I meant earlier," I admit, swallowing a lump in my throat. "When I asked if you knew why they did it. I meant this time. Because I know. They did it because we hung out that day."

She nods, looking so sad it breaks my heart. "I figured as much."

She's a smart girl, so I'm not surprised. I am surprised that she sought me out. I hung out with her guy. And then I got him beaten to within an inch of his life.

"I'm sorry," I say again. "If I'd known… I mean, I should have. I just didn't think they'd go that far."

"Colt's a big boy," she says. "Maybe you should have known, but he for sure *did* know. If he wanted to play with fire again, that's on him."

That's what he said to me when I asked about his hand—that some people liked to play with fire. Maybe once before, he'd fought back in his own way, and they hadn't liked it.

"Well… Thanks for being cool, I guess," I say. "Most girls in your position would have it out for me."

"Maybe I'm not most girls," she says.

"I know."

"People underestimate me all the time," she says. "Like because I'm fat and have a soft voice, I must be this timid little mouse. It used to bother me, but not so much anymore. There are lots of ways of being strong. Crystal taught me that."

I think of the stiletto-wearing, street-racing, head cheerleader queen bee finding me about to leave school and challenging me to stay.

"I thought I was strong," I say. "But now I'm not so sure. They've really gotten to me."

She nods solemnly. "That's what they do. They don't start with a beatdown like they gave Colt. They start small, and they slowly but systematically destroy you. What they did to Colt, that was the grand finale for him. I thought it was his finger, but I guess they had more in store. This time, I'd bet money they never bother him again."

"Unless he plays with fire again," I say with a shudder, remembering the sound of Royal's fist connecting with Colt's face, how it didn't crack like bone anymore. I have to squeeze my hands into fists to keep them from shaking. I *was* strong when I started here, but they're breaking me down. They're making me doubt myself, question whether I was ever strong to begin with. But I know I was. I still am. I'm losing it, though, and that scares me more than anything they've done.

Dixie's right, though. It all adds up and wears me down, exhausting my energy.

The bullying, made worse because they got everyone on board with it.

The blowjob, made worse because it was all for nothing when they broke their promise to give me something in return.

The video, made worse by the fallout and the constant barrage of sexual harassment when I walk down the hall.

And witnessing the horror of what they did to Colt, made worse by the guilt and the threat that they'll do it again if I dare to talk to another guy.

"You shouldn't be out here," I say to Dixie. "The Dolces have it out for me. If they're going to destroy me, I'm not taking anyone else down with me."

Dixie gives me a long, calculating look. "I already offered, but I just wanted to tell you again, that I'm here if you need anything. I know I'm a gossipy bitch and some people don't like the blog, though most of them still read it. But I know things, Harper. I've been here the whole time."

I nod. "Thanks, Dixie."

She blows out a breath, puffing out her cheeks, and then stands. "You know, they told you to stay away from guys," she says. "We can still be friends, Harper. You're going to need them. No one can survive a Dolce targeting alone. Having friends doesn't make you weak. It makes you stronger."

It may not make me weak, but it makes me vulnerable, and that might as well be the same thing. But I'm not going to convince her, so I just shrug. "Look what happened when I made a friend."

"You made friends with their enemy," she says. "With the only Darling left in this school. The one person that would piss them off the most."

She's right, of course. I didn't do it intentionally, not at first. But I kept going after they told me to stop, when all along, Dixie was right here, offering the same information Colt had. I could have walked away from him, but apparently I have a soft spot for lonely rebel boys, and there he was. Or maybe it's the tortured souls that pull me in, and that's why I'm drawn to Royal even as I despise him.

I stand to go in with her. I'm not going to skip classes all day. I'm lucky I'm still here, but I'm sure eventually, even the admin will find out about that video, and they'll probably kick me out for tarnishing their reputation. Until then, I'm going to get as much out of this opportunity as I can.

"Hey, Dixie," I say as we start for the main building. "I know it's a little late to say 'off the record,' but can you just keep this conversation off the blog?"

"Of course," she says, looking hurt. "I'm not a total bitch, you know."

"I know. I just… Seem to end up in there a lot."

"Look, the way I figure it, people are going to talk. If it's something people saw, it's going to get around school. I'd rather get first-hand accounts and sets the record straight before the gossip gets all twisted around. If anyone doubts something, they go consult the blog. It helps rumors from getting out of hand. That doesn't mean I don't have my own private life. I'm not a reality show."

"Sorry." It's true that a part of me doesn't like the whole blog thing Dixie has going, even though it's useful as fuck to an outsider like me. I can imagine how helpful it is for people coming into the school as a freshman, who want to climb the social ladder or even just survive. I probably should have scanned through it more than I have, just skipping anything about me, but it sits funny with me.

I know that makes me a complete hypocrite. I spill the fucking tea every week to Mr. D, including this weekend after I got my laptop back. That's no different than what Dixie's doing. Sure, I have a reason for it. I need this scholarship, and that's how I'm paying for it. But maybe that makes it worse. Dixie doesn't hide what she's doing. She's sharing gossip with the whole school, making it public knowledge, helping out newbies who find themselves suddenly navigating the dangerous waters of WHPA.

I'm sharing personal information with one person who wants to ruin the Dolces. I do it in secret like a rat.

When I think of what happened to the last person who ratted on the Dolces, my skin gets cold all over again. The cops didn't do anything. Colt says they're paid off. Which means that even if they find out who attacked Colt, they probably won't do anything. That comes as little surprise to me. No one on my side of town calls the cops. We know not to expect them to serve and protect us. The only thing they serve in my neighborhood is warrants, and the only people they protect are those on this side of town from people like us.

The gangs deal out justice in my neighborhood. If you don't join a gang, you're on your own. No one has your back.

But that doesn't mean I can't fight injustice on my own terms. Just because I can't have friends, that doesn't mean I can't have allies. Colt told me there were people in this town who still supported the Darlings. And once, I thought Dixie couldn't help me just because she couldn't protect me from the Dolces. I don't need protection, though. I need allies who have cultivated their own protection already, who aren't a liability and who won't be hurt by their association with me.

She might know more Darling allies as well. In fact, I already have one. A guy who has a shitload of money and the same goal I do—taking down the Dolces.

Maybe it's time I become more than a spy for him. Maybe it's time I become a soldier.

*

The Monster

The monster under the bed
And hiding in the basement shadows
Watching in the hotel shower
Crouching in the closet corners
Isn't the beast they make him out to be.
He didn't intend to rampage through the palace halls
And terrify the kingdom.
He came to protect
The Little Royal.

ten

Harper Apple

BadApple: I think its time we meet

MrD: You do, huh?

BadApple: Yes

MrD: And why is that?

BadApple: We both want the same thing.

MrD: I knew you liked older men.

Barf. I fight the urge to write back something snarky or ask if he's seen the video. It's probably left the confines of Willow Heights by now.

BadApple: Do men rly only think about sex 24/7?

MrD: Closer to 23/7.

BadApple: Good 2 kno.

MrD: What about you, Harper? Do you think about sex a lot?

BadApple: As much as the next girl

MrD: Do you touch yourself when you think about it?

My skin gets crawly, and I shake my hands out, trying not to gag as I picture some old guy like Mr. Behr leering at his phone screen with one hand down his pants. But I suck it up and dive in.

BadApple: As much as the next girl

MrD: Do you think about me while you touch yourself?

BadApple: I'm not having chat-sex w u right now

MrD: But you will later?

BadApple: Depends

MrD: On what?

BadApple: u told me u like negotiations. Whats in it 4 me?

MrD: If we could send pictures on this app, I'd show you.

Does he really think I want a dick pic? Gross. But I have to play my cards right, and flirting with an online creeper isn't the worst I've done to get what I want.

BadApple: What if u showed me in person?

MrD: Greedy little thing, aren't you?

BadApple: Cut the bs. You want 2 take down the Dolces. I want 2 take down the Dolces. Lets work together n get it done instead of playing games.

MrD: I like how you put it all out there, Harper. Not a great move in a business negotiation, but I respect the direct approach in a woman who knows what she wants and will do whatever is necessary to get it.

BadApple: So…?

MrD: Will you do anything I want if I agree to meet you?

BadApple: once only

MrD: You'd let me fuck you however I want?

I've never felt more disgusted with myself. Am I really going to whore myself out for an ally? That makes me no better than what Royal has said I am all along. Guess he was right about me.

But maybe it's not so bad. Mr. D is not just any ally. He has money. Power. Things that turn me on anyway. Maybe he's not old and gross at all.

I wish I'd asked Dixie about the Darlings who remain in Faulkner so I could narrow it down, but it's a little late for that now.

BadApple: Not 4 a meeting. Only if u agree 2 help.

MrD: And what exactly is your plan to take down the Dolces?

BadApple: Whats ur plan? Besides ur little acts of voyeurism thru me. What r u doing w the info i give u?

MrD: All things in good time.

BadApple: u wont work w me even if I let u fuck me?

MrD: Games are so much more fun, don't you think?

BadApple: I don't like games. Im doing it with or without ur help. Just thought ud want in.

MrD: I want in you.

I stare at the screen, swallowing several times to keep my disgust down. Guess I'm not the only one laying it all out there today.

BadApple: So u'll help me or not?

MrD: Patience, my little darling. If I can wait for you, you can wait for me. It makes the payoff that much sweeter.

BadApple: I'm basically offering 2 whore myself out 2 u, n ur saying no?

I'm so frustrated I could scream. My body is my only currency. I have nothing else to offer.

MrD: Don't be discouraged. We will both get what we want.

BadApple: How do u kno?

MrD: You want out. I want in. It is inevitable.

BadApple: When? I don't have all the time in the world.

MrD: You have another year and a half before you graduate. Don't rush this. For now, keep giving me what I want, and I'll keep giving you what you want. When the time is right, we will meet. I will fuck you, my little treat. I promise.

BadApple: I want 2 meet n make a plan 4 this

MrD: You want too much. I gave you a scholarship. That's what you asked for. You haven't repaid that debt. Don't ask for more.

BadApple: k

I slam my laptop and jump up to pace my room. That did not go as well as I'd hoped. I thought the old perv would be slobbering on himself for a chance to fuck me. Guess even my body's not that valuable.

But of course not. Rich guys get all the pussy they want.

Do I want too much? Ask too much?

Of course I fucking do. I have nothing, after all. I'm starting from miles behind. I have to work for every fucking clue, and all I have to offer is my one possession, all the more precious to me because it's all I have. But my body isn't precious to him or to any guy who can get laid whenever he wants.

So what is precious to him? What do I have to bargain with?

Nothing. Not now.

He has everything he wants except one thing—information on the Dolce boys. That's the key. That's the one thing I can provide that he can't get for himself. And I've already promised it to him for something else.

Okay, then. Moving on. I struck out there, but that doesn't mean I have to give up. I'm used to fighting my own battles. I can still take down the Dolces myself, all the while getting Mr. D his information as I go and keeping my scholarship. He can do whatever the fuck he wants with the useless tidbits I give him. If that keeps him happy for now, I'll keep providing. Meanwhile, I'll find the key myself.

I can't afford to enlist friends in anything dangerous. But I can enlist myself. No one gets that powerful without making enemies. No one can be that dirty without leaving a trail. I just have to find it. Not the little info that keeps Mr. D satisfied, but something big. A scandal. A secret they don't want the town to know, something big enough to bring them to their knees. Something like the letter the Dolce sister wrote, but with proof. Or that they killed her to shut her up.

That's the kind of thing that can take down a family like the Dolces. It has to be a scandal, not just illegal but shocking and salacious.

And I know how to find it. It might take time, but I might have that now. I might even have a way in. I don't know how Royal feels about me now that I pushed him off a bridge, but I know not to assume he's done with me until he tells me he is. I made that mistake before.

I won't make it again. I'll assume what he said on that bridge is still in effect. I can't change the fact that he's psychotic and has me in his sights. All I can do is work that to my advantage. Being his toy isn't exactly prestigious, but it gets me closer to them. And that's exactly what I want. I want to become one of them, someone they trust. And I'll do whatever it takes to get there, to get that secret, something so good Mr. D can't just sit on it. Together, we'll expose them for the monsters they are, and their crowns will roll.

What's my plan? It's simple, really. Obedience is my plan. I can't change overnight, in a way that makes them suspicious. But I will let them win every battle after a little struggle to make it believable. If Royal wants me on my knees, I'll kneel. If he wants to own me, I'll tie a fucking bow around myself and deliver myself to his doorstep. If he wants to fuck me… Well, I already offered my body to a creepy online predator. Why wouldn't I give it to Royal?

If that's the price of admission, sign me the fuck up. No matter what it takes, I'm getting in. I don't want to be just a Dolce girl. I want to be one of them. To be their female counterpart, the piece they didn't even know they needed until they realize too late that they can't live without me. One way or another, I'm getting in. Nothing can stop me. After all, I'm a fighter, and I won't give up until I've walked in their world, been swallowed into the belly of the beast, and touched the beating heart of the Dolce monster. Then, I'll destroy them.

*

Darling Girl

Plain Jane
Red apple
On teacher's desk
Blonde hair to shoulders—
Proper length—
Everything in its place.

SELENA

A column of A's down a page
A book in one hand,
The other tucked behind your back.

But I know your secret.

In the hand they cannot see,
A noose.
Between the pages of the book,
The Marquis de Sade.
Less than a perfect score deserves a spanking—
Will he enjoy it as much as you?
Your proper place,
Bent over teacher's desk,
A hand fisting your tangled strands
Lift your head and let them see
There's no Jane here
Only

Mabel.

eleven

Harper Apple

The moment I park my bike on the rack on Wednesday, I know the Dolces are back. I can feel it in the air, a current of nervous excitement. The kings have returned to the castle.

I skipped the vigil on Tuesday night, partly because I didn't want to see a bunch of fakes pretending to care when they never gave a fuck about him while he was at Willow Heights, and partly because I was afraid of what the Dolces would do if I showed I still did give a fuck. Nothing in this school goes unnoticed by those boys, and I wouldn't put it past them to find Colt in the hospital and finish the job.

I will do something better than light a candle for him or go visit him. I'll avenge him and all the other girls and boys in this school they've ruined. I'm ready to play my part as the lowly peasant who serves the royals, not a princess or even a lady who might grace the throne beside them, but a whore they'll visit a few times on the side. I'm secure enough in my worth to play the part and know I'm only playing. They're the ones who can't see the value of a girl without a pedigree, or, as Royal said, a golden pussy.

It doesn't bother me. I need a way in, and if this is it, so be it. I spent the past few days doing my homework, and not just the stuff for class. I've studied up on the Dolces, reading everything I could find on them online, most of it boring news articles that didn't tell a quarter of what I know must have gone down in the past two years. Still, I know a little more than I did before. I'm educating myself, and I have no plans of stopping. I'll find what Mr. D is missing, the key he needs to take them down. Then he can work on the parents. The boys are mine.

I'm so caught up in scheming that I almost forget reality. When I walk in the door, I'm quickly reminded.

"Sucky, sucky, five dollar," a guy calls, making a lewd gesture at me while his friends laugh.

"Keep your five dollars," I shoot back. "You couldn't begin to afford me."

They follow me down the hall like a cloud of bad body spray. "Hey," one of them says, grabbing my arm. "We know you're a whore. We want in on it. Name your price."

I give a quick jab to his nose, not enough to break it, but enough to make him bleed. He drops his hold on my arm, stumbling back, looking so shocked its comical as he blinks past the pain. Adrenaline and sweet satisfaction courses through me. I missed the fight on Friday, and damn did I *miss* it. I stick around just long enough to see him touch his nose and see his fingers come away bloody. I'm a bloodthirsty bitch sometimes.

"That's the price of touching me without permission," I say, then turn and walk away.

I open my locker and get my books, ignoring the other comments and snickers as people stream down the hall past me. I wore Mabel's clothes again yesterday and today, despite the girls giving me shit. After the video, I'm glad to have something concealing to wear. I get enough guys ogling my body as it is. About the only guys who have left me alone, to their credit, are those in the Dolce boys' inner circle—DeShaun, Dawson, and Cotton.

SELENA

As I close my locker, a bespectacled little dude who must be a freshman sidles up, clutching his books to his chest. "So, is it true?" he asks, licking his lips nervously.

"Whatever it is, I'm sure it's not," I say with a sigh.

"Is it really you in that video?" he asks. "It's hard to tell because of the angle, but if you pause it at just the right moment, there's a pretty good profile shot with only a little hair covering your face."

"Sounds like you've got it all figured out," I say, imagining this asshole in his basement replaying the video over and over, watching Mr. Behr's cock going into my mouth a million times over.

"Get lost, asshole," says a big beefy guy, shoving the kid aside and throwing an arm around my shoulders. "So, here's the deal, ho-bag. You're going to come service me and my boys after school today, or we're going to send the video to your mom."

I snort and duck out from under his arm, stopping at the door to my first class. Every day, the same damn shit. It's a relief to get out of the hall and into class, where the bombardment dies down to a couple lewd comments per hour. "Y'all just go right ahead," I say with my most winning smile. "After she has a good laugh, she'll probably invite y'all in and service you herself."

Suddenly, the voices in the hall die down, and I see the three kings flanked by their three dukes heading our way, their eyes locked on me like predators who've singled out the weakest antelope from the herd. I sigh. Jesus fuck, it never ends.

My eyes meet Royal's dark gaze, and tension crackles between us for a moment before I tear my eyes away.

"Well, if it isn't big George Tanner," Cotton drawls, strolling up to the guy who accosted me.

George Tanner looks bewildered and a little freaked out as he glances behind him to see the Fear Squad blocking his retreat.

DeShaun boxes him in on the other side, so he can't make a quick escape. "Or should we call him Little George," he says, rubbing his knuckles against the big guy's scalp like he's a kid. His words are taunting, but the look in his eyes is pure viciousness. "We all know your brain's not the only thing the size of a peanut around here."

"Are you fucking with my toy?" Royal asks George, his voice low and so incredulous it sounds like a death threat.

"N-no," George manages, his hammy neck still clutched in DeShaun's muscular arm. "I mean, I didn't know! I'd never disrespect you, bro. I've got your back on the field every week. You know that. I'm your boy."

"No, we're his boys," DeShaun says. "You're a slab of meat who takes a pounding like a bitch every Friday night. If you were his boy, you wouldn't have your hands on his girl."

Royal doesn't react to the mischaracterization of the situation, to DeShaun calling me his girl. He doesn't seem to notice his boy is there at all. He's glowering at George like a snake preparing to strike. "I'm sure you've heard since Friday what I do to people who touch my things," he says quietly.

I start to edge backwards into the classroom while poor George begs for mercy, but Baron's eyes fix on me, and he steps around Cotton to grab me and wrench me back into the hall. "What the fuck are you wearing?" he demands, fisting a handful of my blouse.

"You, too?" I ask, rolling my eyes. "It's one thing for the fashion-obsessed Bitch Pack to give me shit, but why would you care? Or even notice?"

"Because it's fucking noticeable," Baron snaps, his eyes burning into me.

Duke steps over to us, looking me up and down. He swallows, his eyes going wide. "Are you wearing Mabel's clothes?" he asks, his voice low.

Royal may be making a scene to make a point, but his brothers aren't.

"What do you care?" I ask again, shooting them a defiant grin. "They barely fit me. There's no way you could squeeze your ass into them."

"Take. Them. Off." Baron grits out the words, his fist twisting in the fabric until it strains around my ribcage. The motion brings us closer, until I'm almost flush against him, only his fist keeping our bodies apart. I stare up into his blazing eyes, and something snaps into place.

Guys might notice I've changed my look, but this isn't that. I glance at Duke, just standing there gazing at me like a wounded puppy who just saw a ghost, or some such mixture of emotion. That's what this is about. Not what I'm wearing, but their feelings about it.

"You cared about her," I say, my voice barely above a whisper.

"What the fuck are you talking about?" Baron demands.

"Mabel Darling," I say. "You didn't just ruin her life. You liked her."

I know Colt's on the other side in the war between families, and I only heard his perspective, but it still rattles me to realize that it was more than them bullying her to the point of suicide. There's a lot more to that story than he told me.

"Mabel Darling was a fucking cum dumpster," Duke snaps. "Just like you."

But they're wrong about her, just like they're wrong about me. They may not admit they have feelings, but they wouldn't flip out about me wearing her clothes if they didn't care. Hell, they probably wouldn't even recognize her clothes.

"Understand this," Baron growls, dragging me even closer, leaning down so we're nose to nose. "We don't 'like' Darling girls. They're no more memorable than a used condom. Once you've cum inside them, they're worthless. We threw her away like the trash she was. You're no different, so don't go thinking you're special just because Royal wants to wreck your ass before he tosses you in the dumpster for good."

His eyes glitter with a twisted malice, and I wonder if maybe he is the most dangerous one. I've seen Royal's dark side, seen his eyes go ragey or hollow, and I've understood him. I understand murderous rage. I understand detaching from your body so you don't freak the fuck out. I've spent enough time locked in closets to do some self-reflection.

This manic, sadistic gleam in Baron's eye is beyond my scope, though.

I swallow hard and force my voice to come out light. "Never in my life thought I was special to you."

But she was. Mabel Darling, a girl whose colorless wardrobe seems like an attempt to disappear long before she graduated. She did graduate, though, and she left behind more than her tormentors. She left three broken boys who are still tied to her in some way. Did Royal pull her out of the river because he loved her? Is that why he no longer dates high school girls? I'm not sure if it's better or worse if they loved her, that their love was so toxic she wanted to die rather than endure it.

But I understand why she changed her name and vanished.

"Why are your hands on my little jailbird?" Royal asks, stepping up beside Baron. He doesn't sound like he's going to kill him in the next ten seconds, but his nickname for me sounds forced, like he's straining to hide his annoyance. The bell already chimed, and the other guys have slipped into class, leaving me with the three Dolce boys. Our annoyed English teacher swings the door closed, giving us a sour look as she leaves us in the hall.

"My hands aren't on Harper," Baron says to his brother. "They're on her clothes—Mabel's clothes."

Royal glances over me like he's just noticing that I've changed up my look. Today I chose a pair of beige linen pants that are probably out of season for people who care about that stuff, and a pale blue blouse with tan flowers and too many ruffles, which is now clutched in Baron's death grip.

"Are those Mabel's clothes?" Royal asks, sounding genuinely curious for once, like he's actually going to take my word on it.

"What about it?" I ask, trying to play it cool.

"Are you trying to piss off my brothers, or are you just that fucking stupid?" Again, he sounds genuinely open to hearing my answer.

"I didn't know," I say quietly, not dropping my gaze from his. "So I guess I'm that fucking stupid."

I really must be, too, because I can't summon the rage and hate I've felt for them while they were gone. Now that they're here, in the flesh, looking at me with real emotion, they're just boys again, not monsters. I don't even care that they're telling me what I can and can't wear. It's not like they're telling me how to dress. I'm walking around in a painful reminder of what they lost, and I feel ashamed of it and angry at Colt for not telling me the whole story. I might as well have shown up to school in their dead sister's clothes.

"Go change," Royal orders.

I wrap my fingers gently around Baron's wrist since he's still holding my shirt. "No one told me. I'm sorry."

He pushes me back against the wall, but Duke holds up a hand. "Wait," he says, narrowing his eyes at me. "Where did you get those?"

I glance from one boy to the next, my mind racing. I may be pissed at Colt, but no fucking way am I making things worse for him, even if Dixie's right and he knew what was coming if he fucked with me.

"I don't want to say."

"I didn't ask what you fucking wanted," Duke snaps, stepping forward and looming over me, his eyes stormy and dark. "Tell me where you got those clothes."

"From the thrift store." It makes sense. She left, and she's never coming back. Why wouldn't they donate her clothes, make her room into the guest room that it looks like, as if no one ever lived there at all?

"Which one?" His hands are balled into fists, and the vein in the side of his neck is popping.

I open my mouth to make some smartass comment about him deigning to set foot in a thrift shop, but then I decide I like my teeth where they are, so I shrug and answer. I give them the name of a cute little resale shop called *Lexi Lands It* where the clothes are a little more upscale than where I actually shop. Second-hand designer clothes are more likely to be found there than anywhere else in town.

The twins exchange a look. "Guess we have our afternoon cut out for us," Baron says before turning back to me. "You better hope you're not lying."

He turns and walks off, and Royal shakes his head at me like I'm too pathetic for words.

"I'll take her to change," Duke says. "I've got class with her, anyway."

"Fuck no," Royal says flatly before I can even get a word of protest out.

"Aw, come on, I've already seen her naked," Duke says.

"Remind me of that again and I'll rip your eyes out of your head and strangle you with your optic nerve."

"You're going to throw her to us when you're done with her, anyway."

"And until then, you don't touch her," Royal grinds out. "You don't even *think* about her."

"Chill the fuck out, she's just a piece of ass," Duke says, raising both hands in surrender. "I've seen a million. I don't even remember what she looks like."

"She's *my* piece of ass," Royal growls out, staring down his brother.

I clear my throat. "As much as I enjoy being fought over like I'm one bone between two dogs, I should probably interrupt this little display of alphaness to let you know I don't actually have a change of clothes."

"I've got, like, ten pairs of panties in my locker," Duke says. "And probably a couple other pieces of clothes."

I start to tell him I'm not going to wear the clothes his hookups wore, but since I'm already doing exactly that, I don't have much ground for argument.

"I'm not wearing her underwear," I say, glaring at him.

"Are you sure?" he asks. "Because you wouldn't know they were hers, right? When you were digging through the bins, hers would have been the nicest ones."

"I didn't get my underwear there," I grit out. Not that I'm above such things. When you're fourteen and no one will give you a job unless you want to whore yourself out to truckers, and your mom hasn't gotten out of bed for two months, you eat out of dumpsters and wear secondhand underwear or go without. But I'm not going to tell these guys anything to make them think I'm more disgusting than they already do. What do they know about desperation?

Royal tells Duke to go back to class and then drags me down the hall and out a side door. Another building sits off to the side, a gym that I've never been inside, since I don't have PE or play sportsball. I eye the wall, thinking it would be a fabulous canvas for one of Zephyr's masterpieces. I wonder if he knows it's here.

"Were you in the hospital?" I ask as Royal pulls me across a stretch of dead grass. "Is that why you were gone the past two days?"

"No," he says. "But I missed the game on Friday, thanks to you."

I roll my eyes. "I seem to recall you stuffing me in your car and driving me out there. I have a right to defend myself."

"You tried to fucking kill me."

"Then I guess we're even."

He pulls open the gym door and roughly pushes me inside. "I say when we're even."

"Well, thanks for bringing me my stuff."

"I didn't bring you shit," he snaps. Which is probably true. If he was in the hospital, his brothers brought it.

SELENA

We step inside the cavernous building where a group of basketball girls are practicing, the squeaks of their shoes and the sound of the ball hitting the floor and bouncing off the rims echoing off the high ceilings.

"What are we doing here?" I ask, jerking my wrist free of Royal's grasp. Without answering, he strides across the room, right through the middle of the court where they're playing. He knows they'll drop everything for him. Of course they do. They all gape at him with expressions ranging from exultant to wary. But they're all watching. He's Royal fucking Dolce. I wonder if he ever gets sick of it.

With a sigh, I follow him. He unlocks a wooden door at the side of the gym, and I can't help but wonder how he has keys to everything. But I don't bother asking. At this point, I'm not surprised by much that they have access to.

He steps into what looks like a storage room and opens a few boxes, rooting through what must be gym uniforms. "Are you wearing a bra?" he asks without looking up from his search, like he has every right to know that.

"Are you wearing boxers or briefs?" I shoot back.

160

He glances up, frowning. The asshole doesn't even know he's being invasive. He sizes up my chest. "It's hard to tell," he says, scrutinizing me. "Your tits are so small you probably don't need one."

"My tits are not that small," I protest before catching myself buying into his bullshit. "Not that it matters. Last time I looked, I was a lot more than my chest size."

"You'd better be," he says, flashing me a smile. "Otherwise you'd fit in the palm of one hand."

"Jerk."

"Thumbelina."

We stare at each other for a second, and then we both laugh. I think it's the first time I've ever heard him laugh, and even though it's barely more than a chuckle, it makes my chest fill up like a fucking helium balloon.

"Just tell me if you're wearing a bra," he says, turning back to the boxes. "Because if you're not, I'm not giving you a white t-shirt. I don't need every guy in this school popping a semi because they can see your nipples through it."

"I'm wearing a bra," I say, rolling my eyes. "And it's funny that you care about them seeing my nipples, but you don't care about them seeing your creepy porn video of me giving head."

He throws me a white T-shirt with the WHPA crest on the front. "Do you want them seeing your nipples, too?"

"No," I say, crossing my arms over my chest and scowling.

He pulls out a pair of grey sweatpants and holds them up to my hips before going back to the boxes. Finding another size, he hands them to me and leans his elbow on the top box in the stack. I can't help but marvel at the extravagance of every single thing in his world. There must be twenty boxes of brand-new clothes here, just waiting to be handed out as PE uniforms next semester. I can't remember the last time I wore something that wasn't owned by at least one person before me.

"Look, Harper," he says, then licks his lips and glances at the door behind me. "I…" He shakes his head, like he's decided against whatever he was going to say.

"What?"

"Go change your clothes," he says. "The girls locker room is the next door on your right."

"You're not going to watch me change like a pervert?"

162

"Do you want me to watch you change?"

I'm taken back to that day in Mabel's room, which feels like weeks ago even though it was only days. How it felt to have Colt watching me, to tease him a little and know he liked it. But Royal is not Colt. Just thinking about his eyes on me makes me have to swallow past the butterflies in my chest.

"No."

"I told you I have no interest in your dirty cunt," he says, his voice hardening. "Why would I want to see it?"

"Riiight," I say. "You like the dry, hard ones, made of solid gold. I'm too soft and wet for you."

He swallows, but his eyes stay hard. "Stop talking like a whore."

"Oh, but what else could I talk like?" I ask, batting my eyes at him and slipping my thumbs into the top of my pants, like I'm going to pull them down and change right here. "According to you, that's all I am."

He strides across the closet and grabs my arm, spinning me around and marching me out the open door. The basketball girls watch him march me to the locker room. "Get off my dick and go put some clothes on," he growls, shoving open the door and manhandling me inside.

He doesn't follow.

My heart is pounding in my chest as I change, and fucked up as I am, I can't help but picture him watching me the whole time, even though he's not here. Every time I get close to him, I feel like I'm balancing on a precipice, and if I fall, I'll either soar like a fucking phoenix in a shower of sparks that light up the sky like fireworks and make every single person on earth stare in wonder, or I'll plummet straight to the depths of hell.

When I've changed, I fold Mabel's clothes, but even seeing them doesn't bring me down to reality. I'm high, intoxicated by Royal's power, his danger. My insides are full of quivering, fluttering butterflies, and my mouth won't stop smiling even though I'm as scared as I am exhilarated.

My hands are shaking and my stomach feels funny, like the time when I was a kid and I picked up a plate off the coffee table, and I thought my mom and her boyfriend had eaten something with powdered sugar, so I licked it. Mom and the guy came running when I screamed, and they laughed their asses off for the next fifteen minutes while I freaked right the fuck out because I couldn't feel my throat and thought I was smothering.

As disturbing as that situation was in retrospect, this one feels equally fucked up.

I step out of the locker room and find Royal surrounded by four girls in basketball uniforms all staring up at him like he's the lovechild of an ice cream sundae and Brody Villines. They all burst into a squeal of giddy laughter at something he says, though his expression is somewhere between bored and annoyed. I swallow my ugly thoughts and start toward him, determined to keep myself under control.

I'm not some starry-eyed little fangirl going to hover around giggling at his every word, though I understand the rush they must feel when he gives them attention, and I have to admit, it's a bit tempting to join them. Instead, I set the clothes into his hands and head for the door. I don't need a fucking escort, and I don't like myself very much right now. Too many unwelcome feelings bubbling up inside me.

"Harper," he calls after me, but I don't turn.

Fuck him. I did what he wanted.

He catches me halfway out the gym door and spins me around to face him. "As much as I enjoy looking at your ass, don't walk away from me when I'm talking to you."

"Fine. Then say what you need to say. I'm missing class."

He examines my face for a second, then smirks down at me. "You're jealous."

"Not even a little."

We stare at each other a long moment, my foot already out the door, the damp air sweeping into the gym where all the girls are standing around just watching us, like they have nothing better to do than gape at the girl in the blowjob video and the guy they all worship. By the end of the day, the rumors will probably say he made me change because I had cum on my clothes.

"You said you were wearing a bra," he says at last.

"I am."

"I can see your nipples."

I look down. "Yep, it's winter and I'm in a t-shirt," I say. "Good thing I have my own little thermometers on my chest to remind me when it's cold."

The bra hides the color of my nipples so they don't show through the white tee, but there's not much I can do about the rest. You'd think guys would get over the fact that girls have nipples, since they have them too, but I guess it's a big fucking deal.

Royal considers for a minute and then nods. "Don't fight this, and I'll go easy on you this week," he says, shrugging out of his letterman jacket. Twin instincts to preen and recoil tug at my body from opposite directions. He swings it around my shoulders, and the smell of him engulf me like a mixture of warm grass in the sun and his iron grip pulling me down into the depths of the icy river.

I hear the rush of whispers in the gym behind him, the hiss echoing up into the ceiling above. Something about the moment feels so surreal, I detach from my body for a second.

"What are you doing?" I growl through clenched teeth. For a second, all I can think about is how they said they let Colt keep his letter jacket. I wonder where it is now, if he burned it like I would have if I had a constant reminder that I'd been part of a team, something I loved, and that I'd never be able to play again.

An ironic smile tugs at the corner of Royal's lips, not making it to his eyes. "Didn't you know, everything I do and say is scrutinized and psychoanalyzed until everyone's sure I'm making point whether I want to or not."

"I wondered if that bothered you."

"Why would it bother me?" he asks. "I fucking love it. Look, it's that guy who was kidnapped and rose from the grave like a demon to rule the whole shitty-ass little town, like that's an actual accomplishment. I wonder what he'll do next. Let's lock him up, not in jail but in a cage at the zoo so we can come by and stare any time we want. Maybe stick a needle in his brain and poke around in there, too. I bet he's super fucked up."

"Are you?" I ask, sliding my arms into the sleeves of his jacket. "Or do you just do all that shit to shock people because you're pissed that they treat you that way?"

"Everyone wants a ticket to the Royal show," he says, pushing open the door and ushering me out with a hand on my lower back. "Gotta give the fans what they want, keep 'em coming back for more. Empty seats don't line pockets, and unlined pockets don't grease wheels."

I hear the soft chime of the bell, and Royal shoots me a grin. It's not the bitter one or an authentic one, but an unhinged kind of smile that reminds me of one of his brothers. "Watch this."

twelve

Harper Apple

Royal shoves Mabel's clothes back at me and pushes open the door to the main building, holding it while he nudges me in with that possessive touch on the small of my back. We enter the hallway as everyone is filing out of their classes. I don't know what I'm watching for. I start down the hall, feeling the heady tension of Royal's presence behind me. Someone catcalls me, and Royal steps over and clocks the guy. He goes down like a ton of bricks.

"What the fuck," I ask, spinning on him. I'm just in time to see a guy making a lewd gesture at me, and Royal decking that guy, too.

"Keep walking, sweetheart," Royal says. "I'm just getting warmed up."

Everyone crowds around the guys who fell, and we keep walking, until we reach the next group who doesn't know what just happened, and someone pinches my ass. Royal spares a minute to grab the guy by the collar and punch him in the face four or five times before I grab him. He lets me drag him off and shoots me a crooked smile. "By the way, you look absolutely fuckable in my jacket. Don't ever take that off."

"Are you fucking crazy?" I snap. "I don't need you to pull this shit, especially because you're the one who caused it to begin with. Seriously, Royal. Stop."

He crowds in on me, his hands landing on my hips as he walks me backwards down the hall. "They're the ones who need to stop," he says. "Their playtime is over. You're mine now, and they need to know it."

"Trust me, they'll know it. Just let the word get around. I can handle a few days of catcalls. I'm so used to it, I don't even hear it most of the time. It doesn't bother me."

"Yo, Royal," someone calls. "You gonna test her out and see if she's as good as she looks in the video?"

Royal releases me long enough to punch out the guy, who stumbles back and crashes against the lockers.

"Yeah, well, it bothers me," he says, raking his hand through his dark hair and adjusting his sleeves before giving me a grin that is positively devilish.

Damn him. My panties are wet in one second flat when he looks at me like that, but my heart is also breaking. His eyes are alive and shining, the way I've only seen them after the car race. I wish I'd known the boy he was two years ago, the boy who probably always smiled like that.

"That's why you fight, isn't it?" I say, halfway to myself. "Not for the money. You enjoy it. You need it. It makes you feel alive."

"You make me feel alive," he says, sliding a possessive arm around my waist and pulling my body flush against his. He flattens one huge hand against the small of my back, sliding the other one under the front of his letter jacket to squeeze my breast. "This is why they call you Appleteeny, isn't it? Your tits are like two little apples."

I stare up at him, my heart pounding as we stand in the middle of the crowded, noisy hall, confessing that we know this about each other. He's admitting he fights. He knows I fight.

He takes his hand out of my jacket and runs it roughly up the back of my head, making a mess of my hair as he fists a handful of it and presses his forehead to mine. "I want to pin you up against the lockers and fuck you right now," he says, bending me backwards as he crushes my body against his with one hand and leans in like he's going to kiss me, his other hand still cradling my head. "Let me feel that wet pussy you like to brag about so much."

"Royal, what the fuck," I say, my voice breathless. "What are you doing to me? You said I was your toy, and you were going to ruin me."

"So be my darling doll and let me have a little fun while I play with you," he says, his voice rough with desire. "I want to hurt you so good you can't stop moaning for more."

"I can't do this," I say, trying to keep my feet under me and my head on my shoulders. It's all too much. I wonder who he fucks after his fights on Saturday, because if punching out a few guys got him this horny, he'd better have someone on standby at the Slaughterpen.

"You're not a virgin," he whispers against my lips. "You can take me."

Heat ripples through me, and I grip his shoulders. "We're in the middle of the hall."

His eyes snap open, and he straightens, his huge hand swallowing mine as he pulls me down the hall and into the darkened library. This is not what I meant. I wanted in, but it's way too fucking fast, the way he's trying to consume me like the demon he calls himself. I balk, trying to break his grip, but he drags me across the room and pulls open the shelf that hides the door to the basement. My blood runs cold, and my legs shake for a whole new reason.

"Stop," I say, my voice so loud it echoes through the empty room.

He pushes me against the inside of the door to the basement, his hips pinning mine. "I can't stop," he whispers, brushing my hair back and kissing my forehead. "You make me lose my fucking mind, Harper Apple."

"I thought you were disgusted by me," I say. "Not half an hour ago, you said I smell bad and you wanted nothing to do with me."

He rests his forehead against mine, his eyes closed, his inky lashes casting shadows over his chiseled cheeks. He's so beautiful I could cry.

"Can't you tell when a man is lying through his teeth?" he asks, his voice rough with desire, his hand gripping my hip painfully even as his face remains so gentle.

"No," I admit, a tremor in my voice. "Despite your constant shaming, I know very little about men, and nothing about ones like you."

"Then know this," he says, turning his face so his skin brushes against mine, sending a wave of erotic energy rushing over me. "When we go down those stairs, I'm not going to make you fuck me. But I'm going to make you wish I had."

Before I can ask what the fuck that means, he pulls the door closed and scoops me up in his arms.

"You're going to fall," I cry, throwing my hand out.

"Not before you, baby," he says, his feet rasping on the stone steps as he takes careful steps down into the pitch black where he forced me onto my knees. I swallow hard, my heart racing so fast I think I'm deprived of oxygen and can't think straight. My hand gropes along the dirty stones of the wall beside the stairs, sure he's going to pitch down them at any moment. But he sways to a halt when we reach the bottom, then fumbles forward.

His breathing is ragged and uneven, and I'm suddenly scared of more than him forcing himself on me. He's unraveling, unhinged, and I remember how dead-eyed he was when he was beating Colt. Did he even know who he was hitting?

I don't think so. But I think he would have killed him if I hadn't stopped him. If he got pissed enough, would he beat me to death down here?

He stumbles against something and then lowers me into an armchair. "I just want to make you feel good," he mumbles against my mouth. Then he sinks onto the floor in front of the chair, pulling me so my back is flat on the cushion, and my legs are on either side of him. I struggle to sit upright, but he pushes his mouth between my thighs, inhaling the scent of my arousal, his warm breath heating me through my sweatpants when he exhales.

"Royal," I say, pressing a palm against his forehead, my voice strong. "I don't want you to do that."

"You smell so good," he says, rubbing his face against me, then pushing it over the front of my pants and onto my lower belly, his hands bracketing my hips.

"It's too... Intimate," I say, my heart racing in my throat. I hate the darkness here, the way it makes me feel trapped and detached from my body, like I did in those closets my mother shoved me in.

I wait for him to laugh or make some derisive comment. Instead, he slides his body up onto the chair on top of mine, and kisses me. "Let me make you cum," he murmurs against my lips. "I want to feel your cunt squeezing my finger when you make a mess all over my hand."

He kisses me again, sliding his hand down the front of my pants. I struggle to position myself better on the chair, and he takes it as an invitation and sinks his fingers into my slippery slit. He moans when he finds me wet, thrusting his tongue into my mouth with slow, aching strokes as he pushes his hand deeper, slowly pushing a finger into me. My core clenches, and I gasp as the pleasure of his touch overwhelms me. I try to breathe, but his smell is everywhere, and the smell of my arousal, and god, I'm hot all over...

"Fuck," he groans, breaking the kiss and dropping his forehead onto my chest as he scoots lower on the chair. "You feel so good, baby, you're killing me. Tell me it feels good to you. Tell me you like it. Tell me you want this."

"I do but—"

He kisses me again, little distracted kisses, and I know he's not here, that if I turned on the lights, I'd see it's not Royal at all but that dead-eyed doll version of him.

"Tell me again," he says. "Say you want it, Harper."

"Royal," I say, pushing at his chest. God, he's so fucking hard, so wide, it's like pushing against the ceiling. "Can you turn on the light, or… Slow down or… Something. I can't fucking breathe. You're drowning me."

"Drown with me," he whispers against my lips, stroking my hair gently back from my forehead with his thumb. I can feel him just inches from my lips, like he's staring into my eyes, but it's too dark to see one goddamn thing. I wonder who he's seeing behind those blind eyes. His finger moves inside me, slow and strong, his thumb stroking my clit. His lips press gently to mine, and he rests his weight on his elbow, so he's not

178

crushing me. But I know he won't stop now, that he's somewhere else, where he can't stop.

"Let go," he says, his voice this hypnotic, lulling murmur. "Just stop fighting it and open your mouth and let the water in. It's easy. As easy as breathing air. Sink to the bottom with me. It's cold at first, but don't be scared. I'm right here with you, baby. Nothing can hurt you in the dark. Let go and let it in. Let me in." His finger keeps stroking just the right way, and I know I'm going to have to let go because I can't help it, despite the distracting words he's breathing on my mouth, peppering the sentiments with kisses. He presses his hips against me, and I can feel his thick, hard length against my hip as he sinks his finger into me in a slow, maddening rhythm.

"It's so dark," he whispers, his lips brushing my ear and sending shivers of pleasure through me. "It doesn't hurt anymore."

He presses his hips against me again, and the sensation of his hard cock against me and his finger inside me and his thumb on my clit pushes me over the edge. His name falls from my lips, and I press my hips up, opening my thighs for him to push as deep as his finger will reach. My walls clench around him, and he moans, slowly massaging my clit while my core pulses around his finger. He waits until every last aftershock throbs through me before sliding his finger out and pulling his hand from my pants.

His head rests so heavy on my shoulder I could almost believe he'd fallen asleep if his hand wasn't still moving.

"You're really fucking fucked up, you know that?" I ask.

"Shhh," he says, putting his finger to my lips. It's wet with my cum and smells like pussy. He slides it along my lower lip, coating it with wetness. "Taste it."

I squeeze my eyes shut, suddenly grateful the lights are out, and let him push his finger between my lips. The moment my tongue touches his finger, he comes alive, rolling onto me and pressing his mouth to mine, his tongue battling mine for the wetness coating his finger. A moan escapes him, vibrating into my mouth and down my throat, igniting my core. I'm so fucking turned on and turned around and disgusted and aroused that I don't even know what's up or down.

When his hand is clean, he finally pulls it from between our mouths and strokes my hair back, his mouth taking command of mine, his tongue moving against mine in the way I know and crave, the dominating rhythm of his usual, starving kiss. He kisses me so long I'm dizzy, and I've forgotten why I ever wanted him off me. All I can feel is his body on mine, and that it's not close enough. His cock throbs against my abdomen every few minutes, and every time, my clit throbs hard in answer. I think I'm going to cum again just from kissing him.

I reach for his pants, my fingers wrapping around the thick ridge I can feel through them. He groans into my mouth, and heat shimmers through my core. Reaching for his zipper, I slide it down and dip a hand inside. His boxers are damp, and under them, his bare cock is so hard, his skin so soft, I can hardly breathe. Bliss wraps around me as I run my hand down his full length.

He breaks the kiss, his wet lips skimming over my cheek and caressing my neck as he kisses me there, his breathing labored and hot against my skin. I drop my head back, closing my eyes and giving in to every bit of the pleasure that's drowning me. Using my free hand, I push down the top of my sweats, then drag the thick head of his cock through my wetness from my clit to my opening and back. My core trembles with heat, and I think I'm going to cum again before he's even inside.

His breathing is so rough he's almost choking against my neck.

"Put it in," I whisper against his ear.

Suddenly, his head snaps up, and his fingers spread across my face, feeling roughly over my features like he's trying to remember who I am. "You're fucking stupid to be doing what you're doing right now," he snaps, and he slides off me, onto the concrete floor in front of the chair.

For a minute, I just lie there catching my breath, the sweat on my body feeling suddenly clammy and grimy. I climb off the side of the chair and stumble around, barking my shins on things and running my hand along the wall until I finally find a switch. All the while, I can hear Royal sitting there just breathing in that hiccupping way that makes me wonder if he's crying. At last, I turn on the light. He's sitting there with his elbows on his knees and his head hung down between them, not moving.

I'm not sure what to do. I force my feet to move as I make my way across the room and sink down beside him. "Are you okay?"

"You should go," he says, his voice cold.

I lay a tentative hand on his shoulder. "I don't want to leave you here."

His muscles tense under my hand, and I draw away. I know when I'm being told to fuck off. But I also know when someone is hurting so much it hurts me, too, as if he can't contain it all no matter how big and strong he makes himself. I can feel it seeping through the air between us like the damp in the basement.

"Royal," I say, knowing I have to try, even if it breaks my heart. "You can let me in, too, you know."

"I said go."

"Okay," I say. "If it's what you really want, I'll go."

I stand and go to the bottom of the stairs, trying to make sense of what just happened between us. I can't seem to walk away. If I was unsure whether I'm in with them before, now I know for sure that I am. Royal is going to use me up until there's nothing left to use if I let him. Which means I have to find out something good enough to break him and then get the fuck out while I can.

But right now, being in isn't about getting even or playing games. It's about having to bear witness to whatever messy, fragile, fucked up pieces of his tortured soul that remain. So I sit on the bottom step, and I just wait. After a long while, he gets up, and without even looking at me, he walks to the door on the far side of the room, wrenches it open, and disappears, slamming the door behind him. Only then do I go upstairs and go back to class. I may as well not bother. My mind is in a daze and I don't hear a word anyone says to me all day.

thirteen

Royal Dolce

I pull up behind the three cop cars in the driveway, my fingers tight around the wheel.

"What the fuck do they want now?" Duke asks.

"I don't think they're here for Dad," Baron says, nodding at the house.

Duke swears and jumps out. How he missed the vandalism, I'll never know. That dude's mind is a strange thing. Baron and I climb out, too. There are cops standing around on their walkies, someone taking pictures, a few more filling out a report. A couple are talking to Dad and the house manager, who will lose his job for this one. He should have been here all day. To miss this, he must have been either out of the house, passed out drunk, or off fucking the cook in a closet somewhere.

That, or in the Darlings' pocket.

Ignoring them, I start across the lawn. The rage inside me simmers quietly, coldly. I don't need to talk to the cops. I know who did this. We may have beat back the Darling tide, but it never really ends. Not as long as a single Darling breathes air in this town.

Red paint drips down the two curving staircases on the front of the house that Crystal said look like arms. He must have stood up there and tipped over a paint can at the top of each. The paint doesn't follow the curve all the way around, but it's enough. It drips through the steps like blood, splattering the white gravel below.

He left the lower level alone, either because that's where the staff was working or because he wanted to broadcast his message. Along the top floor, his words are painted eight feet high, like a billboard to every car driving into the neighborhood. Ours is only the third house down, which means everyone else in the gated community passes our house on their way home. No doubt some of them will snap pics, and this will be all over the internet by this evening.

I pull out my phone.

"It's gotta be Preston," Baron says quietly as he and Duke step up beside me. "Just because someone disappears, that doesn't mean they're gone."

The words hang heavy in the air. Even Duke doesn't pop out a smart-ass comeback.

"I'm checking with Gloria now," I say, shooting her a message.

Royal: u ok?
ThatsLo: yeah why?
Royal: where r u?
ThatsLo: omw home
Royal: stop at my house 1st
ThatsLo: k

"Preston," I say quietly, staring up at the words.
BLOOD MONEY
They're messy, a single stroke for each line, but it still would have taken him a while to do this considering their size.

"Think about it," Baron says. "We fucked up Colt, and a week later, they fuck up our house."

"But any of them could do that," Duke says.

"Would any of the adults do this?" Baron asks, gesturing. "Or key our cars like a little bitch?"

"If they want to die," I say, thinking of what I did to the Darling men who chose to stay in Faulkner. Even my brothers don't know about that. Only me and Dad know that dirty little secret. Well, us and the dickless Darlings walking around town. It gives me a small moment of vindication when I see one of them and know. And then the shame sets in.

Of course, some of them scattered like roaches, and like roaches, they could have returned.

Devlin's parents, for instance. I frown at the empty house next door. I keep a close watch on it, and so far, no sign that they ever intend to come back and tear down the eyesore.

"Let's burn down Preston's house," Duke says, bouncing up and down like a boy about to get his first box of matches. He must have seen where my attention was focused.

"That's one way to flush out rats," I say, turning back to our house.

"Preston doesn't live there," Baron points out. "We've got to think about this logically. Have a strategy. Driving by and tossing a flaming bottle of gasoline is too obvious."

Trust Baron to be the levelheaded one.

"Then let me finish off Devlin's house," Duke says. "It'll let them know we're onto them, but it gives us time to find out where he lives, what he drives, all that shit."

"You'll be doing the neighborhood a favor," I agree. The fuckers love rubbing shit in our faces. Not only does that burnt shell bring down the value of the neighborhood, as Dad likes to point out, but we have to look at it all fucking day.

Duke rubs his hands together in anticipation and gives an evil laugh, mimicking some cartoon villain he's seen. He may be clowning, but I see the truth behind it. He's about to cum his pants just picturing the blaze.

I leave them when Lo's Mustang pulls up at the end of the drive. I jog down and meet her.

"Oh my god," Everleigh says, rolling down the window. "What happened?"

"Probably some punks skipping school," I say with a shrug, like it doesn't matter.

189

"From our neighborhood?" Eleanor asks. "Do you think our house is okay?"

I could kiss the idiot for giving me such a good opening.

"I'll run by and check," I say, opening the passenger door.

Everleigh slides out, pretending to trip and fall into me. Lo rolls her eyes and grins. I help her sister into the back and then slide into the passenger seat. "You really think they hit more than one house?" she asks.

"Probably not," I admit. "I just want to be there when you get home and make sure everything checks out."

"Thanks," she says. "But you know we have Dawson."

I shrug it off. I can't tell her the truth of it, that Dawson's way too soft to deal with Preston Darling, if this was really his doing. None of them have any idea how close he got to Lo last year. I'm not going to give her one more thing to worry about, so I don't fill her in. There's nothing much to tell. I traded her safety for a chance to get Preston once last year, and I'll do it again in a heartbeat. End of story.

Lo is… Rare.

Her grit and tenacity and strength remind me of another girl I know, another girl who showed me it's possible to feel something besides hate for someone who doesn't carry my blood. But that's different. Lo is an honorary Dolce, loyal and brave and fucking fierce, the way I imagine Crys would be if she'd survived the Darlings and come out the other side.

Harper is the enemy.

If it weren't for the fact that we had eyes on her all day, she'd be first on my list of suspects. She loves painting, after all, and she hates us.

Suddenly all I can think about is her breathy whisper in the dark this morning, and my cock throbs inside my pants.

"Put it in."

Christ.

I wanted to. I wanted to see if my cock would even fit in that tight little cunt that squeezed my finger like a vice, like it couldn't take anything bigger. I wondered if all her big talk about fucking that tattoo artist was just a front to make her seem tough because she didn't want to admit she's a fucking virgin. She was tight enough to be one. That's not what stopped me. I wanted to fuck her anyway, to force my cock through that tiny opening, rip her wide open and make her scream. I wanted to make her cum so hard she blacked out, and then fuck her unconscious body until she drowned in my cum.

But not there.

Not where I can feel the ghost, the monster, watching over my shoulder. He's too strong there. I don't know what I might do to her if I let myself.

Gloria's hand falls on my forearm, her wicked nails grazing my skin. "House looks fine," she says, giving me a squeeze, bringing me back.

"I'll go in and check with you," I say. "Just to be sure."

She rolls her eyes, and I know she thinks I'm being overbearing and all that shit. If she knew Preston, and she knew she was on his radar, she'd stop with the attitude. But I can deal with the attitude better than she could deal with the danger, so I shrug it off and go inside with them, noting that the alarm system was on all day and everything looks fine before I'm satisfied. The Walton twins are looking at me all swoony by the time I walk out, and I hear Everleigh whisper, "How does she get him to go all caveman protective like that?"

I shake my head and hold the door for Lo, who steps out under my arm. She's changed into workout gear while I was checking the house, and now she hooks her hand into my elbow, swinging her hair around as we walk down the drive.

"Do you ever stop?" I ask.

"Not when there are people watching," she says, glancing over her shoulder. "Yep, they're at the window right now."

"Sucks you can't be real in your own house."

"That's why I have you," she says, smiling up at me as we start back toward my house on foot. "Now, I know you have a joint on you, so light up before anyone sees me."

I shake my head and pull my little wooden box from my pocket, taking out a joint and lighting it. Lo looks around at all the houses, turning into me to surreptitiously take a hit before pushing it back into my palm.

"Everything okay?" she asks. "You seemed a little... Off today."

"Don't do this, Lo."

"Okay," she says. "You know I'm here, though."

"Same."

I hit the joint and pass it back. She hides behind my arm to inhale, then blows smoke into my shirt.

"Thanks," I say. "I'm going home to talk to the cops smelling like a dispensary."

"You're not afraid of the cops," she says, swatting my arm.

I smirk down at her. "Why would I be?"

"Sooo," she says. "Nothing's wrong? Did you talk to your mom about what happened on Friday?"

I cock a brow at her. "You talked to your dad lately?"

"Touché," she says, grinning. "Fair enough. You going to let me run alone today?"

"Not a chance."

"Perfect. Everyone needs to think we're together if we're going to win prom. Might as well start now."

"Your ambition is fuckin' disturbing, you know that?"

"Do you really want to go there?"

"Not really," I admit as we reach our house and turn into the drive. Only one cop is still here, probably having a drink with Dad. In a town this small, you gotta win 'em all.

"Go get changed," Lo says. "Wear something sleeveless. You know all the neighbor ladies like to watch you run."

I shake my head at her nerve. "Shouldn't you be against objectifying people? Isn't that part of your whole feminist agenda thing?"

"Eh, men have been doing it for centuries. I figure it's our turn. And you know I'm kidding. You're just as hot in a tie as you are in a tank." She gives me a wink.

"Go fuck yourself, Lo."

She glances down the road before leaning into me, standing on tiptoes like she's about to kiss me when Cotton's Jeep appears through the gate. "I just want them to know we exercise together," she says, sliding a hand behind my neck and batting her eyes at me. "Is that so wrong? You never know when someone from school or a relative in the neighborhood is watching out the window."

My fucked up head goes straight to Harper. This will get back to school, and though it's nothing exciting, it's one more thread in the tapestry of lies Lo is weaving about her life, one little piece that makes the whole more credible. If Harper hears about it, will she think it means something? Will she be jealous?

When she goes home at night, does she think about me? Is she at home right now, remembering today, how I touched her, how it felt when I made her cum? Is she touching herself, pushing her own finger into her cunt and wishing it was mine?

The better question is, why the fuck do I care? It doesn't matter how good I made her feel, how hard she came. All that matters is that *she* knows she's mine now, that I control her body, her pleasure, her pain.

And that *I* know that she's nothing but a name to add to a list, a job to do, a plaything to amuse myself with until it's all used up. Enjoying the process is optional. It ends the same either way.

fourteen

Harper Apple

Royal: u will be at the football game fri

BadApple: that wud b a no

Royal: wasn't a ?

BadApple: Still has an answer

Royal: u. will. b. there.

BadApple: sry already have plans

Royal: don't make me laugh

BadApple: not playing hard 2 get. Rly do have plans

Royal: what?

BadApple: u kno wut

Royal: u can skip 1

BadApple: skipped last week.

Royal: there will be no fight. I'll make sure of it.

My heart stutters in my chest. The Slaughterpen is, obviously, an underground fighting ring, considering that there's pretty much zero accountability. Yes, there are rules, but basically you fight until someone can't go on. A quick knockout might be a good thing in other places, but there, it's a good way to get booed out of the ring. The audience isn't there to see skill. They're there to see blood. The longer you fight and the bloodier you get, the more money changes hands. Which, again, isn't exactly legal gambling.

BadApple: u wouldn't
Royal: Try me, cherry pie
BadApple: Shouldn't it b apple pie?
Royal: only if ur referring 2 that scene in American Pie
BadApple: guess I walked into that 1

I shift on the bed, rearranging my two flat pillows to give me more cushioning against the wall where I'm leaning my back. I bite my lip to keep from smiling. I don't want to feel it, the pull of the Dolce boys' power, but I do. I'm not fucking special. I'm just like every other bitch at Willow Heights, drooling over their dicks and dreaming of being a Dolce girl. Not like I'm going to show it, though.

Royal: I want 2 c u dressed like my whore n cheering 4 me. & I want everyone else 2 c it 2

BadApple: don't rly care wut every1 wants

Royal: u should care what I want

BadApple: sry I'm not just getting my fix. I need the $

Royal: how much

BadApple: as much as I can get.

Royal: what do u need money for?

BadApple: lol

Royal: srsly

BadApple: bills n shit. N u wont get the slaughterpen shut down. U need it 2.

Royal: u will b at my game or u will never fight again.

BadApple: R u threatening me?

Royal: no.

BadApple: sounds like it. Isnt that wut the mafia does? Break knees n shit?

Royal: I don't need 2 hurt u. i fucking own that place. u think I can't get u banned? u obey me or u wont make a dime there Friday night. Or ever again.

I grind my teeth, seething with hatred. There's no victory to be had here, only acid on my tongue as I type the hateful white flag word.

BadApple: understood
Royal: Ur boring so I'm out. c u Friday. dress like the slut u r
BadApple: How cud I look like anything else?

As annoyed as I am, that part is true. Thanks to his brothers, I'm back to my old clothes, which Royal despises. After school, I had to race home on my bike, grab anything even slightly identifiable as Mabel's, and fly across town to *Lexi Lands It*. I hope they fucking appreciate it. For all I know, they won't even go. But if they did, and they couldn't find a single item of her clothes and decided I was lying... I don't really want to think about the drama they'll cause.

I kept enough clothes to get me through the week at school—khakis and plain white shirts can't be traced back to her—but I'm not going to go to a football game looking like a preppy little nerd. On Friday afternoon, I ride home on my bike. I think about going next door and asking Blue to go with me, but I decide against it. I don't want to drag her into this ugly mess, and I'm more than capable of walking into the football game alone.

But then I think about Jolene, about how excited she'd be to go to a game at Willow Heights. She was the one who told me about the Dolce boys when I didn't know who they were. I haven't talked to her in months, since I left Faulkner, but she's the kind of friend I can call out of the blue, and it's like nothing's changed. I'm not calling to ask a favor, after all.

I text Jolene, and two seconds later, my phone rings. "Oh my god," she squeals. "I'm on my way over right now. Be there in five. We're already in the car. You still live on Mill?"

"Yep," I say, feeling simultaneously guilty and exhilarated. I should have kept in touch better, even if I'm not the same girl I was growing up with her in the trailer park. Still, hearing her excitement buoys me, as if it's contagious, or at least makes me feel like the long, dark winter of the Dolce reign might not freeze me in the ground like a corpse.

Five minutes later, I hear a sputtering motor and head outside to see a two-tone brown Ford Lariat in the road, the windows down and the back full of redneck boys.

"Hey, it's Fight Club," one of them yells, waving to me.

"How 'bout them apples!" another yells, whooping and raising a coozy that is most definitely hiding a beer, not a soda.

Skeeter Bite hangs out the driver's side window and yells, "Who's dick are you sucking in that video?"

"Not yours, that's for damn sure," I call back, flipping him off.

The guys in the back of the truck bust out laughing, but it's not the same kind of shit I get at Willow Heights. These boys are obnoxious, and I'd get sick of it in the halls, but it's just teasing. There's something darker, more insidious, about the way I'm treated at the prep academy.

"Yeah, because mine's bigger," Skeeter Bite bellows over the laughter.

"Wait, aren't you called Skeeter Bite because that's the size of your dick?" I ask, pretending confusion.

The guys in the back of the truck are rolling with laughter now. Jolene hops out of the cab, then stands on the tailgate flirting with the boys for a minute before jumping down to the cheers of the boys, who I'm assuming are appreciating the lack of support provided by her cheap bra. I grin and shake my head as she skips up the walkway and hugs me.

"I kinda forgot you existed until you texted me out of nowhere," she admits with a giggle, waving to the boys and managing to look both bashful and preening at once. They drive away hooting and hollering.

"How do you do it?" I ask, shaking my head.

"Do what?" she asks, like she has no idea. "Hey, you got a smoke?"

"No," I admit. "But Blue lives next door."

"Oh my god, let's go visit," she says, grabbing my arm and dragging me to the neighbor's before I can answer.

"Y'all are so lucky," she says. "I wish I lived here. So, what's it like at Willow Heights? Have you met the Dolce boys?"

Have I ever. I shiver at the memory of how close we came the other day, the silky smoothness of his skin when I wrapped my fingers around his erection. My clit throbs, and I shove the thought away. I was stupid, burning with Dolce fever, and I got carried away. Tonight I'll have to thank him for saving me from the biggest mistake of my life.

"I've met them," I say with a shrug.

Jolene squeals and grabs my arm. "Tell me everything."

Olive opens the door, saving me from Jolene's appetite for gossip. "Hey, y'all," she drawls, smiling at us through the screen door. "I lost a tooth. Look!" She tilts her head up and pulls up her lip, revealing the gap in her teeth.

"Cool," I say. "Stick it under the pillow tonight and the Tooth Fairy might bring you a piece of candy."

"Is Blue here?" Jolene asks. "We need to bum a cigarette."

"She's working," Olive says. "But I know where the cigarettes are. I don't have to go in her room for that."

"Thanks," I say. "We can share one."

"With me?" Olive asks.

"Not with you, dork," Jolene says. "You're a kid."

"So?" Olive says. "I smoked before once. I wanna look sexy like you."

I shoot Jolene a look, and she grins. "Aw, come on, kid," she says. "You can come with us. But don't run your mouth too much. Us grown folks got some talking to do." She wiggles her brows at me.

Olive returns a minute later with a crushed back of Pall Malls and a lighter. She tucks a cigarette in the corner of her mouth, her lips rolled in completely, and tries with both hands to get a flame from the lighter. After watching her struggle for a minute, Jolene holds out a hand.

"Okay, kid, my turn," she says, taking the cigarette and tucking it between her lips. "Gross, you got it all wet."

She lights up and takes a drag anyway, then passes it to Olive, who inhales and then coughs smoke out of her nose and mouth. I can't help but crack up with Jolene because we were this kid at her age.

"Don't laugh," Olive says, stamping her foot and pouting.

"We've all been there," I say. "That's all."

"I'm not just a little kid," Olive grumbles. "I know about smoking and sex and everything."

Jolene throws her head back and howls with laughter. I put an arm around Olive. "Come on, we're going to make a poster for a football game. Wanna help?"

That perks her right the fuck up. "I've got markers *and* glitter," she says, grinning up at me.

"Well, what you waitin' for?" I ask. "Go get it, girl!"

Half an hour later, we're all sitting on my bedroom floor surrounded by markers, paint, glitter, and glue. I wonder if other girls do this shit, if this is what it feels like to be a football fan. Do Dixie and Quinn make posters for the game? Do Gloria and the Waltons?

"What's a royal ho?" Olive asks, standing back and reading the sign, a frown creasing her brow.

Jolene rolls onto her back, giggling hysterically.

"No, it says Royal's Ho," I correct the kid. "Royal is a boy at school."

"And you're his ho?" she asks.

"He sure thinks I am," I say, replacing the cap on her glue.

"Does that mean you have sex?" she asks.

"It means you have *fun*," Jolene stage whispers.

"Then my sister is a ho, too," Olive pronounces.

"You go tell her that," Jolene says, wiping away tears.

I gather up the supplies and drop them back into Olive's grocery sack. A loud, frantic pounding sounds at the front door.

My heart stammers, and I jump up, my hands balling into fists, sure it's going to be one of those assholes come to make sure I'm obeying their command. When I open the door, though, Blue is standing there, her hair tangled, her eyes wild.

"Have you seen Olive?" she asks before I even get the door open fully.

"She's right here," I say. "We were just making a sign."

"Oh, thank fuck," Blue says, pushing past me and bending to grab her sister into a hug.

"They said you're a ho," Olive says.

Blue straightens and glares at me.

"That's not—"

"You're an asshole," she says. "Leave my sister alone."

I hold up a hand. "Sorry. Won't happen again."

She stands there for a long minute and then nods. "Cool. Sorry, too. If I ever need you to watch Olive, I'll ask."

"Happy to," I say. "Also, she took a drag off a cigarette, just so you know."

She shakes her head and herds Olive toward the door. "This kid'll be the death of me."

"How?" Olive demands as they disappear out the front door.

"Okay, now that she's gone, are you really Royal's ho?" Jolene asks. "I mean, I would so be his ho. Not that I don't love Earnhart, because I do, but I'd totally dump him for a Dolce."

I laugh and shake my head. "And you'd regret it five minutes later."

"You totally fucked him!" Jolene shrieks.

A flash of memory hits me—the sensation of Royal's thick, bare cock sliding through my wetness—and I have to close my eyes and take a breath to get myself under control. But then I'm good. I'm stronger than that shit.

"I didn't fuck him," I say. "He's actually a complete dick, and this is a joke. However, if you could help make me look like the trashiest streetwalker you've ever seen, that would be cool."

An hour later, we're climbing out of the back of the Lariat. Every head turns our way, and it's not because I'm in a free porn they're texting around school. Let them look. I'm obeying Royal like the good little doggie he wants me to be. I hope he likes it.

There are a few football players mingling with parents and cheerleaders and other students outside, not to mention the whole truckload of Jolene's boys sitting there whistling at us as we walk toward the entrance. I turn and give them a saucy little wave… And run smack into a solid wall of muscle. I turn to find Duke Dolce standing in front of me. My tits are practically touching his abs, and considering the size of my tits, that leaves us really fucking close. He's in his football pants and a t-shirt, and damn, does he look good. I've never been this close to him, and for the first time, I notice his eyes aren't quite as dark as Royal's, that little gold flecks are sprinkled through his dark chocolate irises.

"Who the fuck are those guys?" he asks, jerking his chin at them, not stepping back.

"Oh, haven't you heard?" I ask, hooking a finger into the top of his pants. "I'm a whore. Obviously I need clients."

He groans and pulls my hand away. "You just don't know when to stop, do you?"

"Sure don't," I say, batting my lashes at him.

"Baby, I would eat that cherry pie like it's a fucking pie eating contest if I didn't think I'd get my balls busted for it," he says.

"But between you and my brother, I don't know who's crazier, and I like my balls just the way they are." He grabs himself as if to demonstrate, and Jolene lets out a squeak like a mouse.

"Sup?" he says, still cupping himself as he jerks his chin at her.

For maybe the first time in her life, Jolene is speechless, her mouth hanging open.

Duke grins and drops her a wink. "Find me at the after party, and I'll empty these boys between those tits."

"Come on," I say, grabbing her arm and pulling her toward the line for tickets.

"Did you see the size of that thing?" she asks, halfway hyperventilating as she fans herself with one hand and clutches my arm with the other like she's about to faint.

"It's a cup," I say, rolling my eyes.

"I heard that," Duke calls as he saunters past.

"It's still true," I holler back.

"Lies," he yells. "All lies!"

Jolene and I burst into laughter as he disappears through the gate. We get tickets and head inside, our posters under my arm. We stand at the railing in front of the front row, even though some parents give us dirty looks. That's the thing about Willow Heights parents. They'll grumble and glare, but they're too polite to tell us to fuck off.

I don't anticipate lasting too long, anyway.

A little section of girls stand at the railing in the corner, all of them wearing the black-and-gold jerseys of our team, though they're in tiny sizes that are tight on them. "Who are they?" Jolene asks, nodding to them. No one is giving them dirty looks.

"Those are the team's fangirls," I say. "Also known as the Dolce girls. Supposedly they service the team after the games."

Jolene sighs like it's the most romantic thing she's ever heard. "I want to be a Dolce girl."

"You and me both," I mutter, though I'm pretty sure my reasons are different from hers. I want in. If I have to be in their beds to do it, that's a price I'm willing to pay. But my services don't extend past Royal to the rest of the team, no matter how much they defend me in the halls from their own teammates or how good Duke smells when I'm almost pressed up against him.

I hand Jolene one of the posters, and I take the other, and we hold them on the outside of the railing. The cheerleaders read them with mixed reactions. Some of them give us dirty looks, but others giggle and elbow each other. Gloria never breaks her stride, to her credit, continuing her chants. She gives her head a little shake when our eyes meet, but for a second, her smile turns genuine before going back to the plastic cheerleader one she pastes on.

They cede the field to the majorettes, and Gloria drops her pompoms and runs by our spot. "You're crazy," she calls up to me. "Want me to tell him you're here?"

"I think he'll notice," I call back, flashing a grin at her as she dashes away, her blonde ponytail bouncing.

I feel high and free, like I do when I jump in front of a train. That's what I'm doing now. Playing chicken.

Except instead of a train, it's Royal, who might be even more dangerous. Still, it gives me the same rush, the same exhilaration. It's always worth it—until it isn't.

fifteen

Harper Apple

A few minutes later, the majorettes jog off and the dance team races onto the field and takes their positions. It takes me a second to recognize them in their black bodysuits with gold glitter, but then I spot Dixie, Quinn, Gloria, and some of the Bitch Pack girls among them. I wave to Dixie, and then the music starts, and they go into their routine, dancing to some pop song by Isaac Vega. Jolene and I pick up our signs and hold them above our heads, shaking our asses and dancing along.

The team leaves, and the band moves to the sidelines. I'm a little disappointed that the team didn't come warm up on the field, but then, I know zero about how football games work.

"And now," the announcer booms over the PA system. "The moment you've all been waiting for. Let's welcome to the field, from Willow Heights Prep Academy, Royal Dolce and the Knights!"

Our side of the stadium echoes with screams and cheers and stomping feet, and a second later, Royal and the team come bursting through the paper over the tunnel at the end of the endzone and pour onto the field. My heart does a stupid little catch when I see him, but he doesn't see us. The team bounds onto the field and lines up as the announcer calls the other team, the Hellstern Jalepenos.

They take the field, and a referee does some consulting, and then the teams start running at each other. Despite my lack of knowledge about the game, it's not hard to find Royal, since he's the quarterback and a freaking giant. Even though I don't give a hoot about sports, I know our team is undefeated this year. It's hard not to know that when half the conversations at school are about it. But even I can tell his first pass is questionable at best. It's about eighty yards long and doesn't even come close to the guy he's aiming for. The next two are no better.

"Oof," Jolene says. "Someone's off his game tonight."

I've only seen Royal play once, and I remember him being good, but for the first quarter of the game, he doesn't make a single good pass. He throws himself into every play like he's dead set on getting injured and ends up in a pile-up that I'm pretty sure is actually a fist fight at one point. Hellstern's not exactly playing nice, either. At the end of the quarter, they sack Royal so hard his helmet flies off, and when he gets up, he tries to throw a punch, and like five coaches and a ref have to drag him back to the sidelines.

Definitely something going on with him, though I don't think he's even seen us, so I know it's not about our sign. I'm a little guilty about it, and I'm starting to think we should put them away and not fuck with him tonight. Part of me feels for him, and the other part is scared of what he'll do if I piss him off right now.

"Oh, good, he's handing off," Jolene says, pulling me back to the game.

"Is that good?"

"Depends," she says. "When it's a choice between that or playing Russian Roulette with this defense and then throwing Hail Mary's every play, yes."

"Wow," I say. "You're really into this."

"I have a lot of guy friends," she says. "Some of them like sports."

"Do *you* like sports?"

"Mostly for the uniforms," she admits with a giggle.

I shake my head, feeling that pang of regret inside me. If we'd stayed in the trailer park, Jolene would probably be my best friend, the kind I don't have now. Losing that seems far worse than gaining a real house. There's a weird exclusivity to the trailer park pack, though. You can't really be one of them if you're... Not.

We watch the rest of the quarter, which goes better, mostly because Royal keeps handing off to Duke, who runs through invisible gaps between defenders and even literally runs over their backs at one point.

"You think he really meant what he said before the game?" Jolene asks just before halftime, when Duke's just scored his second touchdown and is clowning around in the endzone.

"Hard to know," I say. "He clowns a lot, but he's pretty serious where his dick is concerned."

The whistle sounds, and the crowd starts getting up to get drinks. I'm about to ask Jolene if she wants snacks when I hear something hit the railing. The next second, Royal jumps up and grabs the top bar, jack-knifing his body to swing himself up to standing, shoving his feet onto the edge of the bleachers under the bottom rung. For one split second, all I can do is watch in awe at the power and pure athleticism of the move, like he's a fucking gymnast in the body of a football god.

"What the fuck are you wearing?" he demands.

"Oh," Jolene says, covering her heart and blinking up at him as he towers over us. "You scared me."

He doesn't so much as glance her way. His gaze is on me, wild and ferocious as an animal.

"You told me to dress like a whore," I remind him. "And take out an ad letting the whole town know I'm your bitch."

"I didn't mean for you to show up in a G-string."

"You don't like my shorts?" I ask, gesturing to the denim covering… Some of my pelvic area. True, at least an inch of ass cheek hangs out the back, and they're as high cut as a bikini on the legs and so low rise I had to shave my pubes, but hey, I'm just following orders.

His nostrils flare, and he glares down at me, a vein in the side of his neck pulsing with his heartbeat. His voice is hard and cruel. "You have no class."

I cock a brow. "You sound surprised by that."

"Put the signs away and go put on some fucking clothes," he says, speaking slowly as if he's plum out of patience.

I hold the poster between us and smile up at him. "You don't like it?" I ask. "It says W.A.P 4 Royal. That means—"

"I know what it fucking means, Harper."

"Didn't you want the whole town to know that my pussy's wet for you?" I ask, standing on tiptoes and letting my lips brush his chin. I speak low, so only he can hear, letting my lips linger on his skin. "Or did you think it meant I'm saving this wet-ass pussy just for you? Either way, it's what my king commanded. I simply obeyed. I dressed like a whore and let everyone know it's for you. That's what you said you wanted."

He snatches the sign, drops it on the ground, and hooks his fingers through the crotch of my shorts, which admittedly is really just the seam. I can feel his knuckles pressing against the softness of my mound, and I suck in a breath, but he doesn't seem to notice. His eyes are cold and savage, the way they get when he's dealing a vicious blow. "I already know you're desperate," he snaps. "Everyone in Faulkner knows you're desperate."

"How could I not be?" I ask, gripping his thick biceps and batting my eyes. "Your dick is so impressive, every girl in town is desperate for it."

"Not every girl sucks off old fat men because that's all she can get," he grinds out. "You're not desperate for me. You're desperate for attention and any dick you can get."

The words sting, and my throat tightens.

Royal leans in, getting in my face and pulling my hips toward him so I can't retreat. "Get this straight," he says. "You're worth less than a whore because you give it away for free, and everyone knows it. If I told you I'd fuck you the middle of the field right now, you'd run down there like it's a track meet, spread your legs, and cream a fucking waterfall for me in front of the whole town."

I swallow hard, my heart beating erratically, wondering if he's right, if that's why I'm simultaneously enraged and aroused by his cruel, crude words.

"Consider yourself lucky that I'm even speaking to you right now," he continues, his voice a low and icy. "Consider that being my plaything for even a week is the best you'll ever get in your pathetic little life. And if you can't have any more respect for yourself than this, then consider whether I'll want what's under here after everyone else has already seen it."

My own mother's words echo in my head, so similar to what he's saying. *Don't judge me. Girls like us, we take what we can get. Good men don't waste their time on the likes of us.*

Fuck. That.

Royal releases his hold on my shorts, but I grab his shoulder pads before he can step down. It's my turn to speak my mind.

"And maybe *you* should consider what a steaming pile of bullshit that is," I snap. "I don't consider myself lucky to catch your attention. I consider myself cursed. You think you're so special that girls actually *enjoy* being tormented and tortured by you? The best moment of my life will be when I never have to see your toxic face again."

"Put on some fucking clothes," he growls, getting up in my face until our noses touch. "What's under there is for my eyes only."

"I'm not done talking," I growl back, not backing down a centimeter. "I didn't ask for, nor do I want, to be your plaything. You gave me no choice. But I do still have self-respect— enough to not give a single fuck if you want what's under my clothes, and to know that my value doesn't go down even one miniscule drop whether one person or the whole town has seen my body. It's my fucking body, and its worth has zero to do with your opinion or anyone else's. If it's so repulsive to you, then stop fucking looking."

To my horror, I feel my lip trembling, but I don't drop my gaze from Royal's. He's so close I can feel the heat of his body coiling against me as if seeking a way in, his breaths quick and hot against my mouth, making my blood quiver in my veins.

We're still locked in a staring contest when Duke jogs over and hops up on the railing beside Royal. "Coach is about to have an aneurism over you missing halftime," he says to his brother, clamping a hand on his shoulder. It might look like a casual gesture, but I can see his fingers squeezing until his knuckles whiten. "And there are scouts here tonight, so you might want to stop finger-fucking your toy and start impressing them."

He hands me Royal's familiar letterman jacket and then grabs his crotch. "And you. Go easy on my boy here. You're killing him. You have no idea how much it sucks to pop a boner while wearing one of these things. If you did, you'd have mercy on us all and put this on before you lose us the game in front of a bunch of college scouts. There are a lot of guys on the team who need to impress them if they want to leave this festering swamp."

Shame burns through me, but I only glare at Royal as I slide my arms into the sleeves of his jacket. "You could have told me."

"Like you'd fucking care."

I turn to Duke and smile up at him. "Thank you," I say. "I was actually getting cold, and this asshole failed to mention this was an important night when he coerced me into coming. I certainly wouldn't want to lose you a game because your star quarterback can't keep his dick in a cup."

Duke grins and elbows Royal. "See. More flies with sugar. It's a Southern thing."

"You need to work on your sugar," I say, standing on tiptoes to give him a quick peck on the cheek. "But I appreciate the attempt."

Duke hops down and jogs off. We all watch him go. Then Royal turns back, a frown furrowing his brow. "Don't fuck with my brothers because you're pissed at me," he says. "That's low, even for you."

I swallow hard. "You're right."

He shrugs. "Do it again, you'll pay for it later. That's all the warning you'll get."

"Thanks."

He gives me one more look, shaking his head at my bare legs, then hops off the railing and stalks off.

"What in God's blue blazes," Jolene says. "You been holding out on me, girl!"

"It's not what you think."

"What I think is that *Royal Dolce* wants to rage fuck you six ways from Sunday, and so bad he's throwing away his future for it, too, I might add."

"I never asked him to do that," I mutter.

"Good grief," she says, rolling her eyes. "You don't know anything about boys, do you? Let's go smoke under the bleachers. Got any money? I could use a Coke, too."

I follow her to the concession stand, thinking of those college scouts seeing my tasteless signs. I hope they have a sense of humor. But what did Royal expect? He knows I can't simply roll over and obey. He should have known I'd pull something. Why would he even invite me to a game, let alone a big game where he needs to impress someone?

Unless…

I want to laugh at myself just for thinking it. Of course he didn't want me there for moral support, to be cheering for him and give him confidence when he needs it most. He's got so much confidence he might explode at any minute, like a balloon you keep blowing up until it pops. And he's got a whole gaggle of cheerleaders to cheer for him, not to mention the section of Dolce girls wearing his jersey number, the announcers yelling his plays over the intercom like he's a fucking rock star, and a whole stadium who shriek like fangirls at a *Just 5 Guys* concert when he jogs back onto the field.

Fuck. I rub the bridge of my nose, feeling like the royal asshole that I am. That's a shit-ton of pressure for anyone, and Royal's not exactly the calm and collected type. He's volatile under the best circumstances. Maybe he really did want me here for support. For whatever reason, we have a crazy, intense, soul deep connection with each other, one he's been perfectly clear he feels, too. In fact, he's been far more honest about it than I have, laying it all out there for me.

When he needs someone, someone who understands him on a level that has nothing to do with the logical, he reaches for me. And I can't help but respond, even if it destroys me a little each time. Even if our connection manifests in us trying to murder each other, I get him. So maybe tonight, when he was too scared or overwhelmed or stressed, or just simply couldn't articulate what he really needed, he hoped I'd come through for him. And because more often than not, he's showing his ugliest side when he calls to me, I've built up my own defenses against him, and instead of showing up for him, I humiliated him.

And so goes our vicious cycle. His darkness calls to me, but it won't accept me when I arrive, won't let me in. My darkness answers, but it comes with barbs, ready to defend itself. Instead of letting our darkness merge, we battle each other, hurting each other in ways both subtle and blunt, and we push each other further away. In his darkest moments, he takes out his pain and rage on me, and in return, I become more hardened and more lost to him each time.

That's why we're impossible. Not because I'm poor and he's rich, or even because he thinks I'm trash. We can never be because we understand each other too well, and both of us are too scared to get closer, to let someone in to that extent, and most of all, to lose control.

After all, isn't that why I push his buttons, even knowing how dangerous he is? Because I want to see him snap, to lose that iron hold he has on himself. I want to break down that dam inside him, even though a part of me knows that when his darkness floods out, it will swallow me whole and drown me completely. Maybe, most of all, I want to believe it'll be worth it.

*

Charades

The scouts are here tonight
They say
So make sure you're on your best
Game
The scouts are here tonight
I hear
They're going to be looking for the next
Big Star.
The scouts are here tonight
You say
Let's show them what it means to carry
The Dolce name.

I'll show them what it means
I'll play your games
I'll be their star
Pretend you'll let me leave
With your secrets clutched between my fingers
To play for them one day
But we all know the truth, Dad
If you carry the Dolce name
You won't go far.

sixteen

Harper Apple

After the game, we stand at the edge of the parking lot, Jolene trying to bum a smoke from every passing family as we wait for Skeeter Bite to pick us up.

We're still waiting when a cheer goes up from the small crowd lingering around the entrance, mostly kids from our school. The football team comes pouring out the gate, their hands raised for high fives. The second half of the game started a little dicey, but after Willow Heights kicked away the ball, something happened that I don't want to think about too much because witnessing it felt... Wrong.

Royal was stalking off the field, clearly pissed, when Baron Dolce ran in front of him and grabbed his facemask, right in the front, and pulled Royal's head up. He crammed his facemask right up against Royal's, and they put their arms around each other, and just stood there on the sidelines for the whole next possession. They were obviously talking, but the intimacy wasn't about a pep talk. The way they held each other made me want to cry, the fierceness in Baron's grip on Royal's helmet, the way Royal clung onto him as if all those pads were a life raft.

When the offense went back on the field, Royal seemed more like the last time I saw him—he made risky passes, but they were beautiful to behold, even when Baron didn't catch them. He usually did. Royal still played like he was trying to get himself stomped to death, flinging himself in front of the defense like he was daring them to break his neck, throwing would-be tacklers to the ground like he was unbreakable.

But somehow, the game ended without anyone being carried off the field in a stretcher, though Royal took a beating like I'm sure he's never even gotten at the Slaughterpen. After seeing the game tonight, I'm not even sure why he needs the Saturday night fights. If he does this on Friday, fighting again on Saturday is just plain masochistic.

He ignores the raised hands trying to give him five and heads for his car. Duke soaks up the adoration like it's oxygen, holding up his hands for everyone to slap, running a circle around the group to get more, grabbing a girl to kiss her hard on the mouth, then signing her friend's boobs with a Sharpie. After he's gotten all the slaps on the back he can, Baron tugs him aside and nods to us.

"For fuck's sake," I mutter as they start our way. "What now?"

"You are still wearing his letterman jacket," says Jolene, puffing nervously on the cigarette she finally procured. "He's not going to let you keep that if you're not his girl. That means something, Harper."

I quirk a brow. "Does it, though?"

Duke comes running over, bent halfway over, his arms out like he's a kid playing he's an airplane. He scoops up Jolene, who shrieks so loud half the crowd turns to see—the half that wasn't already watching the Dolce boys' every move.

Baron grabs me and hoists me over his shoulder, so my ass is in the air. "Let's go."

"Put me down, asshole," I say, kicking my legs.

"Your attempts to fight us were cute at first, but they were futile then, and they're futile now," he says. "And they're starting to annoy me."

"Then put me the fuck down."

"Don't you get tired of fighting when you know you won't win?" he asks.

He's right in some ways. This fight with them is exhausting, and he must wonder why I keep fighting when they always win. But sometimes, there's compromise. Sometimes, there's little victories even when the big battle is lost. Poor people know that. That's why I don't roll over. Why I can't.

"Royal told me to come to the game, so I did," I say. "I fulfilled my obligation. That's all he asked."

"There's an afterparty," Baron says, arriving at the Range Rover. "I suggest you behave yourself better there than you have here." He opens the door and stuffs me into the back, where Duke has just deposited Jolene. Duke takes his spot in the front seat, like usual, and Baron slides in with us. Not for the first time, I wonder how the twins worked out who gets shotgun, and if Baron resents that he always literally takes a backseat to Duke.

"Party time is pussy time," Duke hollers, rolling down the window even though the November air is heavy with a damp chill, the kind of cold that settles in your toes and stays there for days, so you feel like you can never quite get warm. Or maybe it's the fact that I just spent hours wearing next to nothing. I'm more than grateful for Royal's jacket.

Duke hangs out the window, whooping and hollering to everyone we pass in the lot, and then flying his hand out the window like a kid playing with the air currents as we speed through town.

"We're going to a party with *the Dolces*," Jolene whisper-shouts in my ear. "I would have worn something else. I didn't even shave my legs today!"

"As long as you shaved your pussy," Duke says, twisting around in the seat and wiggling his brows at her. Jolene goes dead silent, obviously not having meant for the guys to overhear her whispering.

Royal pulls up outside my house, blocking the driveway, where my mom's car and an unfamiliar truck are squeezed in. Great. She has company.

For a second, I think they're going to let me go. Royal has been ominously silent the whole ride. If he's pissed, maybe he doesn't want me at his party after all. I reach for the door handle, but Baron lays a firm hand on my knee. "Go inside and change," he says. "Wear something decent."

"Got it," I say stiffly, jerking my knee away. "And stop touching me like you have the right."

"Do I need to come in with you and pick something out of your trashcan, or can you manage to dress yourself?" he asks.

"Fuck off."

"Don't be a little bitch and come out in sweats, blinking those doe eyes at me and pretending you're clever. A skirt that's just above the knees, a tight top. Not too much skin. Not too little. No turtlenecks. Look like you put a little effort into it, okay, sweetheart? Or is that asking too much?"

I glare at him, wishing I could throat punch the asshole into tomorrow. I don't think that would go over too well, though.

"I'll try my very best, your majesty," I say with my fakest smile.

"If you're not out in ten minutes, we'll come in and help."

SELENA

I think about the Dolces walking into the dump I call home, with the dingy carpets and hideous wallpaper that was ugly decades ago, the dusty blinds and drunken occupants, and my pulse pounds in my temples. No fucking way. It's shameful enough for them to see me and the outside of my house. They don't have to see the whole humiliating inner workings.

"I'll be out in five."

Royal clears his throat quietly, but he doesn't speak. Somehow, it feels like a threat, like he's warning me. Like he might want to come inside and get more ammunition on me.

I hop out, but Baron throws out a hand, stopping me from slamming the door. "And take off some of that clown makeup. Less is more, sweetheart."

I grit my teeth and storm up the walkway, banging through the front door. Smoke envelops me, so thick everything is seen through a haze. Mom sits on the couch between two tattooed men, each of them with a hand on her thigh, all three of them smoking joints. The coffee table is littered with beer cans and overflowing ashtrays and drug paraphernalia. Loud metal music rattles the windows. I shake my head and duck into the hall, hearing my mom squeal with drunken laughter even over the screaming guitars.

I consider coming out in the sweats Royal nicked from the gym and telling them Royal found them plenty sexy the other day, but that would just piss off Baron even more. And yeah, I can be a punk, but I'm not dumb. I know when to quit… At least sometimes.

Instead of blatantly disobeying them and ending up with their polished, shiny rich asses in my house, where they'd see the squalor I come from and probably be hit on by my mother, I yank on my best pair of Levi's, hoping they'll consider tight jeans sexy enough, even though they're high-waisted. Scanning through my closet, I find nothing remotely suitable. In the end, I choose a tight crop top but pair it with a light jacket so I'm not showing too much skin. Then, because I'd rather err on the side of too little rather than too much, I shove my feet in my combat boots, one of my best thrift store scores, since they're real leather.

I don't have time to wash my face and reapply makeup in the two minutes I have left, so I just wash my face, grab a pair of earrings and a tube of lipstick, and then dash to my closet to peel another twenty off the roll. Never hurts to have some cash in case I need a ride or whatever the night brings. Tucking my stuff in my pocket, I head out, ignoring the way one of Mom's conquests eyes my ass the whole way to the door.

The second I step out, I run face-first into the hardened body of Baron Dolce.

"It hasn't been ten minutes," I snap, yanking the door closed behind me, so he won't see inside.

"You said five."

"Even you couldn't change and wash your face in five minutes."

"You'd be surprised how fast a man can undress," he says with a smirk. He reaches out and flicks my jacket open, taking in my bare midriff before scanning the rest of my outfit. "Good enough."

He turns and heads for the car, and I bite my tongue and follow. Duke is in the backseat, his tongue down Jolene's throat, so Baron takes the front while I squeeze in next to the groping couple. Maybe the seating arrangement doesn't mean anything. Maybe my thinking it does says more about me than them. I need to stop this, need to pull back before it's too late. I'm already all tangled up in their shit, even though I still know fuck-all about them.

But I have to remember that I'm not one of them. No matter what happens, even when I get in with them, I'll never be a part of their family, their bond. I'll never fit into their world. I fit in with the likes of Blue and Jolene, with guys like Skeeter Bite and Dodge and Shiner. If I play my cards just right, never making a wrong move, and a little luck is on my side, I can land a guy a little above my class, a guy like Maverick or Zephyr. I don't belong in Royal's world any more than he belongs in mine, any more than he could walk into my living room and walk by that scene tonight and look the other way for me, pretend he didn't see it, because he knows how to let me keep my dignity.

Royal would never let me keep my dignity. And when I'm with him, I don't try. I dress myself up as a skank and make a spectacle of myself, because the truth is, I don't know how to exist in his world, either. And losing my dignity on my own terms is better than him taking it. Than admitting I'm lost, that I'm fucking frustrated as hell and I don't think I'll ever be able to get out from under his thumb, let alone gain his trust or get in with his crowd.

I ignore Duke and Jolene sucking face all the way to the party. I'm not in the mood for any of it. If I had friends who would have my back, I'd get fucked up. I'd drink until I was wasted and puke in the bushes and forget this night and my whole fucking life for a night, just like my mom is doing at home, probably letting those dudes run a train on her and telling herself it makes her a fun girl, that it makes them want her more instead of seeing her as trash. It's not that I don't drink. I just won't drink around these assholes. Too much chance they'll use it to their advantage.

We're not friends. I don't have friends. I have girls like Jolene, who are down to have a good time, but when shit gets real, they split. That's the way I like it. That way, I know who I can trust, and there's never any question who has my back. I have my back. I trust me.

We get on the highway and pass stretches of fallow cotton fields and low-lying areas of trees standing in water from the latest storm, though really, the pseudo-swamp never really dries up. It just doesn't have enough water to have anything cool like crocodiles and be labeled a real swamp. Instead, it's chock full of mosquitos and cottonmouths. For a second, my throat goes dry, and I wonder if they're going to drive me out here and ditch me on the way to the party. I'm sure as shit not going to walk home through those fields.

We turn off at the next exit, and I sit up straight. I may be freaking out a little, but fuck if I'm sitting here moping instead of watching where we're going. Not for a second did I lose track of where we are. I have my phone and twenty bucks to get me home if they ditch me, so I better know where to tell someone to come pick me up.

"Are we going to the quarry?" I ask.

"You know it," Baron says, not turning around in the front seat.

"You guys go to the quarry?"

"Everyone goes to the quarry, Jailbird."

The quarry is exactly what it sounds like—an old rock quarry—but it's also a place Faulkner kids use to swim in the summer, since there's a basin of water. And since it's not at anyone's house, no one's parents have to be out of town for someone to throw a party here, though the cops eventually come bust them up. When there's no party, it's also a good place to park for girls who have the sort of parents who give a fuck about whose dick is in them.

We turn onto the old dirt road leading out there, and I pretend I can't see that Jolene has Duke's dick in her hand and is jerking him off while she sits astride his lap, kissing his neck. He lets his head fall back, rolling it toward me. Our eyes meet, and he does that thing where he slowly wets his lips, a little smile playing over them. He raises his brows just a smidge and glances down at his lap, making the slightest nod with his head. An invitation.

I roll my eyes. Hell no.

Still, it's a dick, and it's hard not to look at it. It's a pretty damn nice dick, if I'm honest, long and full like Royal's. Even though I don't jump in to give Jolene a hand, he keeps watching me, his eyes almost daring me. I stare back at him, refusing to drop my gaze, even though I can feel my cheeks flush when he rolls his hips just a little, pushing his dick up higher, like he's trying to draw my attention, so I'll lose our staring contest.

He should know I'm not afraid of a little dick. Or a big dick, as the case may be. These boys think because they're alphas, because they're huge and dominant, that every girl is going turn into a giggling idiot or a blushing virgin when they get crude. The sight of a dick stopped shocking me before I reached puberty, and fuck if I'm going to be intimidated by one now.

We pull up at the quarry, and Jolene climbs off his lap, blocking our line of sight and interrupting our stare down. I climb out my side of the car and face Baron, who's just gotten out the passenger door. "So, you going to fill me in on my orders, or just let me fuck up so you can publicly shame me when I break the unspoken rules I didn't know existed?" I ask.

He grabs my wrist, his eyes intense behind the lenses of his glasses. "For one, you'll stop fucking with Royal if you know what's good for you," he says, dropping his voice so the others won't hear as they get out their side of the car. "And trust me when I tell you not every girl gets that warning."

"What makes me so special?"

"That's the fucked up part. You're nothing special at all, are you?" he asks, cocking his head and studying me like he thinks I should be easy to figure out. With as many women as he fucks around with, he should know that none of us are.

"Not a bit," I say, giving him a tight smile. "So just tell me what to do, and I'll do it if it means you'll leave me alone."

"Oh, now you're going to obey?"

"For tonight, maybe. Depends on what you ask."

He smirks and lets his eyes rake over me. "Even if you offered me what I want, I couldn't take it."

"Because I'm Royal's toy," I say, rolling my eyes.

"For tonight, maybe," he says, mimicking my words. "But not if you keep this shit up."

I grind my teeth and glare at him. "How can I stop when I don't know what I'm doing wrong?"

He leans in, so close I could stand on tiptoes and kiss this beautiful enigma of a boy. "That's the beauty of the game," he whispers, his warm breath caressing my lips in the cold night.

I'm not sure he's ever talked to me before besides to compliment my street art. He talks to his brothers about me like I'm not there, or he talks to me in this weird way that's really directed at them. I don't know what to make of him. Royal's a mystery, but he's a mystery that's in your face, that you can't help but want to solve, one that you obsess over when you can't sleep at night. Baron's a mystery you didn't see at all, one you didn't know needed solving. And Duke, well, he's a mystery who pretends he's already been solved.

The more I know about these boys, the less I know *them*. It's maddening.

We circle the car and meet Duke and Jolene, who's all flushed and looks so dazed you'd think she had an orgasm just touching Duke's penis. I glance around for Royal, only catching a glimpse of his back as he strides toward the party.

Okay, then. Fuck him, too.

"Guess I'll go mingle," I say. "Considering I didn't even want to come here, and now I have no reason to be here, I'm a bit confused, but I'll live."

Baron grabs my wrist again, his grip strong but not punishing. His hands are big and warm around my bare wrist, almost comforting. After talking to him and being near him, I can feel that pull that I feel toward Royal, though in this case, it's a bit different. Mostly it's curiosity, the thrill of finding a mystery that hasn't been solved. I'm starting to see how a girl could fall for him if he wasn't torturing her.

"Go get him a beer, and say you're sorry," he says, his voice slow and quiet, like he's explaining this to a child.

"Sorry for what?" I ask, though I'm just being a brat. I know what I did. When he doesn't answer but just keeps me fixed in that dark gaze like he's waiting for me to comprehend, I sigh. "Fine."

I jerk my hand, but his grip tightens instantly, pinning my wrist for just a second, like he just wants to see me squirm. But it's over quick enough that anyone watching from the party couldn't tell what's going on. I know, though. He wants me to know I have no choice, no power. That he controls me.

He lets me go, and I turn and walk away, annoyed by his games. I'm a straight shooter. I like to know what I'm dealing with so, like it all laid out before me, so I can strategize and plan. If the rule is, there are no rules, I'm down with that. I just want to know that, so I know how to win.

Trusting that Jolene is more than willing to participate in anything Duke has in mind, I leave her and scope out the situation on my own. Easing my way through the smattering of kids still lingering near the cars pulled up alongside the dirt road, I take in the scene. There are two big bonfires, one set up too close to the edge of the giant pit where they extracted rocks or gravel or whatever the fuck they take out of a rock quarry. The swimming hole is off to the right, out of sight in the darkness, but I know the path there as well as any other Faulkner kid.

There's only so much to do in a small town and even less of it that's free.

I duck some football players who might drag me to Royal before I'm ready. Even though he's being a moody asshole, I'm grateful that I have a minute alone to get my bearings. I like to know what situation I'm walking into before I'm balls deep in it. The guys head toward the fire to the right, so I go left, working my way into the crowd gathered at the smaller bonfire, picking out a few familiar faces. Cans of cheap beer and red Solo cups circulate. The air is heady with marijuana smoke and the bitter tang of tobacco. Someone has a truck backed up close to the fire, the doors open and music spilling out, two kegs in the back. Some guys stand up there filling cups and handing them down. A few girls dance drunkenly in the firelight.

I spot Maisy Gunn talking to a couple art geeks by that fire, and even though we were never friends, relief floods through me at the sight of her familiar face. This isn't just a WHPA party. There are Faulkner kids here. Which means I'm not alone, the only sheep in a pack of hungry wolves. In fact, as I look around, I realize that most of these kids are familiar from

FHS. This is their party, their bonfire. The football players went the other way, which means that's the Willow Heights' fire.

Way to make my first step a misstep. But hey, if Royal gets pissed I'm over here, it's his own fault for not telling me. He should have known I wouldn't chase after him, that when I saw him going one way, I'd go the other. I didn't know this would be another school's party, and even though they're his rivals, I'm from this school. These are my people, even if I don't know most of them, since FHS is way too big to know everyone in one grade, let alone the whole school.

I'm already close enough to the kegs to get a beer, so I step up to the line. I hold up two fingers after catching the eye of one of the guys serving. "Ten or skin?" he shouts over the music.

"What?"

"Ten bucks or show your tits," he says, like it's all the same to him. Probably is.

I pull the twenty out of my pocket and hand it over, and he hands me my change and the beers a minute later. I take a sip and step away to let others take my place. The beer's shit, but at least it's cold. Since I don't want to push my luck with Royal right now, I start in that direction. My absence has no doubt been noted, but showing up with a beer for him might smooth things over.

I'm almost out of the crowd when a guy bumps into me, making my beer slosh over the side of the cup and down his shirt. I'm about to snap at him when I look up and find myself staring into the smoky bourbon eyes of Zephyr Hertz, street art genius, neighbor down the street, and former partner in Dumpster diving and thrift store hunting.

"Damn, if it isn't Harper Apple, my little prodigy," he says, hugging me with one arm while he holds a joint between two fingers of the other. "I was about to bitch at you for spilling beer on me, but I guess you get a pass. Where you been, girl?"

"I was about to bitch at you for making me spill my beer," I say, smiling at him with genuine happiness. "And I think you're the prodigy. Maybe you meant protégé?"

"Still a smartass who thinks she knows it all," he says, toking on his joint.

"And I'm assuming you're still a denizen of the night and the bane of all the cops in town," I say. "I haven't seen you in ages."

"Right?" he says, holding out the joint to me. "You drop out?"

I hold up the cups currently occupying both hands, and he holds the joint toward my lips. My first instinct is to pull back when anyone gets in my space, and Zephyr sees me tense, but he doesn't get all butt-hurt about it. He knows me. He accepts my defensiveness and respects it, the same way Blue does. They get it. They're my people, from my world, people who understand boundaries and don't push them when it's not their place to do it. And yeah, it keeps us all from ever getting too close, but that's our world.

I swallow and meet Zephyr's warm eyes, and I open my lips. He puts the joint between them, and I take a couple puffs and then turn my head away, coughing.

Before I can recover from coughing and answer, a strong arm wraps around me, pinning me to a huge, muscular body. Royal. Of fucking course. He needs to check his possessiveness at the door. He should know he doesn't own me and never will, no matter how many declarations he makes. Just like he can force me to my knees, but I'll never bow to him.

"What the fuck do you think you're doing?" he growls at me, but his eyes are locked on Zephyr.

My former spray-paint mentor is way too cool to get flustered by the fire blazing in Royal's eyes. He takes a puff on the joint and smiles. "Hey," he says, jerking his chin in recognition. "You're Royal Dolce."

"And who the fuck are you?" Royal's words drip with ice, and he tips his head back so he can look down at us through hooded eyes, that asshole move that's meant to intimidate but drives me crazy, so I'm not sure if I want to throttle him or ride him. Preferably both, at the same time.

Zephyr, apparently, does not share those conflicting urges. He only shrugs. "Zeph," he says. "Zephyr Hertz, actually. My dad is Thomas Hertz."

"And let me guess, he's a big fan?" Royal asks. "You're too cool to ask, obviously, so you're going to pretend you want an autograph for daddy?"

"What?" Zephyr asks, his friendly demeanor fading behind a look of confusion and disappointment. Then he shakes his head. "You know what? Never mind. I'm nobody. I was going to talk to you, but I won't bother. See you around, Harper.

Drop by if you need more of this." He raises the joint and then turns and walks away without a backwards glance.

I pull away from Royal and turn to glare up at him. "Are you going to be an asshole to every single guy I talk to?"

Royal just glares back at me. "Why are you talking to a single guy?"

"Um, maybe because he's my neighbor and a friend."

"Did you fuck him?"

I sigh and hand him his beer. "Why are you so obsessed with who I've fucked? I don't ask you every girl at this party you've fucked."

Royal looks around, scowling at the crowd. "You want to know who I've fucked?"

"You know, I really don't. You don't owe me shit. You're a big boy, you can stick your dick where you want. Not my concern."

He looks down at me, an asshole smirk twisting his full lips. "Not what you said when that chick tried to get a ride after the race."

That chick. He either doesn't remember who it was, or doesn't care.

I hate myself for feeling anything about that fact.

"That was a long time ago," I say. "I've come to my senses since then."

Royal steps in so he's towering over me, his eyes burning with intensity, like there's no one else, no party going on at all. Just us. "Deny it all you want, but you're a jealous bitch, Harper Apple. So I'll tell you anyway. I don't see a single girl here I've fucked."

Crossing my arms, I rock back on my heels, cradling my beer. "You haven't fucked a single girl here."

His playful edge disappears behind a scowl. "No. So, did you fuck that guy or not?"

"No," I say. "He's fucking brilliant, and I admire the shit out of him, but we never had that kind of relationship. And who are you to judge? Just because you didn't fuck any of these girls doesn't mean you haven't sucked your way through every girl in Faulkner."

"I don't eat pussy," he snaps.

Duke appears then, slinging an arm around Royal's shoulders, Baron a few steps behind "Don't worry, girl," Duke says, already slurring a little. "I got you. A couple licks from this tongue, and you'll be screaming so loud you break the sound barrier." He wiggles his tongue at me, and Royal shoves him off.

I roll my eyes and address the leader. "Oh, sorry, have you told me that before? I'm losing track of all your rules." I count them off on my fingers. "You don't cum, you don't date high school girls, you don't eat pussy, you don't answer questions… Anything else I should know?"

"You don't need to know anything about me," he growls. "You're not my girlfriend. You're something to play with until it breaks and then throw away. That's it."

"Be that as it may," I say through gritted teeth. "When there are more guys whose dicks I've sucked than girls who've sucked your dick in any given group, you can give me shit. Until then, you might want to reign in the misogyny. Pretty sure that hasn't been cute since the 90s."

"Oh shit," Baron says. "Look out. Here comes the angry feminist. The height of originality."

"You know what's even less original?" I ask. "A man using his dick as a weapon to intimidate women."

"I don't have to use my dick for that," Baron says with a haughty smirk.

"Look, I get it, you're all complete psychopaths," I say. "You've made your point. But maybe you should reign in the Me-Tarzan-You-Jane bullshit every now and then. I am zero percent attracted to Zephyr, but he's a genuinely good human being. He helped try to find your sister."

The air leaves the group. For a second, my breath catches, as if her ghost has sucked up all the oxygen around us. "What?" Royal asks, his voice low and deadly.

"If you'd talked to him for a minute, you might have figured that out," I say. "That's why he told you who his dad was, asshole. He didn't want a fucking autograph. He thought you might remember his name."

For all his faults, Zephyr's dad really did try to help, even if he was really just doing it for the money. Still. Zephyr was the only person on our side of town who seemed to give a fuck about that whole missing rich kids situation. He felt somehow responsible for what his dad did, and he wanted to help make it right because he's Zephyr, and under the arrest record and somewhat surly attitude toward authority, he's got a moral compass made of pure gold.

"What do you mean, he tried to help find her?" Baron asks. "Like, he was in the search parties?"

I shrug. "Yeah. Well, Zephyr was. He didn't expect you to remember him because of that. But his dad was the one who sold a car to a couple teenagers outside the liquor store that night."

"What teenagers?" Royal asks, and when I glance at him, he's got that hollow look in his eyes.

I'm not about to tell him Zephyr's dad was drunk off his ass, since that's the kind of thing you pretend you don't see and definitely don't say about a friend's parent, but these guys act like they've never heard this before. I swallow hard. Shouldn't they know this? "He said he couldn't remember what they looked like, but it could have been the kids on the news—your sister and her boyfriend, I guess. He told all this to your dad when he offered money to anyone with information that might lead to her."

No one says anything for a second. Then Royal tosses his full beer on the ground. "We're leaving."

"Dude, we just got here," Duke says. "And I totally would have taken that beer."

That beer cost me five bucks, but I keep my mouth shut. I know when shit doesn't concern me.

Baron puts a hand on Duke's shoulder. "We've got a ride home," he says, nodding to Royal. "Go on. I'll look out for this asshole."

Their gazes lock for a long moment, and I'm reminded of that moment on the field tonight, when Baron grabbed him and held him steady. I thought in the car that Duke might be the favorite and that's why he takes the better seat, but it's not like that. Baron may not be as loud or flashy as Duke, but that doesn't mean he's not just as connected, as important, to Royal. He just plays a different part in their family.

Without another word, Royal turns and walks away. The twins will probably go home with whatever piece of ass they can pick up, which means I'll be stuck finding my own ride. I'm not too worried about it. With Faulkner High here, someone will have me covered. Duke stumbles off after a girl teetering across the gravel in high heels, and I decide it's time to go find

Jolene. Soon enough, I spot her with a drink in hand and a cigarette between her lips, surrounded by a circle of admirers.

I swear, the girl is magnetic. Can't fault her for getting everything she can out of it.

I grab another beer, figuring the Faulkner side isn't off limits if Royal's not here to see, but not two minutes later, Gloria Walton comes mincing over and links her arm through mine, pulling me out of the crowd. "You just can't help yourself, can you?" she says.

"Really?" I ask, pulling away. "Now it's not just the Dolces keeping tabs on me, it's you, too?"

"I'm not keeping tabs on you," she says. "I'm looking out for you."

"How, exactly, is this looking out for me?"

"Because there *are* people keeping tabs on you," she says. "And Royal won't like you mixing with Faulkner boys."

"What's wrong with Faulkner boys?" I ask, planting a hand on my hip and leveling her with a stare. "If I recall correctly, you asked me for Maverick's number."

"I'm not Royal's... Whatever," she says, gesturing at my body. "There's not a guy at Willow Heights who would touch

256

your ass. Not while you're under Royal's protection. Faulkner guys might not know better."

"Protection?" I ask incredulously. "Is that what you call it?"

"Call it what you want. As long as you're fucking Royal Dolce, nobody fucks with you."

"Except the Dolces," I say, my voice hard. "Don't make it sound like they're doing me a favor. I'd take on the rest of the school if it meant I'd be safe from them."

"You don't get to make that choice," she says, starting across the rim of the quarry toward the other bonfire. "When he's done with you, you can do what you want. For now, I have three pieces of advice for surviving these parties."

"Obey, obey, and obey?"

Gloria stops and plants a hand on her hip. "Do you want me to be your friend, or do you want me to be a bitch and let you find out the hard way?"

"The first one," I say. "Sorry, it's automatic."

She quirks a brow and ticks off on her fingers. "One, never take a picture of the Dolce boys."

"And if you do?"

"You better delete it and hope they never find out."

"Okay…"

"Two, never take a drink from Cotton Montgomery."

"I thought he was your friend."

"He's in my circle, and he lives next door," she says. "He's also a total fucking creep. Stay away unless it's your fantasy to be violated while unconscious, in which case, you do you. No judgment."

I bite back a snarky comment and nod. "Thanks. That's really good info to have."

"Just looking out."

"I'm really grateful."

"Then don't fuck with Royal's head, okay? He may be the biggest bully on the playground, but he actually is my friend. And I won't be so nice if you hurt him."

I snort. "Not sure I'm capable of that. So, what's rule number three?"

"Don't fuck with the enemy. So, if you don't want to start a brawl between schools right now, I suggest you come with me."

I want nothing more than to go back to my people, but I know she's right. If Colt's attack taught me anything, it's not to give the Dolce boys a reason to fight.

We're halfway between bonfires when a group of guys who look college age or a little older intercept me on their way toward the party. "Hey," one of them says. "Are you the girl from that video?"

"That is her, isn't it?" says another one, a thick guy with a trucker hat and a shirt that reads, *Stomp My Flag, I'll Stomp Your Ass*. The sleeves are ripped off, revealing tattoos around bulging biceps.

"Hey, how about that," says a third guy. "It sure is."

There are six of them, all of them looking me over like I'm a rabbit about to run, and they're ready to give chase. Alarm bells go off in my head as I glance ahead to Gloria. The way they addressed me, with their voices sounding friendly but covering an edge of aggression, puts me instantly on the defense. I learned to read men's tones pretty well over the years, and these are just the type my mother brings home. Men who think women owe them their bodies because they give them attention. Men who don't outright grab you but follow you at a distance until you make one wrong turn and you're cornered. Men who don't ask you to sit on their lap until your mom is in the shower and won't overhear them. Sneaky, slimy bastards.

"She's with me," Gloria says, her voice a little too loud. She starts toward me, but I hold up a hand.

"No, I'm not," I say, not taking my eyes off the guys. "Gloria, go away. Go back to your party. I've got it handled."

"Are you crazy?" she asks, her voice rising.

Not crazy, but I can handle myself, and she's nothing but a liability at this point. It'll be hard enough kicking their asses without having to worry about one of them dragging her off and raping her while I'm busy.

"Go," I say sharply.

"Yeah, go on," says one of the guys. "Our business is with this girl. Unless you can suck it like a porn star, too."

Gloria swallows hard, her eyes widening. Then she starts to back away, not turning her back on the guys. I'm glad she's going, that she'll be safe, but being alone with my back to a hundred-foot-deep crater and six predatory men in front of me still makes my heartbeat pick up speed.

"Good move, taking care of that," says the guy with tats. "She looked like a dumb bitch who would call the cops. You look like a smart girl who knows how to keep her mouth shut."

A smart girl who knows how to kick their asses. Adrenaline spikes through me, and I toss my beer, glad I didn't drink it even if it means another wasted five bucks. I'm plenty clearheaded to fight these assholes. My hands ball into fists, and I take one step back, glancing over my shoulder to gauge exactly how far I am from the edge.

Bring it, bitches. I've been missing my Friday night fights, and this is as good a way to get my fix as any. I can't wait to feel the sweet ache of my knuckles or the satisfying crunch of bone when I break their noses. I bounce on the balls of my feet, excitement mixing with just the right amount of fear, the level that keeps me sharp but doesn't make me stupid.

"Now, where were we," says the first guy, prowling forward. "How about it, girl? Want to give us a little demo? Show us you're as good as you look in that video."

"Oh, trust me," I say, backpedaling toward the edge, my fists raised in front of me. "I'm better. Come and find out."

seventeen

Royal Dolce

I'm halfway home when my phone chimes, and fuckwit that I am, my first thought is that Harper is texting me. But no, it's just Lo.

ThatsLo: Where r u?
Royal: what do u need
ThatsLo: nothing asshole harper is in trouble
Royal: Whats going on?
ThatsLo: Some guys have her surrounded I'm scared 4 her

I slam on the brakes and yank the wheel hard, flying across the median and doing a one-eighty to head back the way I came. Fuck. It'll take me at least five minutes to get back, even doing over a hundred. I floor the car and grab my phone.

Royal: Fucking do something
ThatsLo: I tried.
Royal: Try harder asshole
ThatsLo: fuck u im not a martyr I'm helping more by txting u than making myself a victim 2
Royal: bitch

Fuck, fuck, fuck. Why did I leave her at that fucking party? Every time I turn around some guy has his hands on her. I should have known she couldn't be left alone for five minutes, let alone the whole night. I curse my brothers for not keeping eyes on her, but I'm the one who should have been watching. If something happens, it's on me.

A sick feeling grips my insides, twisting them all up into something I don't want to look at, something weak, disgusting, that won't go away no matter how hard I try to crush it into a fucking diamond with the force of my hatred. I know not to walk away from someone I—

I stop that thought. I don't give a fuck about Harper. Still. She's mine, and you don't leave something that's yours and expect it to be there when you go back, not when it's something precious.

Royal: What is she doing?

ThatsLo: idk

Royal: TELL ME

ThatsLo: She knocked 1 out and kicked a guy in the nuts, but theres like 8 of them. U need 2 come back

Royal: WTF do u think I'm doing?

ThatsLo: then stop txting

Royal: no stay on I need 2 know she's ok

ThatsLo: She's not

ThatsLo: hurry k

I hit the dirt road too fast and almost spin out. Anyone who says you can drive fast on gravel has never tried it. But I do my fucking best, and if I slide in the ditch a few times, it's nothing the Rover can't handle. Thank fuck I'm not in Baron's Tesla. I roll up to the party and hit the brakes, sending up a spray of gravel as I pull the brake and bust out of there without bothering to kill the engine or shut the door.

I see Gloria first, over toward the Faulkner side but not at the party. Of course she's fucking on their side. Everyone on our side knows better.

I sprint across the gravel to where she's standing a ways off from a small crowd gathered at the edge of the pit. Harper is standing with her back to the edge, not two steps from falling. Her tiny shirt is torn down the front, her hair's a wreck, and her mouth is bloody. A couple guys are facing her, while two lie on the ground and another kneels nearby, holding his dick and groaning. About a dozen people stand around not doing shit but watching it all go down.

"Out of my way," I growl, shoving through, not bothering to look who I'm pushing to the ground on my way. I grab the two guys' heads and smash them together, feeling the satisfying crunch of their skulls connecting. Without bothering to see if they're conscious, I step past Harper and toss them into the pit.

That gets the crowd going. A couple people scream.

"What the fuck?" Harper yells, wiping her mouth with the back of her hand. "I had it handled."

I'm too pissed to find the words for her, so I grab her and throw her over my shoulder. She struggles, but I ignore her futile attempts. They're just a show. Even she knows she can't get away. She's doll-sized compared to me.

I turn to the little crowd, wanting to hurl them all over the edge, too. Some of them have the balls to look pissed or upset.

"I'm calling the cops," a girl says, her face all twisted up and covered with tears. Apparently she liked that douchebag who was hitting a girl. Good fucking luck to her.

"Do you know who this is?" I ask, moving forward a few paces toward the dozen people standing there gaping. "Do you dumb fucks even know who I am?"

A few shake their heads, but the others just stare. They know.

"I am Royal Dolce, and this is mine," I say slowly, my voice trembling with rage. "If you have something to say about that, I suggest you say it before you join those carcasses in the pit. If you don't, then get the fuck out of my way. But don't ever disrespect me and what's mine again."

They all scuttle back like cockroaches when I approach, so I shove past. Gloria hovers, her phone in her hand. "I tried to find your brothers, but I don't know where they went, and they didn't answer," she says, sounding panicky and close to tears.

I want to tell her to go fuck herself for not helping, and I'm too pissed to thank her even though some part of me knows I should. Ignoring her, I go straight to the Range Rover and yank open the passenger door. Harper is making herself as heavy as humanly possible on my shoulder, which only makes me want to laugh. I could bench press her ass.

I set her in the seat, battling the rage that's simmering up inside me like black clouds, trying to churn over my mind.

"I had it handled," she growls again, shoving my chest. "I didn't need your help."

I barely feel her little hands pushing at me. I grab the seatbelt and yank it around her, snapping it into place. She reaches for it, like she's going to jump out and make a run for it while I head for the driver's side. I grab her hand, my grip crushing until I see her chest swell as she sucks in a breath. Though her bra is completely exposed, I barely notice her tits. I loosen my hold, but I don't release her hand. I want her to remember what I can do to her.

"You want to try something?" I ask, low and menacing. I hear my own voice through the rushing in my ears, but it sounds like a stranger. I don't know when I started to sound like a dangerous man.

Harper swallows and relaxes her hand, and I drop it and slam the door. We peel out in another spray of gravel, but this time, I control my speed and the vehicle on the gravel road. My fingers ache with the force of my grip around the wheel. I don't speak. I can't. Everything in my body is charged with rage so deep it pulsates in my veins, sinks into the marrow of my bones. I know this place of darkness well. I have a fucking timeshare here.

We turn off the dirt and onto a paved road, and Harper speaks at last. "You didn't have to do that."

"Like hell," I growl.

"I only had two left," she says "I can take care of myself."

"You're fucking welcome."

"What, I'm supposed to get on my knees and suck your dick with gratitude that you swept in to rescue me like some gallant knight? Fuck you, Royal. I wouldn't have been in that situation if it weren't for you."

"Every time I turn around, you're surrounded by guys. I leave for five fucking minutes to deal with family shit, and they're on you like flies. If you'd stop putting it out there that you're a whore, maybe I wouldn't have to keep rescuing your ass."

"*You* put it out there that I'm a whore," she says quietly. "You put the video out there. They saw it, and they wanted what he got. That's on you, Royal. Not me."

"They said that?"

She gives a little snort of breath. "Yes, they said that. You didn't have to kill them for it."

I want to rip the steering wheel off, tear the car to pieces, go back and drive over every single one of those assholes. I should have killed them. They won't die, though. The edges of that mining pit aren't ninety-degree angles. They're more like seventy-five. They'll roll down the hundred-foot gravel slope, and even if they weren't knocked the fuck out, there's nothing for them to grab onto to stop the slide. By the time they reach the bottom, they might wish they were dead.

"And what was I supposed to do?" I ask.

"Let me deal with my own problems," she says, throwing up her hands. "I was doing fine. I would have gotten the last two."

"You shouldn't have to," I say quietly. I'm the one who fucked up. But saying that part aloud is impossible.

She just shakes her head. "You don't get it. You have brothers who always have your back. No matter what you say, they respect it. They've got you. Not everyone has that luxury just built into their lives, automatically, without question. Some people learn early to look out for themselves, because they know damn well that's the only person who will."

I'd feel like a whiny little bitch if I said anything about my brothers now, if I said they're a responsibility and not just backup. But she's right. At the end of the day, I'm fucking lucky.

"You have your mom, though, right?" I ask, even though I shouldn't give a fuck if she has someone or no one. It doesn't matter. Nothing about her matters. She's something to take the brunt of my rage when I need to destroy something beautiful. That's all. It's all she can ever be.

She snorts and turns toward the window. "Yeah. Sure."

I don't push for more. I know better than anyone that parents and even siblings aren't always there when you need them. Sometimes, they disappear without a trace. They blow you off. They move on with their lives. They only care when there's something in it for them.

"I see your shitty mom," I say, glancing over at her. "And I raise you one dead sister."

Surprise flashes across her face, and then she laughs. She fucking laughs. It about does me in, that throaty, genuine laugh from this tough-as-nails, pain-in-the-ass, don't-need-anyone bitch. I should pull over and strangle the life out of her for that, but as I adjust my grip on the wheel, I realize that I'm not pissed. Somehow, I'm calmer, the rage sinking back to the usual simmering level. I don't know how she did it. I even crack a little smile.

I don't know how she got me to talk about Crystal, either. It's still raw as a pulled tooth to mention her, even after two years. In those two years, I could count on one hand the number of times I've heard her name. People tiptoe around it, like if they mention it, I might remember that yeah, I once had a sister. Like I could forget. Like it's not always there, her absence like a tumor pressing against my lungs, so I can never breathe again, not the way I used to.

I've never talked about it to anyone, either. What would I say? That I disowned her and told her she was dead to me, and then she was. That those were the last words I ever said to her. That if she could see me now, she'd be disgusted and devastated by the person I've become. No one needs to hear that shit, and there's nothing else to say.

Though I should keep going until I reach the exit that leads to the shitty, derelict part of Faulkner where Harper lives, I pull off the highway on the exit to the winding road toward our neighborhood. I don't want her hearing the shit I have to say to Dad, but I also don't want to waste another thirty minutes. This needs to be said now. She can wait in the car.

After a long silence, she shakes her head. "Damn. I can't beat that. All I've got left in my hand is a dad I've never met."

"I wish I'd never met my dad."

Another silence falls.

"What was she like?" she asks quietly.

That's her fucking question. She could have asked where I'm taking her or demanded a ride home. But she wants to know about Crystal.

And I want to know why.

When I look over, she's staring straight ahead, working over her split lip with her tongue. I watch her wet, pink tongue teasing the ragged, bloody cut and my cock throbs in my jeans, and I almost miss a curve and run off the fucking road. Taking her to my house is a real fucking bad idea.

I jerk the car straight and check to make sure she didn't notice. She didn't.

"She was… Everything," I hear myself saying.

"Was she a lot like you?"

"A monster?"

"Your words, not mine."

"No," I say quietly. "She wasn't like me."

I wait for her to say she's sorry, the way everyone does when they hear I have a dead sister. But she doesn't say anything. She's still tonguing the slit on her lip like it's a fucking cunt.

Instinctually, I know this is my only chance, the one time I'll allow myself, the one time anyone else will allow me. I have no right to say her name after what I said to her last. I took her family, her name, and I told her it was no longer hers. What right do I have to speak it now?

Once we leave this car, reality will slam us back to being what we are—enemies.

So I try to think of something to say, letting my foot up on the gas a little to make it last longer, to keep the illusion just a few more seconds. But everything I could say to describe Crystal would take longer than we have or sound cliché as hell—that she was soft but strong, innocent but smart, giving but selfish, eager to please but defiant, clever but gullible.

Before I've found something real to say, we're at the gate to our neighborhood. "She was… A contradiction," I say, hitting the gate code.

"Most women are," Harper says simply.

I don't say anything as we pull onto the white gravel road through the neighborhood. I hate that she makes me think of her as a woman, as human, as someone whose life is as complex—as important—as my sister's. Seeing the burnt rubble of Devlin's house after Duke's latest fire and the gaudy antebellum monstrosity that Dad bought brings reality back like a slap. We didn't even get to climb out of the car before it hit.

"Stay in the car," I say. "I'll take you home in a minute."

She gives me a look. "You know me better than that."

I close my eyes and rest my head back against the seat, summoning my patience. She's right. She's going to go snooping around no matter what I do. "You can get cleaned up in my bathroom," I say at last. Maybe she'll be too busy getting the blood off her face to eavesdrop on my conversation.

She shrugs and climbs out of the car, and I do the same, stepping in front of her to unlock the back door. Thank fuck it's late enough that the maid isn't around to hover. I start for the stairs, but just as we reach the bottom, a door opens in the hall behind us.

"I thought I heard a car in the drive," Dad says, sounding so fucking normal you'd think he wasn't the worst of all of us.

I turn around and grab the front of Harper's jacket, pulling it closed over her exposed skin. "Keep that shut," I mutter to her, but my eyes are on Dad, who's busy eye-fucking her from behind.

"You're home early," Dad says, giving me a knowing look. "Twins still out?"

"Yeah," I say. "I'm just taking Harper upstairs to get cleaned up."

I put an arm around Harper, who tenses but turns reluctantly to face my father, holding her jacket closed.

"Ah," Dad says, coming along the hall to meet us. "So this is the girl you've been spending time with."

"Stay out of my business," I snap.

He smiles and holds out a hand to Harper, who awkwardly shifts her grip on the front of her jacket from her right hand to her left so she can shake his hand.

"Hi, Mr. Dolce," she says, and damn if she doesn't sound nervous. Never thought I'd hear that tone in her voice.

"Tony's fine," he says, still holding onto her hand. "That's some nasty bruise on your face. I hope my son didn't do that." He chuckles, like it's fucking funny, and raises a brow at me, like I need a reminder not to punch a chick in the face.

Harper glances up at me and extracts her hand from his. "No, I just fell."

Dad drags his gaze over her. "Well, if there's one person who knows how to take care of a bloody nose, it's my son," he says, smiling like he's some kind of proud papa and not a piece of shit father.

"That's what I'm trying to do," I say.

"You might need stitches for that lip," Dad says, reaching out like he's going to touch her face, turn it toward the light to examine the wounds.

I block his hand, pulling Harper halfway behind me. "Keep your hands off her," I growl.

Dad holds up both hands and laughs. "You kids know where the ice and bandages are," he says. "I guess you don't need me to patch you up anymore."

Anger pulses in my temples, and I grab Harper and drag her up the stairs. All the lightness from the car ride is gone, and I just want to get this over with and get her out of my house.

"Your dad seems nice," she says, her words measured.

"You're just his type," I snarl. "Almost legal." I pull her along the hall to my bedroom, unlock the door, and pull her in.

"You have a lock on your bedroom door?" she asks. "That's… Interesting."

I flick on the bathroom light and pull her inside. "All the other doors have locks, too, so don't bother trying to snoop. Clean up. You might shower, too. You smell like garbage."

She rolls her eyes. "Got a T-shirt I can borrow?"

I grab her a school shirt and hand it into the bathroom. "I'll be back in ten minutes. Don't go anywhere else, and keep your hands off my shit. I don't need your greasy fingerprints all over everything."

I find Dad downstairs in his office, a shot of whiskey in a glass in his hand as if he's waiting for me. "That one's a looker," he says when I walk in.

"Who's Thomas Hertz?" I ask.

Dad frowns. "Who?"

"Thomas Hertz," I grit out. "Some asshole who sold a car to two teenagers the night she disappeared. Apparently he came to you with that information, so why the fuck haven't I heard about it?"

Dad swishes his whiskey around in his glass, his eyes never leaving mine. "Oh," he says at last, leaning back in his chair. "One of those."

"One of what?" I ask, fighting the urge to throttle him across his desk.

"One of the vultures," he says flatly. "Do you know how many people came forward with worthless tips when we offered a million-dollar reward? Hundreds of unscrupulous conmen came running with bullshit stories that led nowhere. Did you expect me to share every single one with you boys? You were grieving. I had to protect you."

"I deserved to know," I growl at him. "She was my twin."

He shoots to his feet, slamming his glass down on the desk. "She was my daughter," he shouts. "I followed every dead-end tip as far as it would go, and they all led nowhere. You want to stand here and tell me I didn't try?"

He's breathing hard, raging at me across the desk, his own temper meeting mine and dampening my impulsive outburst. Of course he looked. Of course he followed the tip, even though it was some poor asshole from Harper's side of town who was only after a quick buck. Just because he didn't share every detail with us doesn't mean he didn't fucking try. He's not the person I'm really pissed at, anyway. As always, that honor goes to my own damn self.

"I know you tried," I say quietly. I barely remember a thing for the six months surrounding her disappearance. Dad and King took care of everything. I was worthless. Before and after, I was living in some kind of autopilot nightmare. I remember looking, how desperate and immediate everything felt at the time, like every moment was a punch in the gut. Now it's just a dark blur, a ruined page in the story of my life where the ink runs together and bleeds into all the pages after.

Dad sits down heavily, pulling the cork from his whiskey to pour himself another shot. He grabs a glass from the liquor cart and hands me one, too. "I don't remember the names of any of them," he says. "I offered a reward for information that led to her recovery, and none of it did. If it had, I'd have written someone a check for a million dollars, and you can bet your ass I'd remember it."

"And she'd be here," I say, sinking onto the edge of the chair next to his desk before downing the shot and reaching for the bottle.

For a rare, peaceful moment, we sit in silence, not blaming each other for tragedies that don't make sense, that have no ending, no villain, and no winners. When there's no one to blame, but the weight of it is too great to bear alone, we each find someone to point fingers at.

I remember a fuss when some of the people who had tips didn't get paid, that a couple of them got together and tried to sue Dad, because that's the kind of assholes who live in this town. The kind who would sue a father who just lost his daughter because he didn't hand over money for worthless information and lies. Dad won that one when they dropped the lawsuit, and a lot of people in town rallied behind us because everyone loves a good tragedy, and we had so fucking many.

No one wants to be known as a tragedy, especially a man as proud as Dad. As any of us, really. No one wants their pain on display for the town to walk by and marvel at, offering sympathies while secretly relieved it's not their life behind the glass. Maybe we're all just doing the same thing Duke does, creating a chaos around us so great that the true moments of hurt aren't standing out for all the world to see. Instead, they're buried in a hundred other tall tales and true stories. If we keep giving them shit to look at, to distract them, they'll stop quenching their thirst for gossip in the endless well of our pain.

Dad's the one who breaks the silence. He jerks his head toward the ceiling, gesturing with his eyes. "You enjoying the girl?"

I push back and set my glass down, avoiding his shrewd gaze. "I'd better go check on her before she plants a bug in my light."

"Just watch what you say around her," he says. "Everyone's after something."

Don't I fucking know it.

eighteen

Harper Apple

In Royal's bathroom—yeah, he has his own fucking bathroom, and I'd bet every other room in the house does, too—I take care of my lip as best as I can. There's not much I can do about it but let it heal on its own. If I were rich like the Dolces, I'd probably go get stitches like their dad said. But I've had worse, and they've healed, so I know this one will, too. I think about skipping the shower, since being naked in someone's house is too fucking vulnerable, but I'm pretty sure our water got shut off at home today, so I might not get a shower for a few days if I don't take one now.

A little thrill goes through me when I peel off my clothes. I try to crush it back down, to stop imagining him walking in, the way his eyes would darken with desire when he sees my body bared to him for the first time. I shake the thought away and shower quickly. When I finish, I pull on his t-shirt and my jeans and leave the bathroom.

I'm surprised to find the room still empty. My brain tells me to take this opportunity to go through his shit, but in truth, I'm intimidated as hell. It's one thing to know he's rich, to see his fancy car and clothes, to look at his house from the balcony next door. Being inside it… It's like I've been swallowed by the beast. I'm in the belly. I'm *in* at last, at least physically.

Instead of wanting to poke around, I find myself wanting to get the fuck out of there, to run away from this reality slapping me in the face. His room is huge, with a giant bed, two chests of drawers with mirrors, an armoire, two bedside tables, a computer desk with a laptop on it, another long desk in front of the window, and a small table in the corner with two recliners and a TV mounted on the wall. It's practically as big as my house. On the way in, he rushed me through the back door and down the hall, but I caught a glimpse of the living room, all high ceilings and leather furniture that probably costs more than my house would sell for. It's too much. I'm out of my element, practically dizzy with the reek of wealth around me.

Before I can get my head on straight, footsteps thud in the hall, and the door opens. I jump, even though I heard him coming. This place has me crawling out of my skin. Royal stands there, fixing me with an accusatory stare. I feel suddenly guilty, as if I really did go through his shit instead of just thinking of it. This house is so rich it makes me ashamed for just existing inside its walls.

He steps inside and pulls the door closed. His expression is unreadable.

"How'd it go?" I ask, edging away from him. I can smell whiskey on his breath, and I'm not sure if I want to see what Drunk Royal is like. Sober Royal is scary enough.

"It was nothing," he says, his voice flat. "A false lead like all the others."

I want more details, but I know better than to expect them. Royal doesn't share personal shit. What he told me in the car is like a fucking revelation, way more than I hoped for. I still can't quite believe it was real, that any of this is real. I've fallen down the rabbit hole into Wonderland tonight, and I'm not sure I like it.

"You ready to take me home?" I ask.

"I'll take you in the morning," he says. "I'm going to take a shower."

He grabs the bottom of his shirt and peels it off over his head, and even though I've never wanted to have babies in my life and probably never will, I swear the sight makes my ovaries seize up. Or something a hell of a lot deeper inside me than my pussy. My brain shuts down, all reason disappearing as he drags the hem over the deep, thick ridges of muscle in his abs. And then the absurd slo-mo porno soundtrack in my head screeches to a stop when he pulls it over his pecs, each one a slab of muscle the side of a fucking dinnerplate.

One of them being a commemorative plate with the face of a gorgeous girl on it. Just as I'd recognize Zephyr's art without seeing his tag, I recognize Maverick's work when I see it on someone's skin—the painful attention to detail, the emotion captured in every line. Her face is delicate and ethereal, strands of hair floating around it, her full lips slightly parted and her haunted eyes staring out at me from the canvas of Royal's chest.

He smirks when he sees me ogling his body like a fucking creep. "Enjoying the show?" he asks, slowly tugging his belt loose with one hand.

I tear my eyes away and feign nonchalance. "I just didn't expect you to be the kind of guy who tattooed a chick's face on his heart."

"Heart's in the middle, Cherry Pie," he says, touching the center of his chest, over his sternum, and running two fingers slowly down the center of his abdomen between his eight-pack abs, toward his belly button. His belt is open, his jeans slipping dangerously low on his hips, until I can see the muscles that bulge over his hip bones, the sharp V carved below them, the point leading toward the hint of dark hair peeking out above his jeans. His skin is smooth and dark but ridged with veins, and a light trail of hair leads from his belly button downwards, as if every line on his body leads the eye straight to his cock.

I swallow hard, remembering the heart-stopping heat of it, the size of it in my hand, the way he tasted when I ran my tongue over his skin. My pulse throbs, and heat blooms in my cheeks and between my legs when he reaches for the button on his jeans, slowly undoing it and letting them fall. Even when he's not hard, it's impossible not to stare, not to marvel. Every inch of him is intimidating, commanding, and dizzyingly masculine.

He chuckles quietly. "Get in the bed if you want me to fuck you."

He strides into the bathroom and closes the door in my face. My heart is stutter-stepping in my chest, and I shake my head, trying to clear it. What the fuck. I need to get myself together, not act like my mother, seduced by her own desperate fantasies to escape the hand she's been dealt. Yes, Royal radiates power, oozes sex appeal, and would probably blow my fucking mind.

He'd also obliterate my heart, take my life, and walk away unscathed. Even if I made it out alive, he's the kind of man you never forget, the kind who changes you so deep it's in your DNA. The connection I feel with him, the obsessive pull of his magnetism, the knowledge that clicks in my brain, my heart, my bones… It tells me this is it, that this kind of thing is rare and comes along only once, if ever.

It also tells me not to be stupid, and there's a reason it only comes along once—because if you give in to this, let it wash you away, you never recover. You never feel that way again because after the devastation, you're incapable of feeling that again. Your soul knows you won't survive it again, that the part you gave to him died when he walked away.

Because he will walk away. Men always do. They've been doing it all my life. Hell, before I was even born, they were already walking. And me, I'd end up just like her, a broken woman who chose the wrong man, one who never looked back, who left her to clean up the mess he'd made of her life. She never quite recovered, never found her feet or fit the pieces back together, and though she doesn't hate him for it, sometimes I do.

I sit down at Royal's desk and consider my options. This is one of those moments when my decision to not have friends seems really fucking stupid. I could call Jolene, but I don't really want her truckload of rednecks coming here to gape at Royal's house. He gets that shit enough at school. I could wait for the twins to get home, assuming they're coming home tonight at all. Or I could go downstairs and ask Mr. Dolce for a ride.

Considering Royal was obviously pissed that we even met, I don't think it would go over so well if he came out and found me downstairs with his dad. I could walk, but it's a long way, and I don't have any defense but my bruised fists. It would be pretty fucking stupid for a girl to walk home alone this time of night without at least some pepper spray, and even then, once you cross the tracks, it's not a sure thing.

If he's really not taking me home, I'll sleep in one of the recliners. They're probably more comfortable than my bed, anyway. Was this his plan all along, refusing to take me home so he could fuck me? But that's stupid. He could fuck me and then take me home, or fuck me in his car. Is he really worried about the fact that he's had something to drink now? I wonder how much he drank. Duke's words from the bridge flash in my mind—he doesn't care if he lives. He's the kind of guy who would do something reckless like driving after drinking, so why not now?

Is it because he doesn't want to drive drunk with me in the car? For whatever fucked up reason, he defended me tonight. Sure, I probably could have finished the fight on my own, but he protected me. He came back just to knock those guys out. I'm here because he didn't want to leave me at the party, thinking I wouldn't be safe. Which is so fucked up I can't even comprehend why. His bed is a hundred times more dangerous than a party.

I've already decided I'll sleep with him at some point. It's inevitable. But that doesn't mean it's going to be easy, that it won't mean anything. I'm not sure I'm ready to do it yet, even if it does get us closer.

Whatever his reasons for bringing me here, I need to do something. I'm bursting with energy and nerves, and I'm fucking *in*. Maybe not really, not in their trust, but this is the closest I'll ever get to Royal's outer life. I'm inside his house, his home, his lair. When he was at my house, the thought of him coming inside was instantly abhorrent, and there's a reason for that. People's houses, their rooms, their stuff, it tells you something about them. It becomes part of them, part of their story. Even a room like Mabel Darling's, with no sign of her but what's hidden in her closet, tells you something about her.

I spin around in the ergonomic leather chair and open his laptop, but of course it requires a password, so I close it again. Then I open his desk drawers, not really looking for anything in particular. It's not like I'll find a secret decoder for Royal Dolce's screwed up psyche. Though his room is neat, his drawers are messy and chaotic, like he shoves all his random crap in there when his dad tells him to clean his room—papers, pens, mints, an old cellphone, Chapstick, gum wrappers, a yellowed paperback copy of *The Great Gatsby*.

I pick up the book and fan through the pages, but there's no hidden note, no secret compartment inside. It's just a book about some rich guy with champagne problems.

I hear the water shut off, and I slam the drawer, not wanting Royal to see me snooping.

He emerges in a cloud of steam wearing nothing but a towel around his hips. I gulp at the sight of him, but I'm not about to lose my head again, even if just looking at his body makes me wet. He glances from me to the bed, raising a brow. "I figured you'd be spreadeagle on the bed when I came out."

"Sorry to disappoint," I say with a shrug, my gaze following the path of a drop of water that slips out of his wet hair, tracing the graceful, strong line of his neck to his shoulder, settling on his collarbone. Thirsty bitch that I am, all I can think about is licking the water off his skin.

"Suit yourself," he says, turning to the dresser. Even his back is glorious, with ridges of muscle flexing when he moves, and those back dimples that make smart girls stupid. He pulls out a pair of grey drawstring pants made of T-shirt material and pulls them on, every movement fluid and casual, endowed with the grace of a guy who owns every inch of his impressive body, who recognizes and enjoys its power.

God, it's like he's trying to torture me. Every line of his muscular ass shows right through the pants, and when he turns around, I can see his cock hanging against them, just enough of it to tantalize. The fabric barely hints at the ridge around the head of his cock, but it still makes my knees squeeze together involuntarily.

"Fucking tease," I mutter.

He gives me a cocky grin and shuts off the light, plunging us into darkness. I tense, but a second later, I hear his body hit the bed. My eyes begin to adjust, and I get up and move to the closest recliner.

"What are you doing?" he asks.

"You expect me to sleep on the floor like a dog?"

"Don't be stupid," he snaps. "Get in the bed."

"Yeah, not happening."

He sighs. "We've already established that you're the only one interested in your pussy. Just stay on your side and try to keep your hands off my dick for once, and we can both get some sleep."

"What's that supposed to mean?"

"It's late, I took a beating tonight, and I'm too fucking tired to deal with your drama," he says. "Get in the damn bed, Harper."

I move warily to the bed and climb on, acutely aware that he can flip the script at any moment, that he can claim this is some kind of consent, since he told me to get in the bed if I wanted to get fucked.

His weight shifts on the bed as he rolls over, turning his back to me. I lie perfectly still, wide awake though it must be well after midnight. The room is filled with a silence as heavy as the darkness swallowing us. I blink up at the ceiling, considering whether to let myself fall asleep next to a guy who tried to kill me only a week ago. I can feel him breathing, can hear every rustle in the sheets when he adjusts his position. I wonder if he's thinking about his sister, the pain fresh all over again. I think about how much that must hurt, that they never got closure, and any little comment can open the wound all over again.

This time, however inadvertently, I'm the one who broke the skin on it and made it bleed again.

At last, I roll over to face Royal's back. "I'm sorry," I say quietly.

He's silent for a minute, and I think maybe he's asleep after all.

Just in case, I add, "I know better than anyone that false hope is worse than no hope at all."

"What, you waiting for your darling daddy to show up?"

"Maybe, when I was really little," I admit. "But I never knew him. It was easy to let that hope die. It's the ones that stick around that do the most damage."

"Your mom?"

"Yeah," I say, shifting my position to lie flat on my back. "It's hard to let hope die when the person is still there, and you see the good moments along with the bad. When they do big things every now and then, like get you out of the trailer park and into a real house. You keep thinking maybe one day they'll drop their crutches and make another giant leap forward, reaching for something better."

"Harper?"

"Yeah?"

"That's some poetic shit right there, but shut up and go to sleep."

I laugh quietly, then roll over, scooting cautiously across the bed to wrap my arms around him. I curl my little body around his big one and press my lips to the center of his back. He doesn't tense when I touch him, but after a minute, he rolls over, tucking me into the crook of his body. His arms are huge, and I feel both delicate and vulnerable with all that muscle wrapped around me. Then I feel his cock, stiff against my ass, and I'm the one who tenses up.

"What are you doing?" I ask.

"You did it first."

"Why are you hard?"

"Because you're touching me," he says, tucking his top arm around me so he's cupping my tit in one huge hand. My nipples are instantly, painfully erect, and my clit throbs at the sensation of his warm, whiskey breath on the back of my neck. I once thought a girl would need some massive tits to make a handful for him, and I'm right. My tiny tit doesn't fill half his hand. He doesn't seem to mind, though. He lets out a soft, sleepy moan, running his thumb over my nipple and tightening his hips against mine.

He nuzzles against my ear, and I think I'm so fucked, I'm not going to be able to stop this if it's what he wants. I drop my head back, and he skims his lips down the column of my throat and onto my shoulder, sending spirals of heat coiling through my body.

He lays his head back on the pillow and groans. "Now for the last time, will you please shut the fuck up and go to sleep?"

I can't sleep, though. I'm all keyed up in every way, and as soon as I feel Royal's body relax around mine and his breath go deep and heavy with sleep, I slip from under his arm and lie on the far side of the bed. There's too much in this house, and I'm drowning in it—the shadow of his dead sister, the memory of what I saw the twins doing in another room, Royal's hatred for his dad, and the mystery in all of it.

Finally, I get up and tiptoe to the door, holding my breath. I check over my shoulder, expecting him to be right behind me, ready to grab me, his eyes all dead and empty. But he hasn't moved. I slip out the door and close it carefully, making sure it's not locked from the outside.

SELENA

Morbid curiosity wars with the desire to find out something useful as I stand in the broad hallway, wondering where to go now. Lantern-style lights line the walls between the rooms, but the only room I know is the one I saw from next door, which I'm assuming is Duke's.

Royal told me all the doors were locked, but that doesn't mean it's true. I can't bring myself to go in a dead girl's room, especially when the memory of Mabel's empty, barren room returns to me. I think about snooping in the twins' rooms, but what's the point? I don't even know what I'm looking for. Just something to bring back to Mr. D, since I didn't report back to him today.

But the best place to get information isn't digging through old desk drawers or even logging into someone's laptop. Sure, I could read emails and look at their social media and shit, but that stuff is all meant to be seen, at least by someone. I don't want to know things I can find online. I want to know them, these dangerous, damaged Dolce boys who confuse the fuck out of me, most of all because I can't seem to stay away from them any more than they can stay away from me.

I tiptoe on bare feet back toward the stairs. The house is so big it feels empty, even though I know at least two other people are here. From what I've heard, the twins haven't come home, but they might be downstairs. My stomach flutters at the thought, but I'm not sure if the sensation is fear or excitement, dread or hope.

I step onto the cool hardwood at the bottom of the stairs and turn toward the huge sitting room. I can't see most of the details, but I can make out the stone fireplace in one wall, a chandelier hanging high above, and a lot of leather furniture. On my left is a doorway that leads to what looks like a long, formal dining room with chandeliers above the table and a skylight inset in a ceiling I can't even describe. Where I'm from, ceilings are flat or popcorned. This one has like crazy-ass molding and carvings and gold trim. It makes me feel like I'm dreaming again, like this can't possibly be real. People can't actually live like this.

"Harper, right?" comes a deep, accented voice behind me.

I spin around, my heart thudding. "Mr. Dolce," I say, trying to sound normal, like I wasn't just snooping around his ridiculous house. "You scared me. I didn't hear you."

He's standing outside the open door to the same room he came from earlier, the warm light slanting across the hall and lighting up the edges of his form in silhouette. He slides his hands into his pockets and regards me from the dimly lit hallway. I can't see his face clearly, but I imagine the suspicion etched there. "Are you looking for something?" he asks.

Shit. He probably thinks I'm down here to nick some silver.

"No," I say quickly. "I mean, I just couldn't sleep."

I realize he probably thinks I'm fucking his son. Shit.

I don't do parents. Why am I meeting all the parents of these rich guys, and why do they seem to actually want to talk to me? I've known Zephyr for years, been to his house a dozen times, and I could count the number of words his dad has said to me on one hand. Maybe rich parents actually give a fuck about their kids' social lives. More likely, they're trying to protect their sons from the gold diggers they must attract on a daily basis. When you have next to nothing, it's easy to pick out people who want to use you, because you only have one thing they want. When you have everything...

"I see," Mr. Dolce says.

"Royal set me up in the guest room," I blurt. Surely a house this big has at least one of those. "In case you were wondering."

Even I didn't expect myself to freak out quite so hard when I met his parents. Not that I ever thought about meeting his parents, but damn. I can throw out the bitch attitude to anyone in school, even the administrators and teachers. I'm not the type of person who gets thrown off her game so easily, who gets flustered. But apparently rich parents are a line I can't cross without turning into a complete dumbass.

"I see," Mr. Dolce says again.

God, would he stop saying that? My palms are fucking sweating, and all I want to do is turn and run back upstairs. This was the worst idea ever. Who was I even wanting to meet down here? The twins, yes, but I wasn't sure they were home. I didn't expect their dad to be up so late. Maybe I was just going to walk around, haunting the halls like their sister's ghost, waiting for her to talk to me, to tell me if she really bought a shitty car from a guy outside a liquor store in the middle of the night. Looking around this house, it's hard to believe someone who lived here would want Mr. Hertz's rattly old heap.

"Would you like a drink?" Mr. Dolce asks.

SELENA

No, I don't want a fucking drink. I want to end the painful awkwardness that's humming in the air around us so hard I swear I can feel it making my limbs stiff as I dumbly follow Mr. Dolce into the room he was in.

When I get to the door, I see a large office, the walls lined with books. Now this, I could get behind. Maybe we've read some of the same ones. Fuck knows we have nothing else to talk about, nothing in common. What can I say to a guy who's lost his daughter, whose son hates him, whose wife, if rumors are to be believed, ran off and left him without a word.

I pull my eyes to the long, fancy wooden desk where he's standing, pouring whiskey into two crazy, double-walled, geometric glasses. God, even their cups look like they cost a fortune. That weird sense of unreality sets me off balance again, making me feel like I'm in a funhouse where the mirrors make the floor look slanted. Wonderland is not my jam.

I take the glass without thinking when Mr. Dolce holds it out. I was expecting him to pour me a glass of water and send me off to bed, not give me a real drink. Instinct kicks it, and my focus lasers in on him.

He's attractive in a more seasoned way than his sons, but it's easy to see where they get their godlike good looks. My attention goes deeper than the surface, past his hair that's cut short and combed back to reveal a widow's peak, his chiseled features and sleeves rolled up to show tan forearms sporting a Rolex on one arm and a simple masculine bracelet on the other. I read people—it's what I do. So I narrow in on his eyes, a light hazel color that he obviously didn't pass on to his sons, a slightly unfocused, glass quality to them.

Mr. Dolce clinks his glass against mine and takes a sip. "Like what you see?" he asks.

"I was just noticing how much you look like your sons," I say, forcing a laugh, my whole body on high alert. As well as he holds himself, he's drunk, or well on his way there. Not that I'm surprised—it's got to be around two in the morning by now, and he's sitting up alone. He must have had a drink with Royal earlier, and that's why Royal came back smelling like whiskey. He was probably already drinking, and if I had to guess, I'd bet he hasn't stopped. Suddenly, I'm not just edgy because he's a rich guy and the father of the boys who torment and fascinate me.

He's an intoxicated older man, and though I've had plenty of practice avoiding those, this isn't one of my mom's hookups. This guy has power. Not just because he's an adult or a man, either. He's filthy rich, and more than that, he owns Faulkner. He took down an entire family, the founding fathers of the town, who had plenty of money and power to fight him. And they were a big family, with cousins and uncles and distant relations all over the place. Through bribery and inside deals, he put his own family in their place and claimed the town as his own. He can do anything, have anything, that he wants.

Royal's words flash through my head—*You're just his type. Almost legal.*

If he wanted me... Well, I'm sober and could probably take him, but if I couldn't, there's not a damn thing I could do about it afterwards. No one would believe me. I wouldn't even bother calling the cops whose salaries he pays, taking it to court before a judge he got elected, to convince them. The mayor himself kisses this guy's ass. Maybe he's a mafia boss himself. He's quiet, but power lurks inside him, even scarier because it's hidden like a secret.

This guy raised the three monsters who run the streets and enforce his rule like hired thugs. I know better than to say the apple doesn't fall far from the tree, but I also know that no kid can grow up unscathed by their parents' influence. Even the father I've never met affects me, whether I like to admit it or not. I've internalized his absence, categorized it as part of my worth. Every day I see ways I'm like my mother, and I consciously make an effort not to fall into the same traps. Everything I do is colored by her influence, and at least some of what those boys do is colored by Mr. Dolce's.

The question is, which part?

"Don't be shy, have a seat," Mr. Dolce says in that New York accent that sounds so sharp compared to the southern accents I'm used to. There's something about it that commands obedience, just like his son's. I can see where they got their alpha dominance thing. I want to walk away, but something holds me there, some edge in his voice that says he won't stand for any bullshit. I've never had a problem disobeying authority when I needed to, but this guy... He's not just an adult, an authority figure. He's like a fucking god.

It strikes me, too, that this is a great chance to get a different perspective for Mr. D. I'm not just talking to the sons of his enemy. I'm in the belly of the beast, after all. I'm staring at the living heart, the head, of the family. I sink onto the very edge of the chair, making sure I have a direct line to the door if he makes a move. Instead, he sits down behind his desk, leaning back and studying me as intently as I studied him when I walked in. "So," he says, slowly circling his glass in the air with one hand. "You're Royal's little plaything."

I cringe at the term. It's bad enough when Royal uses it. Hearing his dad use it, knowing that he told his dad something like that about me, is all kinds of creepy.

He chuckles at my expression. "My sons don't do a lot of dating," he says. "Or whatever you kids call it these days. I'm sure you know that by now."

Maybe not dating, but they do plenty of fucking around.

"So being Royal's plaything, that's as close as you'll get," Mr. Dolce says. "It's a privilege most girls at that school only dream of."

I bite my tongue so I won't tell him exactly what I think of his astonishing ability to patronize a perfect stranger.

He stares at me for a long moment, like I'm supposed to answer.

"Well, I'm sure I'm flattered," I say, forcing another smile.

"You should be," he says. "You know, I pictured you as a blonde. You actually look a little bit like my daughter. The hair, I think. Her eyes were dark, though, like Royal's. And she dressed better."

Okay, then. He's a straight shooter, I'll give him that. Considering the mind games his sons play, it's a bit refreshing. Most adults spew nothing but bullshit, empty platitudes and fake niceties. This guy doesn't pull any punches.

"I'm sorry about your daughter," I say, finishing the shot of whiskey and setting the glass on the desk. "I should probably go back to bed."

"Stay," he says, waving a lazy hand and pouring me another shot in the bottom of the fancy glass. "I insist. I usually only see my sons' girls on their way out in the morning."

"Lovely," I mutter.

"Oh, don't get worked up," he says. "Royal doesn't bring girls home like the other two. That's why it's nice to finally meet the one he's been spending time with, see what she's made of. What she's after."

I know he's just looking out for his son, but it's still offensive.

Or it would be if it weren't one hundred percent true. While I'm not after money, I walked my ass down here looking for answers. For dirt. So I can't exactly complain when he calls me on my shit.

"I just want to understand him," I say honestly.

Mr. Dolce chuckles and rises from his chair, coming around the desk. I scoot back in mine instinctually, putting space between us. He stops right in front of me, parking his ass on the edge of the desk, so I'm at eye level with his crotch. Resting his hands on the edge of the desk next to his hips, he leans down toward me. "You darling girl," he says with a patronizing smirk. "Dolce men are too complicated for the likes of you to understand. There's only one thing you need to remember. Give us what we want, for as long as we want it. When we're done, keep your mouth shut, let us forget your existence, and your life can go on as you like."

I swallow hard, knowing a threat when I hear one, even if it comes from smiling lips and is delivered in a purr of a voice. I grip the arms of the chair, cursing myself for sliding back in it, so I can't dive out of it without getting real fucking close to Mr. Dolce, close enough that he can grab me. But if he expects me to give him what he wants and keep my mouth shut, he's in for a surprise. I don't give people anything they haven't earned, and even then, only when I want it.

Mr. Dolce leans back so he's not in my face and picks up his whiskey glass again. "You look alarmed," he says. "Isn't that what all the girls at school do for my boys?"

I want to tell him to go fuck himself, that they're Royal's boys, not his. But they are his boys, Royal included. And he's right. That's all I've heard since I started at Willow Heights—how you have to obey the Dolces, that if they call, you have to let them do whatever they want to you. And though they must have fucked nearly all the girls at school, I really don't hear much of it from the mouths of those girls. So they must be keeping their mouths shut, letting other people do the talking and spread the gossip. Even the Waltons, who are apparently

SELENA

gunning for the position of official girlfriends, have never told me they fucked the Dolces.

The closest anyone's come is when Gloria told me how to recover from a blowjob from all three of them, obviously lying when she said she hadn't been in my situation. And that was a private conversation between the two of us, and she knew I wouldn't talk. Suddenly, I wonder how much of the gossip about the Dolce boys is even true, and how much is rumor and speculation based on what an outsider sees. They saw the Dolces take me to the basement, and everyone assumed they ran a train on me. They did nothing to combat that rumor, even though all that happened was one blowjob. They let their lore grow.

If I hadn't seen Duke and Baron double-teaming a girl, I'd wonder if it was all fabricated. And even that was one girl. One time.

Again, frustration wells inside me, and I get that feeling that every time I find out something, I end up even further in the dark than I was before. Do I know anything real about them at all?

"I should go," I say. "Thanks for the drink."

"Oh, but we've barely started," Mr. Dolce says, leaning forward and bracing his hands of the arms of the chair this time, caging me in. "Just because you're my son's plaything doesn't mean we can't have a little fun, too."

nineteen

Harper Apple

I raise my hands to push Mr. Dolce away, but before I can, a hand shoots in front of me, throwing him across the room. Mr. Dolce flies backwards, slamming into his desk and reeling sideways, crashing to the floor. Royal grabs my arm and wrenches me out of the chair so hard my feet leave the floor. "What the fuck is your problem?" he rages, ignoring the groan of his father from the floor on the far side of the desk.

As he drags me out of the office and back down the hall to the stairs, I consider telling him that I'm not the one with the problem, and he should maybe be more pissed about the fact that his dad was hitting on his girlfriend, but then, he warned me. I just *had* to know more, though, just had to go sticking my nose in his business. It's a curse, really, this wanting to know what makes people tick.

"Are you really so fucking desperate that if I won't fuck you, you'll go hit on my father?" Royal snarls as he stomps up the stairs, dragging me after him. I fight to pry my wrist free of his iron grip, but he doesn't seem to notice as he manhandles me down the hall to his room like I'm no more than a ragdoll.

He shoves me through the door into his darkened bedroom, releasing me so suddenly I stumble forward. Before I can regain my footing, he grabs my arm and drags me backwards. I don't have time to get my bearings before he slams me up against the wall beside the door. His eyes are wild, mad, unfocused as he thrusts a hand between my thighs, his other hand closing around my throat.

"Get away from me," I snarl, shoving at his chest. He doesn't seem to feel it, crowding in closer, his eyes blazing as he yanks at the drawstring on his pants. He slams the door closed with his palm, plunging us into complete blackness.

"What are you doing?" I ask, my breath hitching. I can't tell if I'm afraid he'll listen, or afraid he won't. I'm terrified of what he'll do to me, but at the same time, watching him lose control is addictive. There's a careening thrill to it, like watching a train barrel toward you and knowing you can't stop it, that it's too late to get off the tracks.

Is this what I've always wanted, why I've kept pushing buttons, hoping to find the very one I just pushed?

"I'm fucking you," he says, grabbing my jeans with both hands and wrenching them down with one quick motion.

I start to protest, but before I can even bend to grab them back up, he's pinning me to the wall again, his broad shoulders holding me in place while he yanks my thighs open and rams his cock against my opening.

"Royal, no," I gasp out, shoving at him as my body tightens, locking him out. "I'm not ready."

"You're not wet for that asshole?" he growls, a hint of triumph in his voice. He spits on his hand, slicking it over the head of his cock before pushing it to my opening. A hot throb of desire shoots straight to my core at the sensation of his smooth, warm skin over the unyielding hardness beneath. "If you weren't planning to get fucked tonight, why is your pussy shaved?"

"Wait," I cry, but he thrusts upward, tearing into my resisting flesh. A strangled cry chokes from my throat, tears of pain springing to my eyes as my walls clench around him. He leans his forearm on the wall over my head and drops his forehead against it, his breathing ragged, his body trembling. He doesn't move, but I can feel his thick cock stretching me open, straining against my walls as they spasm around his length. I tremble at the knowledge that he's only halfway in, that the pain is only beginning.

"Oh god," I gasp. "Royal, stop. You're hurting me."

With a brutal thrust, he forces himself to the hilt inside me. "Did you think I was going to be gentle? You know me better than that, Harper."

My body curls in on itself, a sob choking from me, choking off my words, my air. I can't breathe, can't speak. Pain spirals from my core, up through my stomach, wrapping its tendrils around my heart and squeezing until it cuts off all other feeling. I didn't expect gentleness, but I didn't expect this, either. It happened so fast, I can't even comprehend what's happening, that he's fucking me.

He doesn't though, doesn't move further than penetration. He keeps me pinned to the wall like a butterfly, spread open and impaled on his cock. Part of me knew this would happen, was waiting for it, resisting it every bit as much as he was. And now it's happening. I try to breathe through the pain, to adjust to this new world in which I've fucked Royal Dolce.

"This is what you wanted, isn't it?" he ask, his voice edged with taunting. "You're all over my dick every chance you get. You asked for it. Now you're going to get it." He rocks slowly, rhythmically grinding his pelvic bone against my clit as he speaks, until the pain subsides and tingles of pleasure begin to curl out from where he's working me like the pro he is. The stretch of my walls around his thickness makes me lightheaded, and the way he's rocking makes his cock hit all the right places inside me. I hate my body for reacting, for feeling anything but pain. I want to scream, to shove a knife in his fucking heart to show him what it feels like.

But arousal throbs inside me as I adjust to his size, to the sensation of a huge, hard cock buried deep inside me.

"Baby, you're so tight you're going to milk the cum all the way out of my balls," he croons. His voice is completely changed, and if I didn't know him, I might think it was sexy and coaxing. But I can hear the edge of taunting cruelty under it, the bitterness, the hatred. The hollowness.

The words sound as if he's said them a hundred times, to every girl.

"I wasn't ready," I choke out, bracing my hands on his chest to push him away. He shoves them aside, grabs my wrists and pins them to the wall on either side of my head. He pulls out just an inch, then drives in quick and sharp. I can hear the wet sound of my cunt, like a kiss. Royal chuckles.

"You're ready now," he says, that haughty, arrogant lilt still laced through his words. He draws back and slams into me again, crushing me against the wall. I wince when he hits the deepest, tenderest place inside me, where no one has been before. But he's right, my body is ready now, whether I want it or not. I'm wet, and he slides back until only his tip is inside me, then drives in deep again, burying himself to the hilt inside me. I struggle to pull my hands free even as my trembling thighs open for him, craving the contact, the end to the torment of wanting him for so long.

"You wanted me to fuck you, right?" he asks, his voice a cruel taunt, his grip becoming tighter around my wrists the harder I struggle. "You asked for the Royal treatment. If you wanted a pussy, you should have fucked a chick." He punctuates each sentence with a deep, vicious thrust. I asked for it, I did, but I didn't want it like this. He's giving me exactly what I wanted—what I thought I wanted. It should feel good to give in, to let ourselves have what we've been denying ourselves since the moment we met.

But it feels emptier than all the other times put together. I don't know where Royal is, but he's not in this room with me. I try not to care, to tell myself it doesn't matter as he pounds into me hard and fast, slamming me into the wall with bruising force. My breath escapes in little gasps, and he adds a low grunt with each brutal thrust, the wet sounds of our sex the only other noise in the darkness.

I wonder where he is, where his mind is, but not for long. My head drops back, and I close my eyes, giving in. Good dick feels good, and it's dark enough in the room that I can pretend he's someone else, too.

I could if there were anyone else I wanted to fuck, that is. I don't want anyone else, though. I want Royal. I want to touch him, to bring some intimacy to the moment. I want to run my hands over his bare shoulders, feel the power trembling in his chiseled muscles, in his huge body that dwarfs mine and looms over me, trapping me as he owns me with each stroke, controlling the depth, the pace, the rhythm that sings through my blood and binds me to him in some dark, sick pleasure.

At last, he releases my hands, gripping my thighs instead. His thumbs cut into my flesh as he rotates my thighs, grinding into me. Then he grabs me around the waist, lifting me and slamming me down on him. He grips my ass hard enough to leave bruises, forcing me down hard as he grinds upwards into me with a guttural groan. I cry out in shock when he pulls out, pressing his wet, hard cock to my bare skin. The sensation fills me with an erotic thrill of wet heat. For a second, a minute, we don't move. I can feel his heart hammering and the rapid rise and fall of his chest as his breaths come short and fast against my neck. His cock throbs every few seconds, sending a pulse of heat into my center, and I wait for the liquid fire of his cum to spurt against me, but it doesn't come.

Reality comes back slowly, my senses returning. I can smell the sweat on his skin, and the whiskey on my breath, and the scent of our sex in the air around us. I rest my hands on his shoulders as if to steady myself and feel the dampness on his skin, the way little tremors rock through his body. I don't pull away, even though I could now that he's released his punishing grip. I let him fight his internal battle for control.

After a few minutes, he stumbles forward, knocking me into the wall as if he forgot it was there. He lifts a hand and fumbles across my face like a blind man trying to recognize someone he's just met, like he did in the basement.

"It's Harper, you asshole," I say, slapping his hand away. I shove his chest, and this time, he steps back. My body cries out with unfulfilled frustration, like it does every time, but this time, there's sharp pain along with it. I've never taken one that big before, and being dry on top of that...

"I know who you are," he snaps. He turns and strides into the bathroom, flicking on the light before slamming the door behind him.

I pull up my jeans, my whole body suddenly shaking again. When the fabric hits my skin, I suck in a breath. Between my legs is more than tender, it's fucking mangled and swollen, and every move I make sends a knife of pain into me. I cherish the pain, hold onto it. It's only physical, and I can deal with that. I can't deal with whatever fucked up shit is going on in my head. Not now, when he's right here. I'll think about that later.

I open the door to his room, knowing it's impossible to walk back downstairs to call an Uber like nothing happened, but also knowing that's exactly what I'm going to do.

Before I take a step out, the bathroom door opens, and Royal stands there like a giant, taking up the whole doorframe and blocking the light that spills out behind him. The look in his eyes makes me shrink away from him even before he speaks. They're not empty now. They're worse.

"Where do you think you're going?"

"Away from you," I snap. This horrible feeling wells up inside me, and suddenly, I'm sure I'm going to cry if I have to look at him another moment. I dart out the door, slamming it behind me, taking a little joy in the thought that if he tried to follow, I probably just smacked him in the face with it. I don't get two steps before he wrenches it open and grabs my arm.

"Harper."

"Let me go," I warn, yanking at my arm.

Of course he doesn't fucking listen. He spins me around and grabs me by my shoulders like he's about to shake the shit out of me. Instead, he takes a breath, glances at the end of the hall behind me, and lowers his voice. "Harper," he says, his brow furrowing, his dark eyes searching mine. "Were you... A virgin?"

I snort and yank away. "I thought I was a whore who was so desperate for dick I'd get it from your dad if you wouldn't give it up."

He glances behind me again, at the lights lining the walls all the way down to the stairs, where I need to go before I fucking lose it. I need to get out. Now.

Royal swallows. "There was... Blood."

"I told you I wasn't fucking ready," I snap. "Don't you know anything about a woman's body?" To my horror, my lip begins to tremble. I bite down on it fiercely, hoping I draw blood. He'll see my blood before I'll let him see my tears.

Royal's gaze doesn't miss the movement. He stares at my teeth biting down on my lip.

"I—I'm sorry," he says. "Let me make it up to you."

"Why?" I demand. "All you've ever wanted to do was hurt me, so why should this be different? It's just one more way you've succeeded in getting what you want, like you always do."

"I've hurt you?" he asks. He looks so fucking confused, it breaks my heart. How can anyone be so completely clueless?

I sigh. "Of course not. I'm not a person, Royal. I'm just a piece of trash, remember? Trash doesn't have feelings."

I turn to go, but Royal steps past me, blocking my way. I try to duck past, but he rests a hand on the wall beside me, caging me in. "I didn't say that."

"You didn't have to."

"I know you have feelings," he says slowly. "I just didn't know I could hurt them."

"You didn't hurt my feelings," I say, because it's more than that. He hurt something far deeper than feelings. "Just forget it, okay? Let's just forget this happened."

"I don't know if I can do that."

We stare at each other a moment. My heart beats hard, so hard I can hear it.

"Why not?" I ask, searching his eyes, aching to find something that's just not there. It never will be. Just like on Halloween, he couldn't give me a reason to stay. He never will. I don't know if he's even capable of giving me what I need, let alone what I want.

A slow smirk tugs at his lips, and I know I'll never find what I'm looking for in this haunted boy, no matter how much his darkness calls to mine. "I can't let a girl walk away thinking I don't know my way around a woman's body."

"Fine, I won't tell anyone," I say, ducking under his arm. "I wasn't going to, anyway."

Again, Royal grabs my arm. I stop, and for a second, he doesn't pull me back. Slowly, his hand moves down my arm, his fingers lacing through mine. I can't look at him, so I keep my face forward. I close my eyes and take a shaky breath, trying to get it through to my heart that it doesn't mean anything. "Please," he says quietly.

His voice is soft, laced with so much emotion I can't begin to untangle it. All I know is that it breaks my heart. That he said please, and that he was sorry he hurt me. Maybe it will never mean what I want, but it means something. When he pulls at my hand, I relent. He leads me back to his room without a word, pushes the door closed with his foot, and locks it behind us. The light from the bathroom spills out into the room, and when our eyes meet, he steps forward, sliding a hand under my ear to cradle my head. "Harper, I…"

A loud thud comes from downstairs, maybe the front door slamming, and his gaze flicks in that direction before returning to mine.

"What?" I whisper, my heartbeat slamming against my ribs. I need him to give me something, just once, after what just happened. I need him to give me a reason to stay.

"I—I'll get something to clean you up," he says. "Get undressed."

He turns and ducks into the bathroom, leaving me standing there with my mind spinning. I hear the water running, and a second later, he reappears with a cloth balled in his hand. He takes my hand and leads me to the bed, pulling back the blankets and pushing me gently onto the cool, white sheets. I don't protest. I feel numb, and my limbs are shaking as he pushes me back on the bed and lifts my legs onto it. I don't know how I'm going to endure sex right now, but I can't seem to formulate the right thing to say. If I open my mouth, I'll cry.

He pulls off my jeans, dropping them to the floor. My legs shake harder, but he doesn't give me a blanket. He kneels and spreads my knees, pressing the warm washcloth between them. I suck in a breath, the water stinging the torn and tender flesh.

He cleans me up, then looks at the cloth. "Are you sure you've had sex before?"

"If what we just did was it, then yes, I've done it before," I say, defensive at being interrogated for his fuck up.

"Like that?" he asks, his gaze falling on mine.

"More or less," I say, shrugging and looking away.

"How many times?"

"A few," I say. I could ask him the same, but I'm not that stupid. I know I don't want the answer.

"Do you always bleed?" he asks, setting the washcloth on the bedside table.

"No," I say, scooting up to sit against the pillows and watch him. God, he's beautiful, every inch of his body chiseled to perfection as if carved out of marble by one of the great artists. I focus on the sight of his godlike body so I don't have to think about the fact that I'm bare from the waist down while he's still wearing pants. "A couple times, when I wasn't ready, or it had been a long time since... The last time."

He moves forward and reaches for my shirt. "Do you ever cum?"

"No," I admit, letting him pull off my shirt. "I mean, yeah, but not during."

He nods, reaching behind me and unhooking my bra with no more effort than I'd put in. "From oral?"

I swallow hard, dropping my gaze to the front of his pants. He's got me naked on the bed, and he's not even hard. Maybe I was wrong about having the same effect on him. My own heart is racing in my chest, and pressure builds between my legs in anticipation and fear while his eyes move down my body. My nipples harden under his gaze, and hunger builds as he continues to drink me in with his eyes, lingering on the tattoos on my thigh.

"I haven't… I've only given it," I say. I don't want to tell him the truth, that having someone so close to my center makes me more vulnerable than I want to be. So I deflect. "I take care of myself."

"Tonight, I'm going to take care of you," he says, sliding down the bed in one smooth motion.

"Royal, wait," I protest, but he's between my legs, pushing them wider. I don't want him down there, seeing me, smelling me. He hates the way I smell, and even though I showered earlier, I'm still self-conscious. No one's ever been down there, looking at my cunt spread open like a sacrifice. I squirm, but he slides his arms under my legs, wrapping them around my thighs from below. He grips me right in the crease of my hips, spreading my thighs at the very top. He lifts his gaze to mine, and there's nothing empty in his eyes now. They're brimming with heat, with desire.

"I thought you didn't eat pussy," I whisper, my thighs shaking in his hands.

"This isn't pussy," he says. "It's you."

He drops lower, and I grab his shoulders, suddenly more terrified of this vulnerability than of an angry Royal. I'd rather him fuck me again, no matter how much it hurts, than have him make me vulnerable like this.

"You don't have to—" My voice catches, breaking off as a shock of pure, erotic bliss rocks through me when his mouth touches me. His warm, wet tongue slowly strokes my clit, and all reason leaves me. All that's left is the painfully exquisite sensation of his skilled, hungry mouth against my bare flesh.

My fingers tangle in his hair, and with whatever bit of brainpower that remains to me, I try to pull him away because it's too intimate, too much, and this is Royal Fucking Dolce, my enemy to the death.

"Just relax," he murmurs, kissing me gently. "Let me make you as crazy as you make me."

Without waiting for an answer, he dips lower again, letting out a sound that's half sigh, half moan as his tongue slips between my lips, toward my entrance.

"Don't," I breathe, but I barely hear the sound because I'm melting, weakening, as his lips and tongue and breath combine forces, overwhelming me. I drop my head back on the pillows, gripping his hair as if it can anchor me to this world even as his mouth moves against me like magic. He explores me slowly at first, tasting and sucking, his teeth nibbling gently at me, his tongue stroking me until I can't breathe, and my hips start jerking involuntarily against his mouth.

He grips my thighs harder, his fingers cutting into my flesh, holding me still while his tongue moves faster. I let out a soft cry when his rough tongue breaches my opening, rasping against the raw, broken skin. But his mouth is wet, and I'm wet, and soon the burning sensation is too entwined with the swirling pleasure to tell where one ends and the other begins.

"Royal," I gasp. "Stop, it's too much, I can't—"

He lets out a rough groan and squeezes my thighs harder, opening them wider, his whole body writhing in the bedsheets as he pushes deeper, thrusting his tongue into me until I'm dizzy with it. I buck under him, grabbing at the pillows, at anything, because I'm going to explode if he doesn't stop. But he doesn't stop. He goes on and on, moaning into me, eating me, until I can't hold back the soft, breathy cries that have been building inside me with the pleasure. He fucks me relentlessly with his mouth, his tongue, until he pushes me over the edge.

It's like nothing I've ever felt, not even when I've given myself a good one. This one is different, unwillingly almost as he drags it from my helpless body. A rush of wet heat flows from me in a way I've never felt, and I cry out, humiliation burning through me even as the orgasm clenches me in its grip. He moans deep in his throat, pushing his tongue deeper even as I cry out wordlessly, not sure if I'm telling him to stop or continue, not sure of anything except the waves of bone deep pleasure and release bearing me away on a current that I know will take me over the edge of the world into the abyss of Royal's darkness, to be swallowed by his world, his soul-sucking emptiness.

When it ebbs, his mouth is still on me but moving slowly, his tongue lazily answering each pulse of my flesh with one of its own. I want him out, in case he didn't notice how I came, so much it almost felt like I pissed myself, so much it's unladylike and humiliating and like everything about me, too fucking much. I made a mess no girl should make, and the shame aches behind my eyes as I wait for the gloating, the degrading taunts. This is Royal. There will be triumphant smirks and bragging that he proved he knows a thing or two about my body after all, followed by scathing words about how I'm a disgusting freak who cums like a man.

He lifts his face at last, his lips shiny, his eyes wild and unfocused. "God, you taste so fucking good, Harper," he groans, his breath coming as quick as mine. "I want to bite the fuck out of your pussy."

"No," I cry, shoving at his forehead.

He unclamps his hands from my aching things, which will surely be bruised to hell tomorrow. Instead of climbing on top of me as I expect, he braces his hands on my inner thighs and spreads them wide, staring down at me with that hazy, transfixed expression. There's no way he can miss what I did now. When he leans down, I tense, trying to twist away.

"I'm not going to bite you," he snaps, forcing my legs wide. "Let me lick the cream out of your cunt." His tongue is gentle this time, slowly winding a spiral of pleasure deeper and deeper into my core as he laps up the mess of cum from my wrecked pussy until I swear even my heart is quivering for him. When I think I can't take it another second, he slides a long finger into me. "Cum in my hand this time, Cherry Pie," he murmurs. "I want to feel you gush again." Then his mouth descends, stroking me toward an edge I know I can't come back from. This time, I don't even try. I let him carry me over.

*

When She Comes

When she comes
Mountains tremble
With her cries
With her thighs
Opened wide

BRUTAL BOY

Begging me to come inside.

When she comes
Her rains awaken desert blooms and
Oceans turn their tides
To see her arrive
To see the divine
Sunset inside.

When she comes
All the world loses its mind
Setting suns rise
In stormy skies
Stars in velvet night
Forget to shine.

When she comes
I come undone
and tell her the truth:
Wherever you're going,
Take me with you,
I want to come, too.

twenty

Harper Apple

When Royal's finally done with me, I don't think I could get up from the bed if I tried. I'm a giant pool of jelly, and when he pulls me back into the crook of his body and curls around me, I offer no resistance. He sighs, long and deep, like he's the one who just had six orgasms in a row, and buries his nose in my hair. I'm too exhausted to think about getting up again, so far beyond contentment that I'm actually guilty for how good I feel, how much pleasure I let him give me.

I'm not someone who normally wallows in pleasure or has an easy time letting go, but I couldn't help myself. It felt too good—he felt too good. Not just the skillful way he touches me, but the way he talks to me, the way he seems to somehow enjoy it as much as I do, like he can't get enough, is addictive. More addictive than any drug, I think as I fall toward sleep hard and fast. Maybe this is what my mother's really after, why she chases men and does drugs and doesn't give a fuck about anything else. For the first time in my life, I think I really get it. I understand how chasing this high could take over your whole life, become the only thing you wanted or needed until it was all you had left.

*

I wake before Royal. Sunlight streams in the window, and I turn away, hiding my face in his chest and trying to block it out, to block out reality. In the light of day, it comes screaming toward me like a train.

I fucked Royal Dolce.

I may have gotten in at his house, but he got in *me*. I let him go down on me. And not just go down on me but make me cum. Afterwards, I shamelessly let him do it again and again.

I start to get up, and his arms tighten like he can't let me go yet, even though he hasn't opened his eyes or moved. I pry myself free and use the bathroom and freshen up, using mouthwash to get rid of the whiskey and beer breath from last night. Even as I'm doing it, I know I'm being a dumb bitch. There's only one reason to clean up in the morning before he gets up.

So yeah, maybe I am a whore. I like sex. It feels fucking amazing, even when I don't get off. And last night... Well, Royal's the only guy who's ever bothered. So if I want a little more before I go, fuck anyone who judges.

I slide back into bed and throw my leg over Royal. He may still be mostly asleep, but his cock isn't. It throbs against my bellybutton when I slide in close, already standing straight up and proud, making my core tremble. I wrap my fingers around it, my eyes nearly rolling back in my head it feels so good. I stroke my hand over it a few times, and he gives me a slow, sleepy moan, still not bothering to open his eyes.

I remember how rough he was with me, the way he touched my face like he didn't know who I was, the emptiness in his eyes when he turned on the light. But this isn't a rage fuck. This is a lazy Saturday when we slept way too late after staying up until probably 4 A.M. Royal is calm now, and even though I'm sore as fuck, I'm aroused just looking at his body, every inch of it bare and beautiful and breathtaking.

I shift around on the bed, pushing him onto his back and straddling him. His eyelids flutter, and his thumb moves absently against my calf, but he doesn't make any move to rouse himself. I grip his shaft and lift up, rubbing the head along the seam of my lips. His cock throbs, wetting my skin, and my core pulses with wetness in response.

His chin tilts back, and he lets out a deep sigh of arousal, his hands fumbling until they lazily land on my hips. I open my knees wider, letting his tip touch the swollen, wet flesh of my bruised entrance. He shifts a little but doesn't take control, letting me sink down onto him slowly. When the pain subsides and I've adjusted to his size inside me, I begin to move, watching his enormous body like a mountain under mine, his impossibly broad shoulders, his olive skin and dark nipples, the muscles etched so deep in his skin they're like their own landforms on the world of his body.

But the highlight, the most beautiful part of him that I can't tear my eyes away from for more than a moment, is his face. It's relaxed, peaceful, even blissful as I ride him slowly, drinking him in like it's the last time I'll ever see him. His jawline could cut glass. His thick, dark lashes cast shadows over the hollows under his eyes. High cheekbones frame his strong nose and full, masculine lips that gave me so much pleasure last night that I couldn't take it anymore.

"That's right," he mutters as I start to move faster. "Fuck me, my little slut."

Again, I wonder who he's thinking about, if he's as far away as he was last night.

"Royal," I say, wanting to see his eyes, to know if it's even Royal that I'm fucking.

"Hmmm?" he says, his hand giving my hip a little, encouraging squeeze.

I don't go on, though. I lean forward and brush his dark hair from his forehead, running my fingers over his brow and cupping his cheek. "Open your eyes," I whisper, brushing my lips over his.

Slowly, his lids lift, and I see it's not Royal at all, just that hollow shell, the doll boy with nothing inside. It breaks my heart that he's not here, that he can't enjoy this.

I move slowly on top of him, keeping my eyes locked on his. My hands find either side of his face, as if I can hold him here with me, anchor him somehow. "Where are you?" I ask, my

338

voice barely above a whisper. "Come back to me, Royal. Be here with me."

For a minute, I just move on top of him, holding his face and feeling our bodies fit together, if just barely. I keep talking to him, saying his name, and after a bit, the darkness in his eyes fills up, and he's with me, and all the heat in that dark gaze devours me in a way the emptiness never can. His hands leave my hips, and he buries them in my hair, his gaze wild and almost panicked.

After just a few seconds of him being present, right here with me, moving with me, he sits straight up, grabbing my hips and bucking his hips up under me so hard I cry out. Liquid heat bursts inside me, spreading through my core and making my walls clench with bliss despite the tenderness inside. "Ah fuck," he groans breathlessly. "Fuck, I'm sorry, Harper. I'm a piece of shit. I can't believe I did that."

"It's okay," I say, laughing as I catch my breath. "That's kinda what you're supposed to do, right?"

"Yeah, but not before you," he says, lifting me off him and slipping off the bed. "God, I'm such a fuck-up. I swear I've never done that before. You make me look like a fucking virgin again."

"I mean… This isn't porn," I say, pulling his sheets over my lap as he paces into the bathroom. "These things happen. Sex is messy. I don't expect you to be perfect."

He closes the door in response. Okay, so not the fantasy I might have had when I woke up, but whatever. I'm a big girl. It's not like I've never had a quickie before.

He comes out of the bathroom a minute later, his expression stormy. "Sorry I'm fucking worthless when it comes to you," he says, grabbing his pants and jerking them on. "Get dressed. I'll take you home."

"Royal…"

"I said get dressed," he snaps, turning away to tie his pants, his whole body a coil of angry tension, like a snake getting ready to strike.

I've felt his venom before, and I lived through it. I climb off the bed and wrap my arms around him from behind, kissing the center of his back. "Royal. You're spiraling. I need you to fucking stop. Okay?"

His body remains tense, a giant wall of tight muscle, but he doesn't pull away.

I press my lips to his warm skin again. "This isn't a big deal. Seriously. Yes, I was enjoying that, and I would have kept enjoying it, but considering I can't even cum during sex, it's not like I really care how long it takes you."

I feel his ribs expand as he takes a deep breath, and then he starts to relax against me. "You should care," he mutters. "You deserve more than five minutes."

I roll my eyes behind his back, wondering when he started thinking I deserved anything but the worst life has to offer. I run my nails down his chest and abs, lightly scratching them over the sexy trail of fine hairs below his navel. "If you're really sorry, you could make it up to me like you did last night…"

"You want me to go down on you?"

I run my palm lightly over the front of his pants. "Or maybe you could let me show you what a real blowjob feels like?"

He chuckles and pulls my hand away, turning in my arms to look down at me with those hooded eyes that make me all ragey and hot at once. "You think I don't know what a blowjob feels like?"

I smirk up at him. "You don't know what one of mine feels like."

He bites his lips together, and I can tell he's hiding a smile. "You're a thirsty bitch, you know that?"

I sit back on the bed, slowly undoing the knot in the front of his pants. I slide them over his hipbones, running my fingers over that ridge of muscle above them that makes my head spin. And maybe he's right about my thirsty bitch status because my mouth is positively watering as I lower them until I can see the dark hair on his pelvic bone, those veins in his lower abs, and then the base of his cock. I hook my hand into the top of his pants and look up at him. "Before I do this," I say. "I don't fucking bite. Frankly, it's offensive that you'd accuse me of that shady shit. If you need to fuck my throat raw, do it, but keep your damn fingers out of my mouth. I will bite those."

"Damn, Cherry," he groans, circling his hand around the back of my head and bring my head down. "Put that mouth to good use."

I duck my head and smile, letting his pants fall. His cock is hard, full and long and mouthwateringly primal. I wrap my hand around his shaft and pull my hair to one side before running my tongue along his length, wetting him with my mouth. I can taste myself on his cock, and a dirty thrill runs through me. I get on my knees and elbows on the edge of the bed, holding his cock as I circle the head like an ice cream cone, letting him feel the flat of my tongue before I bring my mouth down over the tip. I'd almost forgotten about my split lip, since we've done almost no kissing up until this point, but now it burns when it stretches around his girth.

Royal buries his hand in my hair, taking control like I knew he would. He rocks his hips in rhythm with his hand, pulling my head up and then pushing it roughly down until I'm deepthroating him with each stroke. I don't mind. It's easier, and more than that, I know it's exactly what he needs right now—to feel powerful, to be in control, and to dominate me. That's why I offered.

"Christ," he breathes, pounding into me roughly while I try to breathe between thrusts, and not gag or choke as tears blur my vision. "Your throat's so fucking tight."

I moan in response, and his cock throbs inside my mouth, salty precum wetting my tongue. His taste send a thrill of pleasure and triumph shimmering through me. Was he lying about never coming? Or was it a line that gets girls, a challenge? Either way, I feel pretty fucking special that I made him cum and that I'm about to do it again.

Heat pulses between my thighs at his words. I slide a hand under my body, sinking it between my legs, working my clit with my fingers while he uses my mouth for his pleasure.

My lip splits open again, blood leaking out along with saliva, running down my chin, but I focus all my willpower on not gagging while he plunders my throat, rougher with each thrust. Tears drip down my cheeks as I fight my gag reflex, letting him go deeper, forcing himself down my throat.

"I'm gonna cum down this pretty little throat," he growls, running his fingers down the side of my neck and letting them rest lightly on the front, so he can feel himself fucking me deep.

I bob my head in a nod, all I can manage.

"Are you touching yourself?" he asks, yanking my head back, giving me a chance to breathe. His eyes burn with primal, fevered lust, and his cock stands glistening in front of my face, precum leaking from the tip. A shudder of desire goes through me, and I sink a finger deeper inside myself and close my eyes.

My voice is nothing but a throaty whisper, choked with desire and hoarse from the bruising force of his domination.

"Yes."

He drags me up and flips me onto my back in one motion, plowing his cock to the hilt inside me with one brutal thrust. I cry out at the sudden, painful invasion in the soreness from the night before, my back arching and my heels digging into the edge of the bed. He grips my hip with one hand, resting his weight on the other as he slams into me again. I'm beyond ready this time. His size is painful but deliciously so, and I'm so wet I can hear the slippery sounds of his cock slicking into me, the slapping of his balls hitting my ass as he begins to pound into me hard and fast.

I reach up, pushing my fingers into his mouth. "Taste me," I breathe, wrapping my legs around his hips, wanting more after each punishing stroke. He sucks my fingers, his tongue flicking between them as he fucks me harder, crushing me into the bed.

I hear myself begging for more, and he gives it, picking me up and slamming me down on him. We fall back onto the bed, rolling over so I'm on top.

"Your tits are so fucking perfect," he growls, grabbing my tits and squeezing my nipples until I cry out. "I want to cum all over them and your face. You'd like that, wouldn't you, my little slut?"

"Yes," I gasp, bouncing on him hard and fast, relishing the aching depth he can reach inside me while our eyes are locked together, our bodies warring to make the other break first. "I want to swallow you until I choke. Drown me in your cum, Royal."

"Shut the fuck up, you dirty whore," he snarls. "You're going to make me cum again."

I grab his chin, my nails digging into his cheeks. "I'm your whore," I say between panting breaths.

"Fucking cum," he commands, grabbing my hip and crushing me down onto him.

"I'm fucking trying," I growl back at him.

"Your mouth is bleeding," he says. "I'm going to eat your blood, Harper."

He rolls us over again, pinning my knees together with his and lifting up onto his fists. He leans down, clamping his teeth on my bleeding lip and sucking hard. Something about the angle, the way the head of his cock pushes back and the base grinds up toward my clit, combined the pain of my lip that pulls my focus away from trying to cum, undoes me. My control, the one I've been trying to let go of even when one stubborn part of me clings on, shatters. I hear myself cry out wordlessly, feel my body arch up, every muscle tensing as if electrified, like it did last night. My nails rake through his skin, my toes curl, my head drops back, and orgasm sucks me under. My walls clamp down around his cock, and he sucks in a loud breath, grinding deeper while his cock throbs thicker, his cum pouring into me in pulsing waves of heat.

When at last my vision clears and I can breathe again, I stare up at Royal. His massive chest is rising and falling as he pants quick breaths, his lower lip shiny with my blood as he catches his breath. For a minute, we just watch each other. My legs are still locked around him, and I can feel his cock jerk inside me every few seconds. I clench my walls around him, squeezing him in response, relishing the way his eyes widen and he sucks in a quick breath when I do it. I do it again, and he grinds his pelvic bone slowly against my tender clit, making my core tremble around him. His eyes are full of heat, and desire, and *me.* He's here with me all the way, watching my face, licking my blood off his mouth.

I never want to let him go.

"Watching you cum is the hottest thing I've ever seen in my life," he says, lowering himself onto me. His forehead is beaded with sweat, and I can feel my own skin glazed with moisture from the exertion.

"So, that's what all the fuss is about," I say, laughing through my labored breaths.

"Nah, babe, that *is* the fuss," he says, running his tongue gently over the split in my lip. "Can I stay inside you forever?"

"Fuck. Yes."

He lays his head in the hollow of my shoulder, his arms folded to bracket me in. Neither of us move for a long time. I can feel his heart hammering against mine, can smell the sweat misting his skin, making me hot all over again.

"Harper Apple," he breathes into my neck at last. "When I feel you cum, I absolutely come undone."

I swallow hard, poking at the hurt that little lie caused. Maybe I'm not so special at all. "I thought you didn't do that."

He laughs quietly against my ear, and I have to close my eyes and take a deep breath as a hot shiver races through me. "It's been a long time," he admits, rubbing his nose lightly along the shell of my ear.

"Why?" I ask. "Is it, like, a control thing? Or a physical thing?"

"No questions, remember?" He blows softly against my earlobe, and my skin prickles deliciously. "But fuck, Cherry Pie. Even before… I've never cum like that."

"Like what?"

"That hard," he says. "And inside you…"

I feel his cock throb inside me at the words, but my brain has come to a full fucking stop. A bucket of ice water couldn't have cooled me off faster. I freeze under him, my blood running cold.

twenty-one

Harper Apple

"Fuck," I whisper, panic slamming into my chest. I shove Royal's shoulders, and he sits up. I push up on my elbows and look down, as if I might be wrong, as if a condom might magically appear on his long, thick, perfect cock. Damn him and his flawless body. Damn his father and those shots of whiskey last night. Most of all, damn my poor, weak, animal self that lost her mind at the first sign of good dick and did exactly what I've always sworn I would never do—exactly what my mother did.

"I've never fucked anyone without one before," Royal says, obviously taking my stricken expression for a question about his reputation. "I should be clean. You?"

I shake my head, trying to clear the spiraling, panicked thoughts. I cannot get pregnant, oh my fucking god, I just can't.

I can't be stuck with this psycho forever. I don't even like him. Good dick does not make a good man. I know that for fucking sure.

When I just keep staring at him, shaking my head slowly back and forth, the truth dawns in his eyes. "You're… Not on birth control?"

He must know before he even asks, because he grabs his hair with both hands. "Fuck," he yells after a minute, turning and slamming his fist into the pillow beside me.

I jump involuntarily, and his gaze moves to me, angry and calculating, as if he's trying to think of a way out of this. Of course he fucking is. It's not his problem, after all. I'm literally living proof that's how guys think.

"Obviously I'm not on fucking birth control," I snap, sitting up and yanking the sheet over my body. "I'm a poor piece of trash, remember? I can't afford birth control, let alone a doctor visit to get a prescription. What's your excuse?"

He gives me a sour look. "You make me fucking crazy, Harper," he says. "You make me every kind of stupid. I was so pissed last night, I wasn't thinking. And this morning, *you* climbed on *me*."

"Oh, so it's my fault?" I ask, tossing off the sheet and standing. I can feel his cum still inside me, leaking out of me, a drop trickling down my thigh. Shame and disgust washes over me. It was me. It's all my fault. He didn't use one last night, but he also didn't cum. The chances are slim. This morning, he came inside me twice. Because I fucking climbed on him like the horny bitch I was raised to be. What have I done?

"I didn't say that," Royal says, looking up at me from where he's still sitting on the bed.

"You didn't have to," I snap, stalking into the bathroom and slamming the door behind me. I lock it and sink onto the toilet, my legs shaking.

Fuck. Fuck. Fuck. I can feel his cum dripping out of me, and I double over, sure I'll be sick. All I've ever wanted since I was old enough to want anything rational was to get the hell out of this town. Go to college. Not be stuck here like my mother, hopeless and destitute, with a kid I don't want from a man I never knew. The ache behind my eyes becomes unbearable, and a sob wrenches through me before I even know it's coming. I bite down on my fist, smothering it. I'm not going to let Royal Dolce hear me cry.

"Harper," he says from outside the door, his voice sharp. He rattles the knob.

"Go away," I say, my voice harsh with tears. Another sob wracks my body, and I bury my face in my arms to silence my anguish.

"Let me in, Harper," he says, a warning edge to his voice now.

"Go the fuck away!" I yell. Tears streak down my cheeks because oh my god, this cannot be happening. What am I going to do? I can't fucking do this.

A thud sounds as Royal's shoulder hits the door, and the whole room shakes. With a splintering crash, the lock gives way on his second attempt, and the door flies open. Royal stands in the doorway, breathing hard, staring at me. I turn away, but he's already seen. I'm not made of titanium. I'm just a human made of flesh and blood, tears and bone. I'm a girl living her worst nightmare.

"Harper," he says, his voice softer. And then he's lifting me, pulling me onto his lap as he sinks to the floor and cradles my naked and bruised body that is suddenly a ticking time bomb. I don't want his pity, his kindness. I want his violence, his sharpness. I understand that better than softness.

I try to push away, but he holds me tighter, his arms cradling me. "It's going to be okay," he says, pressing his forehead to my damp hair. For a long time, I can't do anything but sob helplessly in his arms. He doesn't speak, just sits and holds me tight as if he could hold me together while I'm being ripped apart inside. When at last I stop, he kisses my bare shoulder. "It'll be okay."

"How is this going to be okay?" I ask, lifting my head, not caring that my face must be an ugly mess. I don't care. I want him to see all the ugliness inside me. To hate me as much as I hate him right now. "You think I want to be here, Royal? You think I like what you do to me? You don't think I'd leave this town the second I get the chance? I can't do this, Royal. I'll fucking die before I'll be the kind of mom my mother is."

"Don't you dare say that," he snaps, grabbing my chin and forcing my gaze to his. His fingers cut into my cheeks, and his eyes blaze with emotion I've never seen in him.

"What am I going to do?" I ask, the fight draining out of me. I'm too desperate to fight him now. The enemy isn't in him anymore. It's inside me.

"I'll take care of it," he says.

"How are you going to take care of it?" I ask. "You think we're going to have a baby together? Or are you going to give me money for an abortion? That's what people in your world do when they don't want a baby, right?"

"No," he says slowly. "I'm going to take you to get a morning-after pill. And then we're going to get you an appointment to get on birth control."

"Why would you do that?" I ask, pulling back and narrowing my eyes. If he's going to hand me a pill, it's probably cyanide.

"Because Harper," he says, still speaking to me as if I might not understand the most basic explanation. "I may be an asshole, but I'm not that kind of asshole."

"Just so I know, for future reference, out of the million ways to be an asshole, which one isn't covered?"

"The one where I walk away and act like this is your problem."

"It is my problem." I glare at him, willing him to contradict me.

He sighs. "You know, it won't kill you to let someone help you once in a while."

"I know you think you're all that because you're richer than god, but you can't just go around throwing money at every problem and thinking it'll go away."

"Not every problem," he says. "But this one? Yeah, that's exactly what I'm going to do."

"I don't want your money."

"You want to raise a kid with me, then? Because those are the options right now."

I hate that he's right, but this time, I'm going to have to give him the win.

"Fine," I say. "Let's go wash down our mistake with a pill, and then we can forget this ever happened."

"Fine by me," he says, roughly pushing me off his lap and standing. If I didn't know better, I'd think I hurt him. If I thought he possessed a heart and the ability to feel, I might be fooled into thinking that look on his face was exactly what it looks like—the bewildered expression of a lost little boy who saw only indifference when he looked to the very ones who were supposed to love him. Suddenly, my throat is tight again, and I have to turn away from him.

It's stupid to read my own lack into his expression. Not just stupid but dangerous.

"I'm going to take a shower," Royal says. "For once in your life, will you just stay put because I asked you to?"

"Fine," I say. "I'll wait in your room like a good little girl."

While he showers, I put on my clothes from yesterday—no use pretending I'm not doing the walk of shame today—and sit in the chair at his desk. After a minute, I pull open one of the drawers I didn't go through last night. It's filled with hotel receipts and betting slips and loose cash. My heart nearly stops. There must be a few thousand dollars in there, twenties and hundreds and a couple fifties, just thrown in there like trash. Guess that pill isn't going to hurt him any.

A picture frame lies halfway buried under other stuff, the kind that folds in half and has two pictures in the middle, facing each other. I pull it out and open it without thinking. My throat squeezes when I see that one side holds a picture of him and the girl from the tattoo, both of them smiling in a way Royal never smiles at me, their cheeks squished together as they grin at the camera. For a second, it breaks my heart. I'm not sure what hurts worse—that he was happy with another girl, or that he'll never smile that way again. That boy is dead.

Royal steps out of the bathroom, and my first instinct is to shove the picture back, but he's already seen me looking. I won't be one of those dumb bitches who assume shit and get pissed about it, running off in a jealous huff because he liked some other girl. I'm a big girl, so I used my words. "Who's this?" I ask, staring at the two of them, both of them so painfully beautiful I don't know who to look at.

Royal's at my side in a second, yanking the frame from my hand and shoving it back into the drawer, which he pushes closed with his thigh. "Keep your sticky fingers out of my business," he snaps.

"Oh, so you can be balls deep in my business whenever you want, but I can't ask about your dead sister?"

"Now you're catching on," he says, smirking down at me. He hasn't stepped away, and his penis is way too close to my face. I swallow hard, trying to keep from salivating at the thought of taking him into my mouth again.

"No deal," I say, forcing myself to sound normal and not like my brain is a scrambled egg. "Tell me who that was."

"You know who it is," he says. "You just said it."

I open the drawer, even though I know I'm playing with fire by pissing him off. I pull out the picture again and flip it open. Instead of ripping it away, he shakes his head and walks away, choosing to get dressed instead of engage with my bratty ass.

I should have known it was his sister. I suspected when I saw his chest, but I wasn't sure. They're both gorgeous, both with the same dark hair and luminous dark eyes, the same thick, dark lashes.

In the other frame is a picture from further away, and I spot the girl in that picture, too. There are five of them in that one, all standing on the grass in front of a church made of stone and stained glass instead of white siding like the ones around here. Their arms are around each other's shoulders, their bodies forming a chain. I recognize Royal to the left of center, looking smaller than now, not as muscular or tall, his hair curling around his ears. To one side of him is one of the twins, though I can't tell which one, as neither are wearing glasses and their hair is cut the same. In the center is a guy who looks almost just like

Royal but taller, and then the girl again, and then the other twin. They're all smiling, squinting into the sun, wearing white shirts with ties and dress pants, except for the girl, who's in a modest dress.

His family.

Now my chest tightens for another reason. I wonder what it must be like to have that much love just built into your life. That many people who have your back, who make it their job to keep you alive, people ready to ride or fucking die for you.

"Ready?" Royal asks, snagging his keys from the pocket of last night's jeans. "Or you want to keep digging through the past like it matters?"

We head downstairs, where Royal drags me into the kitchen. The twins are sitting in a breakfast nook, both of them in pajama pants and nothing else, both looking nearly as gorgeous as Royal. They're both wearing glasses, and for a second, I can't tell them apart. Then one of them looks up and holds up a hand like he's expecting a high-five. I spot a swan tattoo on the underside of his arm and automatically check the other. I can only see the edge of his, but it's there.

Royal doesn't have one. Interesting.

"You finally tapped that," Duke crows, a sloppy grin on his face.

It's in the expression. That's how you know the difference. Duke's the clown. Baron's… I'm not sure what. The serious side, I guess. I remember that scene on the football field, the way Royal held onto him like he was the only thing keeping him from drowning.

Ignoring Duke's hand, Royal plucks a couple bagels from the platter in the middle of the round table and hands me one. "We're going out," he says. "Everything go okay last night?"

"Not as okay as it went here," Duke says, wiggling his brows at me.

"How would you know?" I ask. "You weren't here."

"Because I'm not still with my girl," he says. "You're still here, so by default, your night was better."

If he knew the reason I was still here, and what we're about to do, he'd change his mind. But I'm not about to tell him.

"You done with that?" he asks, turning to Royal. "Because I'm dying to dip my dick in her when you are."

Royal lays a casual arm over my shoulder. "You want to take this one?" he asks, cocking a brow at me.

"You know, I'm good," I say, leaning into him and hooking an arm around his hips. "I'm going to take a page from your book and not engage."

"Damn," Baron says, speaking for the first time, though he's been watching with keen interest all along. "You fucked the brattitude out of her."

"Let's go," Royal says, a little smile tugging at his lips. We turn and head for the door, and despite my earlier freak out, I'm actually smiling.

And then their dad steps in the back door just as we reach it.

"Leaving so soon?" he asks, pulling off his cheesy but expensive mirrored shades.

"I'm taking Harper home," Royal says, his arm tightening around me.

"You know, I can do that for you," Mr. Dolce says. "If you want to have breakfast with your brothers."

"That's not necessary," I say, giving him a tight smile.

"It's not a problem. I'm already heading out," he says, holding up his keys. He drops his voice and gives me a conspiratorial wink. "I'm used to cleaning up my boys' messes."

"Yeah, I'm not anyone's mess to clean up," I say. "But thanks."

Royal chuckles and squeezes me against him, pulling me past his father and out the back door. We climb into the Rover and head down the gravel drive. I cross my arms and stare out the window. "Have you ever had a girlfriend?" I ask.

He sighs and pulls up to the gate. "You're not my girlfriend, Harper."

"I know," I say. "It's just… You seem to know exactly what to do in this situation. And your dad said he's cleaned up your messes…"

"I told you I've never fucked a girl without a condom before."

"You've never had a pregnancy scare?"

"No." We pull out onto the winding, two-lane road. "Have you?"

"No, and I've never had a boyfriend," I say. "If you wondered."

"I didn't." We drive in silence for a few minutes.

"I had a girlfriend once, for like a month," I say. "But I'm pretty sure she just wanted guys to think she was a hot lesbian, because if no one was watching, she wasn't really interested in making out."

"What about Maverick?" he asks.

"Not a boyfriend."

"You know how fucked up it is that I have to look at some other guy's ink all over your body every time I fuck you? Knowing his hands were on you, that he was inside you... It's right there every time I look down at you."

"You know how fucked up it is that I have to look at your dead sister's face every time I fuck you?" I shoot back. "Seeing her big, haunted eyes staring back at me every time I look up at you."

He smirks, his jaw rising in that asshole way of his. "Who says she's my sister?"

I snort and give him a look like, *please, boy. I wasn't born yesterday.* "You're not the kind of guy who gets a girlfriend's face tattooed on his chest. And you told me."

Didn't he? Or did he skirt around the question and let me assume?

He shakes his head and shifts gears, speeding up. "I've never had a real girlfriend," he says after a minute. "But that doesn't mean I'm looking. So stop trying to get me to say something stupid."

"What does 'real girlfriend' mean?" I ask. "Like, not a fuck buddy?"

"Is that what Maverick was to you?"

I shrug. "We didn't really define it. It wasn't the sort of thing that needs a label. It was what it was. Casual. No big deal."

He shifts around in his seat. "Look, Harper. I don't date. I have a lot of shit in my life that has nothing to do with you, or other girls, but it means I can't have a girlfriend. Understand?"

"No," I say. "But I'm guessing you're not going to answer questions about it."

"That is correct," he says, pulling up to a stoplight. "You're just going to have to trust me when I tell you that I'm not fit to be anyone's boyfriend. You don't have to know all my shit to know that."

"True," I say. "And I'm not asking you out, so stop thinking that's what I meant. I just wanted to know why you're Mr. Pregnancy Scare Action Hero right now. It's so unlike you. I thought you must have experience."

He shakes his head. "Just because you made me cum, don't go thinking you're special. And just because I made you cum, don't get attached. Okay? I'm not taking you to the doctor because I'm a decent guy, but I *am* telling you this because maybe I'm not totally hopeless yet."

"And why are you taking me again? You could have just handed me cash. You know, I think you're a lot more decent than you let on."

"I don't trust you," he says, his voice hardening. "You're poor and desperate. You could have taken that cash and told me you went to the doctor. I wouldn't put it past you to trap me in this, so you'll be set for life. That's why I'm taking you."

I swallow hard, turning back to the window, all the flirty fun gone from the car. "Got it," I say, my throat tight. He really thinks I'm that kind of person?

But why wouldn't he? That's exactly what my mother would've done if she could find a rich guy to have unprotected sex with. Instead, she had my deadbeat dad to run off on her, and I guess he wasn't even worth chasing down for child support. At least she got her tubes tied so she didn't have to worry about any more kids ruining her life.

Royal goes on because apparently he has to really drive home the point that he still thinks I'm shit, despite what happened this weekend. "I'm putting you on birth control because I'm going to fuck you again, and I like fucking you raw," he says. "And by not a real girlfriend, I mean not since I was in middle school. Once I was old enough to fuck a girl, I didn't want to be tied down. That's never changed, and it never will. Are we clear now?"

I turn to him and smile, staring him straight in the eyes. "Crystal," I say, biting the word out, my vindictive little heart relishing the way it makes him flinch.

He pulls up and jerks to a stop in the lot of a walk-in clinic, the only ones open on a Saturday afternoon. He leans toward me, his expression almost tender as he lifts my chin and skims his thumb across my lower lip. "Remind me to stop by a sex shop and buy you a gag before I fuck you again," he says, chucking me under the chin. "That should shut you up."

He hops out of the car and heads into the clinic without bothering to check if I'll follow. He knows the limits to my stupidity.

Whatever happened between us, it hasn't changed what we are to each other—enemies. That much is clear. He still thinks of me as trash, and I still know he's a monster who needs to be taken down.

I'm such an idiot. I'm the one who got carried away, who forgot that for a minute. I'm the one who fell under his spell and thought we could be on the same side for once just because he's taking me to the doctor. It's all my fault. He didn't even cum when he fucked me last night. He lost control first, for a minute, but he managed to pull back in time, to keep from finishing and losing himself to me completely.

Was he pissed about giving in first, and that's why he insisted on giving back, to level the playing field? For a moment, I had the advantage. He'd lost control, and I hadn't. He'd hurt me. He owed me. And I didn't even fucking see it.

Instead, I let him have the upper hand again, let him give me half a dozen orgasms, so he has nothing to feel bad about, even after the brutal way he took me against the wall. After all, I enjoyed last night, climaxing over and over, and he didn't. Sure, maybe he broke his rules for me and ate pussy, but I broke mine and let him. I lost control, and he didn't. I gave in, and he didn't.

I let Royal control me, let him make me his plaything, a slave to the pleasure he can give me.

So much so that I lost my head this morning. He said I made him all kinds of stupid, but I'm the one who climbed on his dick without a condom. He was barely awake. And thirsty bitch that I am, I just wanted more, not thinking about the consequences. And here I am the next morning, just like my mother, paying for a mistake because I let my body rule me.

That's why we're here. Not because I was trying to tip the scales back and make him lose control, but because I wanted him with me while I came, wanted the intimacy and connection. That's what made him cum. The realization makes something funny twist inside me, happiness and guilt and triumph all rolled into one. I know how to make him cum. And he wants to do it again. He wants to be with me again, without a condom, enough times that he's putting me on birth control and not just saying he'll pull out.

Could this be the way in I've been looking for? I'm almost afraid to hope as I follow Royal into the clinic. But I do hope. I hope because he's still here. Surprisingly, he didn't kick me out of bed this morning and tell me to get lost. He didn't even hand me off and let his smarmy father take care of this. He's here, and whether he'd admit it or not, he's taking care of me. Could it be that the monster has met his match in the one girl who fights back, a control freak just like him who made him lose control at last? All those people who say the way to a man's heart is through his stomach are full of shit. The way to a man's heart is through his dick. I think I've arrived there at last.

*

Crystal (#396)

She uses your name
As a weapon
Goading me
Daring me
To reach across the seat
And wrap my hand around her neck
And squeeze

Until she's as lifeless as you.

She doesn't say your name
Like a taboo
Like she's the first person
To speak that one word
To my face
Without flinching

BRUTAL BOY

Since I walked away
And let the river take you.

She doesn't know your name
Falling from her lips
Is a gift
That brings equal parts
Agony and relief.
Whatever the intent,
Hearing her blaspheme to speak it aloud
Makes me want to silence her forever
But also command her to say it again
And again
Treasuring even the sweet agony
In the bone-crushing relief.

twenty-two

Harper Apple

Despite what Royal said about not being boyfriend material—and that I wasn't looking for him to be—he acts like one at the clinic. And even though he's right about me not liking to let other people help, it's a huge fucking relief to let him take over while I'm low-key freaking out all over again. Once there are doctors poking around inside me, it feels way too fucking much like all the scenes from TV shows where someone is giving birth.

I'm actually beyond grateful Royal is there, even going into the room with me and respecting my demands for him to stand up by my head while the doctor does his thing between my legs. Royal insists I get all the things at the clinic—the morning after pill, every STD test they have, and a birth control prescription which can be filled for six months at once. He even signs himself up for all the tests without my asking, which is a relief because his penis has seen a lot more action than my vagina, and I might've felt too guilty to ask seeing as how he's hemorrhaging money to pay for all this shit.

Afterwards, we go to the pharmacy, where we sit in the drive-thru line waiting for the birth control pills. "You didn't have to pay for all six months at once," I say. "I could have done it monthly."

"Jesus fucking Christ, Harper," he says, rubbing his temples.

"I'm sorry," I say. "I'm not trying to be ungrateful. I really appreciate everything you did today. I don't know what I would have done without you there. Thank you so much."

"See, that wasn't so hard, was it?"

"I mean it," I say, taking his hand and squeezing. "You're my fucking hero today, Royal."

"Don't be one of those chicks," he says, prying his hand loose from mine and putting it on the wheel, where I can't get it. "I hate those chicks."

"You already hate me, so what's the harm?" I ask, grinning at him. "And I think you like it. Everyone wants to be a hero once in a while."

"I have to be the hero every Friday night," he grumbles. "It's exhausting."

"But I bet you don't get to be the hero every Saturday morning."

He's quiet as we drive up to take our turn at the pharmacy window. He may not admit it, but I'm starting to know this boy, and I think he sounds just a little less bored and irritated as he talks to the pharmacist. It's stupid to think a boy who runs the whole school and has girls dropping to their knees to worship his dick, boys getting in line to be in his posse, and adults holding him up as Willow Heights football savior could need affirmation of his greatness. But being coveted and even admired for greatness isn't the same as being appreciated for compassion.

It scares me a little, how well I've come to know him, how I'm starting to anticipate his moods and give him what he needs when he probably doesn't even know it himself. I wanted to know all his secrets, but knowing him this way kinda freaks me out. Because I may have gotten to his heart, but while I was busy trying to find a way in, to chip away at his walls, he'd already scaled mine and stolen away with my heart.

Fuck.

I can't think that way. I don't want him to figure me out the way I'm trying to figure him out. I'd rather he be an asshole who only wants me for sex.

And maybe he knows me well enough to know that, because as we drive away, he thrusts the white paper bag into my lap and says, "Try not to use that as a free pass to fuck every guy in Faulkner."

"I'll do my best," I say, rolling my eyes. "Although, to be honest, I'm a little surprised you want a repeat. You seem more like the one-time type of guy. Is that one of your rules?"

"I'm the no-time type of guy."

"I thought you were trying to make sure I didn't feel special."

"I fucked you, and I'm going to fuck you again," he says. "Can you just leave it at that?"

"Whatever," I say, turning to the window with a little smile. I wonder how long it's been since he came. Does he do it by himself? Or not at all? That's probably why he shot his load so fast the first time. I feel a little smug about the fact that I unblocked whatever was holding him back. I made him lose control. Yeah, it was scary at first, but so worth it.

Is that the only reason he wants to fuck again—because he thinks I'm the only one who can make him cum? Or is it more that he's already let himself go with me, and he trusts me in some weird way, so he'd rather keep doing it with me than risk being vulnerable with someone else? Or was it some kind of dam that I broke, and now he'll be able to cum with anyone?

Why does that thought bother me so much? I should want him to enjoy sex like a normal person. But the thought of him fucking someone else makes me want to cut his whole fucking dick off so he can never stick it in anyone else.

He pulls up at my house but leaves the engine running. His fucking car probably cost three times as much as my house—when it was built. I could live in luxury in this thing. But it's not the car that's making me linger another minute instead of going inside.

"What are you waiting for?" he asks. "You think I'm going to walk you to the door and kiss you goodnight?"

"I was just wondering if what you did with me… If you could do that with other people now. Like, did I unleash something? Or have you been holding back on purpose?"

"No questions," he snaps. "And get out of my car. If I park here too long, your neighbors will probably dismantle it for parts."

I snort and look around. Blue and Olive are sitting outside in the old woven-plastic lounge chairs from the eighties, and old Mr. Thomas is sweeping his driveway. No one else is out. "Them?" I ask, gesturing before turning back. "Why won't you answer questions?"

"Trust me when I say that if you poke around in my business, you'll find shit you do not want to know." He leans across me to pull the latch on the door, his shoulder pressing me against the seat as he pushes it open. He starts to pull back, then pauses. His face is inches from mine, so close I can see the stubble growing out on his jaw, the intoxicating darkness that swirls in his eyes, luring me in, the fullness of those lips that made me cum so hard I think I cried a little. Suddenly, the air leaves the car, and I can't draw a breath. When I tear my gaze from his lips, his follows, rising from my lips at the same moment. Our eyes lock, and my heart stutter-steps in my chest.

Royal's fingers find my chin, gently lifting it. "Get out of my car," he says again, his voice low and cold now. "You're making it smell like garbage."

I jerk away and slide out the door, grateful that he opened it for me, making the getaway easy. Do I really smell bad? We had sex and fooled around for hours last night and this morning. He took a shower afterwards, and I didn't. Suddenly, I'm sure I smell like a swamp, and he didn't tell me all day until now. "You're a real piece of a shit, you know that, Royal?"

"So I've been told," he says, sounding slightly bored.

"Go to hell," I snap.

"See you there, Cherry Pie."

I grit my teeth, determined not to give him the satisfaction of the last words. "So, I guess fun, sexytime Royal has retired for the day," I say, giving him a cutesy little wave even though I'm seething inside. "If he shows back up, tell him to give me a call, and maybe we'll do it again sometime. If this guy comes knocking, I'm afraid I won't answer." I slam the door, meaning to walk away with a little swing to my hips to give him something to think about tonight.

But the window rolls down, and he tosses the bag out. "Don't forget your birth control," he says. "When I call, you'll have that pussy ready for me. If you don't answer when I come knocking, I'll use the back door."

He shifts into gear and drives off, and I swear I can hear the bastard laughing to himself.

I turn to head inside, but Blue waves. "Who was that?" she asks, cocking her head and squinting up into the late afternoon sun.

I shrug. "Nobody. Just some guy."

The moment I say the words, I know they're a lie. Royal's not just some guy to me. Not anymore. I knew I'd be fucked if we fucked, and here I am. Fucked. Right back where I swore I'd never be. After Colin, I swore I'd never fall for the sweet lies of a pretty sack of shit. After Maverick, I decided casual didn't work for me. And with Royal, I said I wouldn't be his dirty little secret.

And I just broke every single rule for him.

At least I know he's breaking all his for me, too. That's a consolation, as small as it is.

"Some *rich* guy," Blue says. "A Range Rover's like the most expensive car there is."

"No, it's not," Olive says, looking up from where she's driving little knock-off Hotwheels along the arm of her chair.

"I don't know anything about cars," I say with a shrug. It's true. I don't know how much a Range Rover costs because it has zero to do with my life. But from the way it rides, the leather seats and luxury feel inside it, I could have guessed, even if it wasn't driven by Royal Dolce.

"I know lots about cars," Olive says. "A Range Rover is one of the most expensive SUVs, depending on the model. When I grow up, I'm going to drive a Bugatti. That's more expensive."

I lift a brow at Blue, who shrugs. "Is that why you were getting all dressed up last night?"

"Yeah," I say. "He plays football."

"Well, fuck me sideways," she says, pulling a pack of cigarettes out of the pocket of her jean jacket. "Never thought I'd see the day Harper Apple was hanging out with a rich football player."

"Oh, we're not hanging out," I say. "We're just talking."

She shrugs and lights up. "Like a *Pretty Woman* thing?"

"Maybe someday," I say, unable to hide a little smile. That's the fairytale we know. Forget Cinderella. Our kind can't relate to that one.

Blue studies me from the corner of her eye, then hands me the pack. "You got it bad," she says. "You're gonna need one of those."

"Thanks," I say, hooking a thumb back toward my house. "But I better go shower. I feel like I smell bad."

She cuts her eyes toward Olive. "Come talk later?"

I head inside and shower, wondering how pathetic I am right now. On the one hand, Royal had no problem hanging out with his nose all in my business for like an hour last night. He didn't seem to mind my smell then. In fact, he kept saying how good it was, and from the way he acted, they weren't just words. He was the thirsty bitch, not me. He couldn't get enough.

On the other hand, no one wants to smell bad. And when you're a girl, and you can't do much about certain odors that everyone tells you to cover up, it sucks even worse. I keep telling myself he's just being a dick, hitting me with the lowest blow, like if I told him his dick was small. The difference is, he knows his is fine. I don't know if he really hates the way I smell or not. And I fucking hate myself for caring.

I emerge from the shower and go to the kitchen. There's not so much as a single packet of ramen noodles in the cabinet. Mom's friends must have cleaned out whatever was left of last week's grocery haul because the only sustenance in the entire house comes in the form of warm, flat beer in half-empty cans.

I sigh and start picking up. I can't do much about living in a shitty brick house that smells like a bar, but that doesn't mean the inside needs to look like the aftermath of a frat party.

I toss empties, clean the ashtrays, and rub down everything with cleaner. By the time I'm done, the house is put back together, and my stomach is growling like a lion. Since the car is gone, I can't go to the store, though, so I distract myself by sitting down at the computer. Unsurprisingly, I have several message from Mr. D asking why I missed my Friday check-in.

I close my eyes, feeling more guilty than ever as I start filling him in. Every time I do this, it feels worse than the last week. Especially now, when I care about Royal—more than I want to. But he made it clear I was just supposed to be his booty call, so fuck him. He didn't give me a twenty-five-thousand-dollar scholarship. When he's ready to treat me as good as Mr. D, I'll stop owing Mr. D information about him. So, I go through the day on Friday, and the game, and the party. I hesitate before diving into the rest, but I know I have to tell him.

The stuff about Mr. Dolce will be what he wants the most. That's the information that might get the family in most trouble, that could take them down. It's the closest I've come to the beating heart of the beast. So, I keep going, because I'm a fighter and this is what I vowed to do, no matter how much it hurts me. Nobody walks away from a good fight without a few scars, badges that said you were tough enough to take the pain not just from their punches but from your own.

BadApple: he took me to his house n I met his dad

MrD: What was he like?

BadApple: Total creep

MrD: What did he do?

BadApple: Basically said we cud hook up n I should keep quiet about it

MrD: Did you do it?

BadApple: gross no. He's like 40. I'm still a minor ffs

MrD: 17 is legal here.

BadApple: of course u kno that

MrD: Of course I do. ;)

BadApple: maybe u should stop fighting the dolces n join forces. U cud b pervy besties.

MrD: Were you tempted?

BadApple: that wud b a no

MrD: You said you'd let me fuck you, and you don't even know who I am. I could be hideous.

BadApple: there was more 2 that

MrD: What else?

BadApple: He might be a drunk. Def a helicopter parent. He misses his daughter. offered 2 take me home today. Says he cleans up his sons messes. Maybe re: abortions???

MrD: What about Royal?

BadApple: he took me home

I'm not about to go into the pregnancy scare thing. Some things are personal.

MrD: Did you let him fuck you?

BadApple: How is that relevant?

MrD: I ask questions, you answer. Remember?

BadApple: yes

MrD: Yes, you remember, or yes, he fucked you?

BadApple: yes

MrD: Both?

BadApple: yes

MrD: Tell me about that.

BadApple: I just did

MrD: I want details.

BadApple: I'm not going 2 provide u a jerk-off fantasy. Use ur imagination. We fucked. It was good. We both enjoyed it. End of story.

MrD: Is he big?

BadApple: Irrelevant

MrD: Not how this works, Harper.

I close my eyes and take a long breath through my nose. I fucking hate owing people. I should never have done this. But it's too late to turn back now. And telling him about a sexual experience might be skeezy, but it's not like it's going to hurt the family. Information about Mr. Dolce's drinking problem is more likely to affect the family, but of course Mr. D is barely interested in that. He'd rather hear about whether I wanted to fuck both father and son.

BadApple: yes
MrD: How big?
BadApple: Idk, 4got my measuring tape

For a minute, I wonder if he isn't Mr. Darling. If he's Duke and Baron, and they're fucking with me right now. Or if it's Royal, and he's trying to get an honest review. But no. If they knew I was telling someone all this, even if it was really them, they'd fucking kill me. I take a deep breath and wipe my hands on my jeans.

MrD: Did it hurt when he sank it in that tight, young pussy?
BadApple: u need help
BadApple: n yes. Is that wut u want to hear? About another man's cock n how it almost tore me open at the seams, how it was deeper inside me than anyone's ever been, n I screamed when he came inside me?
MrD: Did you?
BadApple: like a pornstar

MrD: Were you naked?

BadApple: yes

MrD: What position?

BadApple: idk don't remember

MrD: Bullshit. I want every last detail. Give me a play by play. Let me picture it like I was the one making you scream.

BadApple: ur as bossy as him

MrD: He's dominant then?

BadApple: yes

MrD: Did he require fellatio?

BadApple: yes

MrD: Did you do it?

BadApple: yes

MrD: On your knees in front of him or on the bed?

BadApple: yes

MrD: I'm so hard right now.

BadApple: isn't that the point of u perving on my sex life?

MrD: Did he fuck you doggy-style?

BadApple: no

MrD: I'd fuck you doggy-style. I bet you'd look good on your hands and knees.

BadApple: amateur hour

MrD: What?

BadApple: Hands and knees. Nobody does that. It's not the 90s.

MrD: You don't do doggy? You don't know what you're missing.

BadApple: doggy but not like that

MrD: How would you want me to fuck you doggy-style?

BadApple: I wouldn't

MrD: Then Royal. How would you like him to fuck you doggy-style?

BadApple: With his hand in my hair holding my face in the pillow

There's a long pause, so I have to assume Mr. D is off blowing his load. I feel dirty and slightly sick. I get up and check the fridge again, debating whether to eat mayonnaise out of the jar. At least I'll know if it's Royal next time we fuck. He'll definitely want to do that if he got off on picturing it. I wander back to the computer. It takes him a full five minutes to write back.

MrD: What position?

BadApple: were still on this?

MrD: You didn't finish.

BadApple: standing, missionary, cowgirl

MrD: You rode him?

BadApple: yes

MrD: Was he good?

BadApple: yes

MrD: Did he make you cum?

BadApple: yes

MrD: How many times?

BadApple: 10

That's an exaggeration, but he'll never know. Unless it really is Royal...

My skin prickles with that creepy feeling again, like I'm being watched. I check the blinds, but they're already closed.

MrD: Did he perform cunnilingus?

BadApple: yes

MrD: Was he good?

BadApple: yes

MrD: Did he get on his knees?

BadApple: no

MrD: Which do you like in your pussy more, mouth or dick?

BadApple: idk both equal

MrD: What about the twins?

BadApple: wut about them?

MrD: Can you fuck them and report back?

BadApple: um no

MrD: Why not?

Is he fucking serious? I didn't fuck Royal to please his pervy old ass. But for some reason, I don't want to tell him that. It's one thing to go through the physical details, but I'm not going to tell him I actually like Royal. First off, he might pull out of the agreement. I'm supposed to be on his side. And secondly, that's just not something I want to talk about, even to Blue, who's the closest thing I have to a real friend. Definitely not to a pervy old dude jerking off behind a keyboard.

BadApple: bc I'm Royal's plaything n he won't let them.

MrD: Ah, yes. That's right. You told me that. Well, I've enjoyed this report immensely. Do let me know how he plays with you next time.

BadApple: Is this just going to turn into me writing free porn 4 u?

MrD: Some people get to do it, others have to live vicariously.
BadApple: Cant u just watch porn like a normal person?
MrD: You're so much better than porn.

Ugh, gross. I sign off and go take another shower, feeling dirtier than when I had Royal's cum dripping out of me. Maybe I should just make shit up in advance next time. I really don't want him all in my business, especially now. And I feel weird telling him about Royal's dick. It works. Why does he need to know more than that? For that matter, why does he even need to know that much? Why is he living vicariously through me instead of going out to get some for himself? Even if he's hideous, as he suggested, he's rich. No matter what he looks like, he could hire a prostitute for a hell of a lot less than twenty-five grand. Hell, for that he could probably buy a whole sex slave on the human trafficking market.

I shiver and turn off the water, an idea coming to me as I climb out of the shower. What if he can't hire a hooker where he is? There's one place where even a rich guy can't get a girl, and I'm pretty sure Mr. Dolce has sent some Darlings there. My hands are shaking as I pull on my pajamas, and it's not just from hunger. It's just a hunch, but it could be the answer. If I'm right, I could find out who he is. All I have to do is figure out which Mr. Darling is in prison.

He has access to his money, somehow, since he provided my scholarship. I can't risk talking to Colt and getting him killed, but there are other Darlings in this town. Colt's dad, for instance. And there's another Darling boy, one who almost no one speaks of. Devlin disappeared with the Dolce sister, but what about Preston, the cousin Dixie said it was easy to label as evil? Could he help me? If I gave Mr. D the information he needs, and he really is in prison, who would do the actual dirty work of taking down the Dolces?

Does he expect me to do it? Or does he have someone on the outside to act for him?

Because I think... I really dare to hope... That I'm finally in.

Royal let down his guard. He trust me enough to let me sleep there, in his house. If I go back, I'll have access to his father again, to him, to his brothers. He may not think he trusts me, but he's starting to.

I unlocked something and made him cum, and now he wants to keep me. That's exactly what I wanted—to get close. Sure, I had to give up my body and probably my heart for it, but it will be worth it in the end, when I win. Even when we're fighting, even though we're still enemies, something's changed.

Royal took care of me today so that he can have me again. As long as I keep him coming back for more, I can find out what I need to know about him. I'm in his house. In his bed. It's only a matter of time until I'm in his head, until I gain his trust and his secrets. Then, he'll be mine for the taking down.

twenty-three

Royal Dolce

"So let me get this straight," Duke says on the way home from school on Wednesday. "You're going to ruin Harper all by yourself? We don't get to help *at all?*"

"If I need help, I'll let you know."

"She's getting to you, man," Baron says, shaking his head. "You almost fucked up with the scouts because she wore some slutty outfit. You missed a game because of her."

"So did you," I point out.

"Because you almost fucking died," Duke says. "That could have waited until Sunday."

"No," I say. "It couldn't."

"Fine," Baron says. "But just know you can't keep her. She's not your Darling Doll."

"I know that," I snap. "Let it go."

He and Duke do that twin exchange of glances. I want to fucking murder them every time they do it. If I hadn't already murdered my own twin, we'd be looking at each other, knowing what the twins don't.

I want to be left alone, but the moment I walk in the door, the fucking maid is on my dick.

"Mr. Dolce," she says, fluttering her invisible blonde lashes at me and twisting her hands in front of her like something out of a cartoon. "Do you require food?"

"I require some fucking peace in my own house," I snap. "And I'm not Mr. Dolce. That's my father."

"Some water, then?" she asks, looking so hopeful I give in with a sigh, and she scurries away.

Duke slugs my shoulder. "Throw poor Helga a bone," he says, stifling laughter. "She gets her twat in a twist every time she sees you."

"Does Dad require her to wear that ridiculous uniform?" I ask. "She looks like she's auditioning for a St. Pauli Girl ad."

"And we all benefit," Duke says, throwing an arm over Baron's shoulder. "What do you say? Want to put in your contacts and pull the old switcheroo on her? Or the double-team?"

If Dad would stop hiring hot foreigners under twenty to work in our house, he'd have lower turnover. With these two around, none of them last long. But then, I'm sure he's fucked as many of them as the twins have. Hell, it's probably part of the interview process.

After getting the water from Helga, I go upstairs, kick my shoes under the bed, and stretch out. I've been off my game all week. *Fucking Harper.* Even though everyone knows to leave her alone now, and they know she's mine, I still have to think about what she does when she leaves school. Who has seen the video? Who knows it's her? Are people fucking with her, the way they did at that party?

It's my fucking fault. That's the worst of it. I fucked up, and now I'm paying.

And if I'm paying, she's paying ten times worse.

I press my thumb and finger into my eye sockets, trying not to think about the shitty thing I did to her. The thing is, I'm supposed to do shitty things to her. It's all part of the plan.

I pick up a pillow and bury my face in it, searching for the scent she left on it on Saturday. I'm not even going to think about how fucked up it is that it calms me. This is not part of the plan. I pull back the blankets and crawl around looking for her scent like a dog sniffing after a bitch in heat. I need her like a fix. It won't stop me from destroying her, but it means I'll love every moment of the destruction, even if it destroys me, too. I fucking hope it does.

I bunch the sheet so I can bury my nose in it, trying to find a trace of her. Yeah, I'm the fucking creep who didn't let the maid wash my sheets after sex because I wanted to keep her on them as long as I could. But she's gone.

I thumb through my phone, opening *OnlyWords*.

I start typing: *Come over.* I stare at it for five fucking minutes, like I just wrote a sonnet and I'm not sure it's perfect. Then I backspace, deleting all the letters. I'm not supposed to want her like this. I'm not supposed to care that I'm lying here thinking about her, and she's probably off doing whatever the fuck poor people do on Wednesday afternoon after football practice is over.

Royal: What r u doing?

My thumbs punch in the words before I think about it. Then I erase those, too.

Royal: What's up?

My phone chimes in my hand, and I fumble it, sure it's her, that she's going to say something about what a shithead I am for not talking to her for the past three days at school. It's just, she surprised me and got all weird and girlfriendy and giggly after sex, and I had to make sure she knew I was serious. I'm not a good guy, and I haven't been for a long time. I'm so far from that it makes me laugh, the kind of laughter that hurts. I have secrets she can't know, that not even my brothers know. And if hurting her now means she'll stay the fuck away, then that's what I'll do. I may be willing to destroy her life and wreck her body and soul, but I won't touch her heart. That's something she should keep for herself, and even a monster like me can recognize that. I just need her to do the same.

Dad: Come downstairs. I need to talk to you.

I sigh and toss my phone on the bed and head down. He's in his office with the door open. I pull it closed behind me. "What do you need?"

He shakes his head and sets his phone face down on his desk. "You make it sound like I only talk to you when I need something."

"You said you needed to talk to me."

He leans back in his chair and links his hands behind his head. "How are things going with the Darling girl?"

"Fine."

"Your brothers," he says. "They got too attached to the last one. You'll make sure that doesn't happen again?"

I glare at him. "I'll make sure."

He works his lips to one side and then the other. "I trust you won't have that problem?"

"Get off my fucking back," I snap. "You got what you wanted. All the dads are out of the way. We said we'd take care of the kids, and we will."

"Okay," he says. "Don't get an attitude with me."

"Then stay the fuck out of my life," I say. "Are we done here?"

He looks at me a long moment, then opens the top drawer of his desk and pulls out an envelope. "I got the DNA results you asked for. Just to be sure."

My jaw clenches involuntarily. I knew it was coming. Dad already told me who she was, the daughter of one of the disowned Darlings who lived in shame in a trailer park seventeen years ago. We knew her lineage. That's why we picked her. Hell, I'm the one who got her DNA for him to send in. But I didn't want to know what it would say just yet.

Dad slides it across the desk, his lips tight. "It's a match."

It's over now. I have to admit the truth I knew all along.

I turn and walk out, not bothering to answer. Helga comes running to ask if I need anything and bat her lashes. I tell her to fuck off. My blood simmers with rage as I stalk back upstairs.

I pick up my phone, ready to text Harper and tell her what's going to happen now.

The app is still open on my phone, my last message still typed but not sent. I erase it before I see there's a message already there.

BadApple: Kno we r not talking but hope ur ok

An hour ago, I would have been as fucking giddy as a twelve-year-old when his crush sends him a nude. But I've had a nice dose of reality since then. Harper is not some girl who makes me feel shit I haven't felt in years. She's the spawn of one of those men. Her family destroyed me, and when I was at the lowest point a man can be, trapped in the darkest hell of their creation, they took my sister, just to make sure I'd never get out.

What happened last weekend… That was a mistake. That's all. She got to me, like Baron said. I was supposed to fuck her and leave her devastated. I wasn't supposed to forget a fucking condom. I wasn't supposed to cum inside her tight little Darling cunt, not once but two fucking times.

How could I be so fucking stupid?

What if she hadn't been willing to take that pill? If there was a Dolce-Darling baby in the world? I sit up, sure I'll be sick. I can't even think about that without wanting to vomit. No fucking way. That can never and will never happen. I would cut it out of her and drown them both before I'd let her bring such a monster, such an abomination, into the world.

Mistakes like that can't happen. They won't happen. I'll be stronger. I won't let myself forget the plan or live in some fantasy where she isn't the enemy. The proof is on Dad's desk.

She can never be anything to me but a possession, a toy that's made to be broken and thrown away, like a piñata.

I hate her not just for who she is but for what she's done to me. She made me lose control. She made me believe she cared, that she saw me. And worst of all, she made me something I swore I'd never be—weak. So I won't make it quick and painless. I'll show her what it means to feel weak. To be vulnerable. And I'll show her what it really means to be an enemy of the Dolces.

If I cared about her even a little, if I were someone merciful, I would destroy her swiftly and never speak to her again. But I'm not merciful. I will extract payment from her slowly, enjoying—no *relishing*—every single moment of her torment like the sweetest candy.

After all, she is a Darling, and every Darling must pay.

*

Will Harper capitalize on getting in with the Dolces, or will Royal ruin her first? Keep reading for more of their story in Book 3, Boys Club, now available:

http://books2read.com/boysclub

Bonus Chapter! Have you signed up for my Exile Reader Army? You'll get a chapter from *Bad Apple* retold in Royal's point of view, notices new releases, and exclusive sneak peeks! Join here:

https://landing.mailerlite.com/webforms/landing/q5z4y6

Also Available from Selena

Willow Heights Prep Academy: The Elite (complete trilogy)
1. Bully Me
2. Betray Me
3. Bury Me

Willow Heights Prep Academy: The Exile
1. Bad Apple
2. Brutal Boy
3. Boys Club
4. Broken Doll (Nov 2021)
5. Blood Empire (Jan 2021)

Willow Heights Prep Academy: The Endgame
1. Mafia Princess (King Dolce)

Say You Remember (A Stand-Alone, Second Chance Romance)

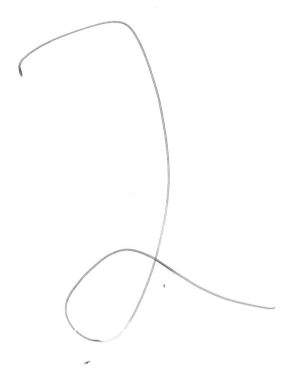

Printed in Great Britain
by Amazon